T0285634

BROADCAST BLUES

BROADCAST BLUES

A CLARE CARLSON MYSTERY

R.G. BELSKY

OCEANVIEW PUBLISHING
SARASOTA, FLORIDA

ISBN 978-1-60809-531-5

Published in the United States of America by Oceanview Publishing

Sarasota, Florida

www.oceanviewpub.com

10 9 8 7 6 5 4 3 2 1

PRINTED IN THE UNITED STATES OF AMERICA

FOR LAURA MORGAN
You will never be forgotten

"The best lack all conviction, while the worst are full of passionate intensity."

—W.B. YEATS

"It's not brain surgery. It's not nuclear physics. It's television. It's only television."

—LINDA ELLERBEE,
Longtime TV Newswoman

BROADCAST
BLUES

PROLOGUE

If you're reading this, I'm already dead.

How's that for an attention-grabbing opening line?

I know, I know . . . it's a bit melodramatic. And I'm not normally the melodramatic type. Really. No, Wendy Kyle is the kind of woman who deals in facts for a living, the kind of woman who doesn't let emotion cloud her judgment and— maybe most importantly of all—the kind of woman who never blindly puts her trust in anyone.

Especially a man.

Hey, I'm not some man-hating bitch or anything like that, no matter what you may have heard or thought about me. I like men. I love men, or at least I've loved a few men in my life. It's just that I don't trust them anymore.

So wouldn't it be ironic—or maybe a little bit fitting, to look at it completely objectively—if trusting a man this one time was what wound up costing me my own life in the end?

Here's the bottom line for me: if I don't succeed in what I'm about to do in the Ronald Bannister case, well . . . then it is important someone knows the truth about what happened to me.

And that it was the lies—all of the damn lies men have told—that were the death of me.

The contents of this document were among the evidence seized by homicide detectives from the office of Wendy Kyle Heartbreaker Investigations

218 West 42nd Street
New York City

This entry is listed as: POLICE EXHIBIT A

OPENING CREDITS

THE RULES, ACCORDING TO CLARE

NORAH O'DONNELL IS fifty years old. Samantha Guthrie fifty-one. Hoda Kotb fifty-eight, Robin Roberts sixty-two, and Gayle King sixty-eight.

The point I'm trying to make here is that TV newscasters—specifically women TV newscasters—don't have to be cute, perky, young talking heads to succeed in the media world where I work.

We've come a long way since the days when a respected newswoman like Jane Pauley was replaced by the younger Deborah Norville on the *Today Show* because some network executive—a middle-aged man, of course!—decided Pauley was getting too old to appeal to a television audience.

Or when an anchorwoman named Christine Craft lost her job at a station in Kansas City after a focus group determined she was "too old, too unattractive, and not deferential to men." She was thirty-seven.

Well, fifty is the new forty now.

Or maybe even the new thirty.

And let's get something straight right up front here. I'm not one of those women who normally gets stressed out over every birthday that passes by or every wrinkle on my face or every gray hair or two

I spot in the mirror. That is not me. No way. I'm not hung up about age at all.

But I am about to turn fifty this year.

The big 5-0.

The half-century mark.

And the truth is I'm having a bit of trouble dealing with that...

My name is Clare Carlson, and I'm the news director of Channel 10 News in New York City. I'm also an on-air reporter for our Channel 10 news show, and I've broken some pretty big exclusives in recent years that have gotten me a lot of attention and made me kind of a media star.

But this whole business of turning fifty still seems odd to me.

When I was in my twenties, I was a star reporter at a newspaper and won a Pulitzer Prize. In my thirties, after the newspaper went out of business, I switched to TV news at Channel 10. And in my forties, I've been juggling two jobs: TV executive as the station's news director and also as an on-air personality breaking big stories.

Turning thirty and then forty never really seemed like that big a deal for me. It was more fun than tragic. Look at me: I'm forty! But fifty? I'm not so sure about that one. Fifty is something completely different, at least the way I see it at the moment. I'm not sure where I go with my life after fifty.

It couldn't be happening at a worse time for me either.

Channel 10, the TV station where I work, is being sold to a new owner—and this has left everyone in our newsroom worried about what might happen next. My latest boss and I don't get along, and I'm afraid she might be looking for a reason to fire me. My personal life situation is even worse. I've been married three times—all of them ending in divorce—and right now I'm not in any kind of a relationship. I have a daughter, but she didn't even know I was her mother for the first twenty-five years or so of her life—so we don't exactly have a traditional mother/daughter relationship.

The only constant in my life—the one thing that I always turn to for comfort when my life is in turmoil—is the news.

This newsroom at Channel 10 where I work is my true home. My sanctuary.

And so each day I wrap it—along with all the people in it and the stories we cover—around me like a security blanket to protect myself from everything else that is going on around me.

All I needed now was a big story to chase.

The bigger the better.

That's what I was looking for right now.

But as the old saying goes: be careful what you wish for—because you just might get it.

And that's what happened to me with the Wendy Kyle murder . . .

PART I

THE HONEY TRAP

CHAPTER 1

Susan Endicott, the executive producer of Channel 10 News, walked into my office and sat down on a chair in front of my desk.

"What are you doing?" she asked.

"Talking to you."

"I mean about tonight's newscast."

"Oh, that."

"Don't be impertinent with me, Carlson."

What I was actually doing at the moment was putting together one of those old David Letterman–style Top 10 lists. I like to do that sometimes. My topic today was: Top 10 Things an Aspiring Woman TV Newscaster Should Not Say During a Job Interview. My list went like this.

10. What's that red light on the camera for?

9. Yes, Mr. Lauer, I'd love to be your intern.

8. I sweat a lot on air.

7. I can name all the Presidents back to Obama.

6. If it helps, I'm willing to get pregnant as a cheap on-air ratings ploy.

5. Katie Couric? Who's Katie Couric?

4. No makeup, please. I want to let my real beauty shine through.

3. My IQ is almost in three numbers.

2. Can I watch TikToks during commercial breaks?

And the Number One thing an aspiring woman TV newscaster should not say during a job interview . . .

1. I have a personal recommendation from Harvey Weinstein!

I wondered if I should ask Susan Endicott if she had any suggestions for my Top 10 list. Probably not. She might call me impertinent again.

"Do you have a lead story yet for the 6:00 p.m. show?" she asked now.

"Well, yes and no."

"What does that mean?"

"The lead story is about a controller's audit raising new questions about the viability of the city's budget goals."

"That's not a lead story for us."

"Hence, my yes and no reply to your question."

"Do you have a plan for getting us a good story?"

"I do."

"What is it?"

"Hope some big news happens before we go on the air at six."

"That's your plan?"

"Uh-huh. The news gods will give us something before dead-line. They always do."

"The *news gods*?"

"You have to always believe in the news gods, Endicott."

Looking out the window of my office, I could see people walk-ing through the midtown streets of Manhattan below on a beauti-ful spring day. Many of them were coatless or in short sleeves. Spring was finally here in New York City after what seemed like an endless winter of snow and cold and bundling up every time you went out. But now it was spring. Yep, spring—time for hope and new beginnings. The sun shining brightly. Flowers blooming. Birds chirping. All that good stuff.

In a few weeks New Yorkers would start streaming out of the city on their way to Long Island or the Jersey Shore or maybe Cape Cod. I thought about how nice it would be to be in a place like that right now. Or maybe on a boat sailing up the New England coast. Anywhere but sitting here at Channel 10 News with this woman. Except I knew that even if I did that, I'd probably wind up sooner or later sitting in another newsroom wherever I went talking about lead stories with some other person like Susan Endicott.

Endicott and I had been at war ever since she came to Channel 10. That was after the firing—or, if you prefer, the forced resignation—of Jack Faron, the previous executive producer who had first hired me as a TV journalist from my newspaper career and had been my boss for most of my time here.

Jack was a top-notch journalist, a good friend, and a truly decent human being. Susan Endicott was none of those things. She was an ambitious career climber who had stepped over a lot of people in her efforts to score big ratings at the stations where she worked before. That's what had landed her the Channel 10 job here in New York, and she was determined to keep her star rising no matter what it took for her to do that. She had no friends that I was aware of, no hobbies or interests, no outside life of any kind. She was completely focused on the job and on her career advancement.

For whatever it's worth, I didn't like the way she looked either. She wasn't fat or skinny, she wasn't pretty or unattractive, she was just . . . well, plain. Like she didn't care about her appearance. She wore drab clothes, hardly any jewelry, no makeup that I could see. It was like her appearance simply didn't matter to her.

Oh, and she wore her glasses pushed back on top of her head when she wasn't using them. I disliked people who did that. I know it sounds crazy, but that's the way I feel. It was the perfect final trait of Susan Endicott though. I detested everything about her. And, as you can see, she wasn't too fond of me either.

There were two things that had prevented her from getting rid of me so far.

I've broken some exclusive stories that got us big ratings. She did like the fact that I was an on-air media star, even if she didn't like me. So all I had to do was keep finding exclusives.

Also, the owner of Channel 10, media mogul Brendan Kaiser, had backed me in any showdown with Endicott since she arrived here. Always good having the big boss on your side when you're at odds with your immediate boss. But Kaiser was in the process of selling the station. We weren't sure yet who the new owner would be. Maybe it would be some great journalist or wonderful human being that would care about more than profits. But people like that don't generally buy big media properties like a TV station. So I was prepared for the worst once the new owner was in place.

That meant I needed to keep on breaking big stories.

And I hadn't done that in a while.

I needed to find a big story in a damn hurry.

"You better come up with a good lead before we go on the air at six tonight," Endicott said over her shoulder as she stood up and started to leave my office.

"Or?" I asked.

"Or what?"

"That sort of sounds like you were giving me an ultimatum. As in 'or you're suspended.' 'Or you're fired.' 'Or your cafeteria privileges are suspended.' 'Or you need to get a permission slip to go to the bathroom.' 'Or . . .'"

Endicott turned around.

She glared at me.

Then she pushed her eyeglasses—which she'd been wearing—back on top of her head again.

A nice touch.

Perfect for the moment.

"Keep digging that hole for yourself, Carlson," she said to me. "It will make it so much easier when the time comes to get rid of you."

"You have a nice day too," I said.

*   *   *

As things turned out, it didn't take very long to find a news lead for the show.

After Endicott left, Maggie Lang—the assignment editor and my top assistant—burst in to tell me there'd just been a big murder.

"Someone blew up a woman's car!" she said excitedly. "On a busy street in Times Square. The victim's name is Wendy Kyle, and she's a former New York City cop and a controversial private investigator who handles a lot of high-profile divorce cases—involving rich people, important people—catching them in sex scandals. Sounds like someone was out for revenge against her. Sex, money, power. This story has everything, Clare!"

Yep, the news gods had saved us again.

CHAPTER 2

It DIDN'T TAKE long to find out a lot of people might have had a motive for murdering Wendy Kyle.

The surprise was that it took so long for something like this to happen.

She was only thirty-two years old, but she'd a made a long list of enemies in that time.

The trouble started when she was on the New York City police force. After graduating at the top of her class from the NYPD training academy, she was assigned to a series of precincts in Manhattan. Controversy followed her everywhere she went. Not on the street, where she racked up an impressive arrest record at each stop. But inside the precincts themselves, where she was constantly being reprimanded for violation of rules and insubordination.

This would probably have been enough to get her kicked off the police force. But, at the same time, she filed a series of complaints with a civilian review board making allegations of sexual harassment and police corruption. The NYPD had to back off from firing her because it might look like retaliation.

But then came the final incident that sealed her fate. She attacked her commanding officer—punching him in the face and then kicking him several times in his genitals. He had to be hospitalized for several days from the injuries that he suffered during the violent altercation with Kyle.

Kyle claimed the commanding officer of the precinct had attempted to sexually assault her first, but he denied it. It wound up being a case of she said / he said. And her actions of physical violence were enough for the NYPD to suspend her and eventually end her career as a police officer.

That's when she became a private investigator. But not just any kind of private investigator. A sexual infidelity private investigator. Kyle specialized in catching cheating husbands for their spouses, and she wound up testifying in a number of high-profile divorce cases. Which resulted in plenty of big money divorce settlements.

The name of her business was Heartbreak Investigations. The slogan was: HEARTBREAK INVESTIGATIONS: WE CATCH CHEATS FOR YOU. She also ran an ad on TV, newspapers, and online, which said: "Think your husband or lover might be cheating on you? We'll catch him in the act." And a New York City newspaper recently did a feature article about her and her business with the headline: "Ex-Cop Wendy Kyle Now Catches Men With Their Pants Down."

The details of the murder itself went like this.

Wendy Kyle drove a 2021 black Toyota Camry that she parked in front of her office in the Times Square section of Manhattan, on West 42nd Street between Seventh and Eighth Avenues. She apparently left her office at approximately 10:30 a.m. that morning, got into her car—and an explosion rocked the neighborhood.

The blast pretty much obliterated the car and instantly killed Wendy Kyle.

She lived in an apartment on East 96th Street, off Third Avenue, that she kept after her last divorce. No one there knew much about her or had any idea of anyone specific who might have wanted to kill her, according to police. They clearly believed the motive for her murder was connected to her job as a peeping eye private investigator who spied on cheating men and their mistresses in the bedroom.

There was a picture of Wendy Kyle that had run with the newspaper article. A couple of videos on YouTube, too, with her talking about her work with Heartbreaker Investigations catching cheating spouses for women.

She had dark hair, striking features, a terrific figure—but also a determined look on her face like she'd seen and done it all as far as men were concerned.

Not the kind of woman you wanted to meet if you were the cheating spouse, I decided.

In the newspaper article, Wendy Kyle talked about a controversial technique that she used called the *Honey Trap*. And why not? It was the kind of sexy, sensational angle that would make more people want to read the story. And probably promote her business with women clients too. The interviewer asked her how the *Honey Trap* worked.

"Simple," she said. "Just like it sounds. The Honey Trap means we set a trap for a husband. In the event I don't actually catch him with another woman, I can make a move on him myself. Make it seem casual, but let him know I'm interested. I act like I want to mess around with him, want to sleep with him. If he bites, well then my client—his wife—knows the worst. Her husband is prepared to have an affair, whether we can document him in the act of cheating or not. Which means sooner or later he will.

"Do I actually sleep with him? No, I don't. I simply ascertain that he wants to go to bed with me and then I extricate myself from the situation. I just want to find out if a client's husband can be tempted to cheat. If he does respond that way, I report it back to my client. That's how the Honey Trap works.

"Either way we get the answer the client is looking for. Although I must say, these things generally turn out badly. Every one of my clients—all the women who come to me—say they want to know the truth. But, once they have it, many times they regret asking the question."

Her own personal life was pretty volatile too. Two marriages that I could find—one to a lawyer and another to a police officer. Both ended in divorces.

Of course, I was the last person in the world to throw stones at another woman over her failed marriages. I've had three of them myself.

But, putting it all together, it sure seemed like Wendy Kyle had a problem relating to men.

And maybe she hated men too.

Enough to lash out at them in both her professional and personal life.

Did any of these men—the ones she exposed for cheating to a client, or someone in the police department that had a grudge against her, or either of her ex-husbands or boyfriends along the way—hate her enough to kill her?

Anyway, that was where we were by the time we were ready to go on the air.

So at 6:00 p.m. that night I was on the set of the Channel 10 News broadcast.

There was the pulsating theme music for the show and then the announcer's voice-over saying:

"This is the news at six with the Channel 10 News team. Brett Wolff and Dani Blaine at the anchor desk; Donna Strickland with sports; Monica McClain with your up-to-date weather forecast; and Vic Zizzo with all the traffic reports in the metropolitan area. And now here's Brett and Dani."

Brett and Dani, the co-anchors, then quickly turned it over to me with the lead story. I looked into the camera and started talking:

ME: *Good evening. A horrific bomb explosion rocked a Manhattan street today, leaving one woman dead in her parked car. The victim's name was Wendy Kyle, and she was a controversial private investigator who specialized in divorce cases. Here's what we know so far . . .*

CHAPTER 3

"ARE YOU STILL thinking a lot about that age business?" my friend Janet Wood asked me.

"No, not at all."

"Really?"

"Absolutely. I'm fine with it."

"Because it can be kind of traumatic for you knowing you're going to be fifty in a few months."

"Two months, one week, and four days."

"Uh-huh. But you're not obsessing about it or anything?"

"Hardly ever even give it a thought."

Janet and I were having drinks at an outdoor table of Pete's Tavern, just off Gramercy Park in Manhattan. Pete's is supposed to be the oldest restaurant/bar in New York City, although I believe there is some doubt about that. People also claim that O'Henry wrote "The Gift of the Magi" here in the 19th Century, although that's never been exactly confirmed either.

But they have a great bar, a decent menu, and the view of the park and neighborhood is cool. It was a beautiful late spring night, and we were people watching and drinking and just catching up. Janet had a daiquiri, like she always did when we went out. I was drinking a Corona from the bottle with a lime. I mix up my drink selection sometimes, but a Corona beer was always my go-to on a nice night like this.

Janet was a successful lawyer with a fancy office in midtown Manhattan. She was happily married, had two wonderful daughters, and always acted in a very sane and logical manner in every aspect of her life. She was like my exact opposite. Sort of a Bizarro Clare. But somehow, we were best friends.

"How are you getting along with that Endicott woman you work for at the station now?" she asked.

"I despise the woman, I loathe the woman, I hate that woman with every fiber of my being."

"And she still doesn't like you either?"

"Hard to believe, huh?"

"What about the new owner of the station who's going to take over soon? How will that change things for you?"

"That's the real wild card in all this. Brendan Kaiser, the media czar who owns us now, is selling out to another company. Kaiser, as you know, has always been on my side. That's saved me so far in my dealings with Susan Endicott. Once he's gone, well . . . who knows what might happen then?"

"You think she'll try to fire you?"

"Not if I can get the new person in charge—whoever that turns out to be—to back me like Kaiser did."

"And you figure you can win over the new owner?"

"Sure."

"How?"

"Because I'm so cute and adorable."

Janet made a face and took a sip of her daiquiri. A medium-sized sip. Not too big, not too small. That was the way Janet did everything. Always under control, always precise, always just right. It drove me crazy sometimes. I took a big chug of my Corona.

Goddamn it, if this woman weren't my best friend, I'd have nothing to do with her.

"How about men in your life?" she asked.

"How about them?"

"Are there any?"

"Not at the moment."

"Any prospects?"

"No, but I have a plan."

"Which is?"

"Wait for some guy to ask me out, and then say 'yes.' No matter who he is."

"You're that desperate?"

"I'm so desperate that I thought the other night about calling up that Sam Bevilacqua guy I was with for a while."

"He lied to you about his real identity, he worked for the mob, and he may well have been implicated in a murder," Janet pointed out.

"Well, if you're gonna be picky about it."

I drank some more beer. I thought about doing it in moderation the way Janet did things. But instead, I finished off the bottle and ordered another. While I was waiting, I grabbed a big handful of peanuts from a dish on the table and began eating as many as I could at once. Moderation is not a strong point of mine.

"I've been thinking a lot about Scott Manning too," I said.

"The cop."

"He's with the FBI now."

"He's also married, last time I heard."

"Well, yes . . . there is that."

"Are you really still waiting out that marriage?"

"Hey, I got time."

Janet shook her head.

"So you're upset about closing in on fifty years old, you hate your boss, and you can't find anyone romantically who is (a) available or (b) interested in you. Anything else I should know about going on in your life, Clare?"

"I have a good story," I said.

I told her about Wendy Kyle, about what we knew so far about her life and her death, about how she might have rattled the cages and upset some rich, powerful people with her investigations into their secret sex lives.

"She sounds like a real piece of work," Janet said when I was finished.

"I like her," I said.

"Wendy Kyle?"

"Yes."

"But you never knew her."

"That's right, but I wish I had. She seems interesting. A real kick-ass woman. Who takes no guff from anyone. Does whatever she wants to do and says whatever she wants to say to people. Or at least she did."

"Sounds like someone else I know." Janet smiled.

"I take that as a compliment."

"Yeah, she sounds as crazy as you."

"I want to find out who killed her. And I want to find out why. And yes, it does make me happy to be doing this story."

"Any big story makes you happy."

"Thank goodness for that."

"So who are you doing this story for?"

"What do you mean?"

"Are you looking for answers about Wendy Kyle or for yourself?"

"Maybe a bit of both."

CHAPTER 4

THE MORNING NEWS meeting had gone off the rails. Big-time. I wanted to talk about the Wendy Kyle story and figure out the best way to cover it. But instead, I had to put out a series of brush fires with the Channel 10 news staff.

"I want a helicopter," Vic Zizzo announced at the beginning of the meeting.

"Why?" I asked. "Are you planning to invade a foreign country?"

"I need a helicopter to do my job."

"Vic, you're a traffic reporter."

"Exactly. And I should be up in a helicopter to report on the traffic."

One of the rival TV news shows had recently started using a helicopter to do traffic reports from the air. It was really just a gimmick. You didn't get better information—maybe you even got less—looking down at cars from the air than you could just taking in information from the Traffic Dept. But it was the same with a lot of things. A reporter thinks they have to stand in front of a crime scene or get blown around in a storm to show people how authentic it is. That's TV news.

"No helicopter," I said.

"But the traffic reporter at Channel 12 has a helicopter."

"If the traffic reporter at Channel 12 jumped off the Brooklyn Bridge, would you jump off too?"

"I'm serious, Clare."

"Okay, how about this? You buy a helicopter on your own, then put it on your next expense account."

I hoped he knew I was kidding.

There was more.

"I plan to stop doing scores and reports on football news," Donna Strickland said when my conversation with Vic Zizzo was over.

"Uh, you're the sports reporter, Donna."

"Right."

"And football is the biggest and most popular sport for our viewing audience."

"I know, but it's brutal and barbaric. Not to mention sexist and racist. If I refused to help spread the news about football, it could be a significant step forward for society. And we would be making news by being the first media outlet to make this stand and help launch this campaign. What do you think?"

I'd hired Donna Strickland about a year ago to give some balance to our sports report. The guy who had been doing it, Steve Stratton, was an old-school journalist who refused to talk about political issues or women's sports or other things that had been a part of the sports scene. All he cared about was football, baseball, basketball, hockey news, and scores.

I figured Donna—a young African American woman who had been a star women's basketball player in college—would provide a nice counterpoint to that. But Stratton was gone now, he retired a few months ago, and Donna Strickland was swinging the pendulum the other way. Heavy politics, women's issues, social justice, and all the rest.

That left me with a tricky situation in which our sports reporter wasn't really talking very much about . . . well, sports.

"Look, I'm a little too busy this week to change the world," I said to Strickland. "I don't know a lot about sports. But what I do know is that the NFL football draft is coming up, and that's one of the hottest topics around. I think it's gonna seem awfully strange if we suddenly stop covering NFL football because it offends you. So . . . no political stances, Donna. Just report the sports news."

I thought I might be done with it, but then something else came up involving Brett and Dani. Brett Wolff and Dani Blaine, our anchor team on the news desk. Yep, there was a problem with Brett and Dani. There always seemed to be some kind of a problem going on for Brett and Dani.

When they started as Channel 10 anchors, Brett was married—and began having an affair with Dani. Now they are married, and Dani just found out Brett was having an affair with a woman journalist who had interviewed him for a magazine article. I found myself having to play Dr. Phil—or sometimes even Jerry Springer—to try to keep them from fighting, on air as well as off air.

"We're getting a lot of feedback from viewers who say you two look mad at each other on air," I told them both now.

"We are mad at each other," Dani said.

"Well, do it—be mad at each other—on your own time."

"I only see her when we're on the air," Brett said.

"You're not living together anymore?"

"Not at the moment."

"But you're still working together?"

"At the moment," Dani said.

"Well, make it work for the camera when you're on the air, okay?"

Finally, we got to some real news. There was a primary election for governor coming up soon. The leading candidate was Jaime Ortiz, a former police commissioner who was leading in the polls at the moment. But a lot of things can change quickly in an election. Meanwhile, a huge fire had wiped out a series of warehouses in the Bronx, although no one was killed or seriously injured so it was mostly just spectacular video. Gas prices were up. So were rents and tax rates for housing. There were more local stories but also some celebrity news involving a new hairdo and fashion look for Rihanna. I threw that into the story mix too. People always care about celebrity news no matter how much they claim they don't.

But it was Maggie who came up with the information on the best story.

The Wendy Kyle story.

"We've got a source who says authorities have some big names they've come up with in her client cases. People—mostly women, of course—who hired her to spy on their cheating spouses. Lots of important people might have had a reason to want this woman dead."

"How soon before we can get some of those names on her client list that she was investigating?" I asked.

"It's totally confidential," Maggie said. "They're not releasing any of it."

"So how long before we can get the names?"

"I'll try to get something." Maggie sighed. "But my source didn't sound very confident he could get any specifics. He said all of this information on Kyle's clients and the people she was investigating is in the hands of the police. Anyone else here have police sources we might be able to ask about it?"

I had police sources. Well, I had *a* police source. A pretty close one too. At least we used to be close. He was once my husband. Homicide Sgt. Sam Markham, who was now my third ex-husband if you're keeping count.

We'd maintained a cordial relationship—well, mostly cordial—since we'd split up a few years ago. He was married again now and had a kid, a young son. I was happy for him, but I'm not sure how happy he is. Every once in a while—usually when he'd had too much to drink—he'd tried to hit on me again. Then he'd get mad at me when I told him to forget about it and go back to his wife.

So I never knew what kind of mood he was going to be in when I went to him seeking information like I was doing now.

I told Maggie that I'd try to reach out to Sam.

"Isn't he still mad at you about something?" she asked.

"He was the last time I saw him."

"And you figure he's cooled down enough now that he'll be willing to help you?"

"I guess we'll find out soon enough."

CHAPTER 5

AT NINE O'CLOCK the next morning, I walked into the midtown precinct where Detective Sgt. Sam Markham worked.

I was wearing a pair of oversized sunglasses along with an outfit consisting of a brown, patterned, ankle-length skirt, chocolate-colored blouse, and a leather vest with rawhide fringe. With it I had on beige cowboy boots and a wide leather belt with a gold Western-style buckle. The cowgirl look. Funky. Definitely funky. A lot more funky than you'd expect from a woman approaching fifty soon. Not that I cared about that or anything.

The midtown precinct where Sam was a homicide detective is in a big red building on the north side of West 48th Street, a few blocks north of the heart of Times Square where Wendy Kyle had died in the car explosion.

There was a cop at a desk by the front door who asked to see my press credentials before letting me in. I showed him my TV media badge from Channel 10 News. He studied it carefully, apparently looking for clues, evidence, or any red flags that I might be a terrorist. Once upon a time, anyone could just walk into a police station, but not in today's world. I don't suppose I looked like I had TNT strapped to my leg or whatever, but you never know.

After checking out my media credentials, the cop handed them back to me. He then directed me to the detective squad room on the second floor. He did not compliment me on my cowgirl outfit. He did not ask me for my autograph. Probably too much in shock and awe after meeting a real-life star TV newswoman.

Like I'd said to Maggie earlier when she'd asked me about my relationship with Sam, I never knew what kind of a mood he was going to be in when I went to him for information the way I was doing now. Sometimes he would help me, sometimes he would refuse—or even worse—be downright insulting.

Worse still was Sam's partner, a smart-ass detective named Larry Parks. Parks didn't like me at all, and he would rev up Sam to give me a hard time too, as a reporter. I definitely was not looking forward to running into Larry Parks again.

Except when I got upstairs to the squad room, I found out Sam had a new partner now.

That was the good news.

The bad news was his new partner didn't seem to like me any better than Larry Parks had.

It was a woman. Her name was Kate Gallison. She looked to be in her early thirties. She was kind of pretty, but a hard-looking pretty. Short brunette hair, muscular, with a piercing stare in her eyes. And she was dressed in the classic female detective pantsuit outfit, clearly a look to let everyone know that she was a very professional and no-nonsense woman.

"So you're the ex-wife," Gallison said after I introduced myself and said I was looking for Sam.

"I'm the ex-wife."

"How's that working out for you?"

"Excuse me?"

"Knowing you lost out on having Sam for your husband."

"Well, it doesn't keep me up at night or anything."

"He's a good man."

"Yes, he is."

"Too good for you apparently."

I really didn't want to engage in a war of insults with this woman.

"That's probably true of a lot of men in my life." I smiled. "Like I said, I'm just looking to talk to Sam. Is he around?"

"No."

"Where is he?"

"Out."

"When will he be back?"

"Whenever he's in again."

This wasn't working out well at all.

"I'll wait for Sam," I told her.

"Up to you." She shrugged.

*   *   *

About ten minutes later, Sam showed up. I asked if we could talk somewhere alone, and we went into a break area off of the main detective squad room. He got himself a coffee from one of the vending machines there, but he didn't offer me anything. Not a good sign either. I wasn't getting a very friendly reception here at all.

"I see you have a new partner," I said.

"Yes. Larry got transferred out to Brooklyn. That's Kate. What do you think of her?"

"Not exactly a people person."

"Kate give you a hard time?"

"She called me the *ex-wife*."

He laughed. "Kate's kinda defensive of me. I guess she's heard me talk about you. But hey, she's okay. Smart, tough, a real go-getter. One helluva cop. One helluva partner, believe me."

"Okay, I'll take your word for it, Sam—she's terrific. What do you know about the Wendy Kyle case?"

"Nothing."

"You won't tell me anything?"

"I can't. I'm not part of the Wendy Kyle investigation."

"You're a homicide detective, right? The bomb blast happened in your area. Wouldn't you normally be the lead detective on a case like this?"

"I thought so too. But I've been pretty much left out of this investigation. It's being handled by people at the top—way above my pay grade. All I know is they're going through all of the records they found in Wendy Kyle's office, looking for some kind of link or motive for her murder."

"I heard there was a client list. Is that what they're looking at?"

"Not so much the clients she was working for, but the people she was investigating for the clients. The word I've heard is that there could be big names involved with her in the past, maybe even some VIPs in the department down at 1 Police Plaza. And, as you know, she had a pretty checkered past in the department. I guess they want to play this one as close to the vest as they can downtown."

"As in a cover-up to avoid some kind of big police scandal?"

"Who knows?"

I figured he was telling me the truth about not being involved in the investigation. I mean if he didn't want to talk to me about the case, he would have just said that. He'd done it before on sensitive cases. But this one seemed too sensitive to even involve a veteran homicide cop like Sam Markham. That was interesting.

"Anything else?" I asked.

He hesitated. I knew that look. It meant he was trying to decide whether or not to tell me something.

One of the advantages I had in our marriage—and I still had in whatever relationship we maintained now—was I could always get Sam to agree to something I wanted in the end. No matter how much he resisted at first. He wanted to make me happy, so he would eventually give in to me. I think Sam was still kind of hung up on me. And I used that to my advantage at times like this. It didn't make me proud of myself. But all's fair in love and TV journalism.

"Sam?" I asked.

"What?"

"Anything at all you know?"

"No, nothing."

"C'mon, Sam . . ."

He sighed. "Look, you can't tell anyone where you got this information. Do I have your word on that?"

"Absolutely."

Sam knew he could trust me on this. I'd never give up one of my sources as a journalist. Especially when that source was Sam.

"Okay, even though I'm not part of the investigation, I did hear about something they found in her office. One of the items looks like the first page of some kind of diary she kept on her cases. Just the one diary page. Wendy Kyle talks in it about her life being in danger. She only mentions one name, but it's a damn interesting one. Ronald Bannister. She makes a reference to the 'Ronald Bannister case.'"

"Are we talking about *the* Ronald Bannister?"

"Yeah, the rich guy."

"Bannister's not just rich. He's very rich. Mega-rich. Like Warren Buffett, Bill Gates, Jeff Bezos, or Elon Musk rich."

"The speculation is that Bannister's wife might have hired Kyle to dig up dirt on her husband."

"Wow! There would be a lot of money at stake in a divorce like that."

"Billions of dollars."

"More than enough money to get Wendy Kyle killed to keep her quiet," I said.

CHAPTER 6

"WHAT DO WE know about Ronald Bannister?" I asked Maggie when I got back to the Channel 10 newsroom.

"He's got a lot of money."

"I know that. What else?"

"I'll have to check."

"Put together as much information on him as you can for me, Maggie."

She came back with a lot of details about Ronald Bannister. It turned out he wasn't quite in the Buffett, Gates, Bezos, Musk stratum of wealth. But he was damn rich.

"Where do you want me to start on Bannister?" she asked.

"The money."

"Okay, the conservative estimate is he's worth at least fifty billion dollars."

"Fifty billion," I repeated.

"At least fifty billion."

That didn't even seem like a real amount of money to me because it was so off-the-charts crazy.

"Where does all this money come from?"

"Everywhere. He's invested in a lot of business deals here and around the world. Oil. Real estate. Pharmaceuticals. Leveraging companies and selling them off piecemeal. Internet and social media sites. You name it, Ronald Bannister probably makes tons and tons of dollars off of it.

"Besides this, he's very involved in politics too. Donates big contributions to both parties on the national, state, and even local levels. He's got big-time connections everywhere, Clare. This guy has a lot of important and powerful and influential friends on his side to help him whenever he needs it.

"He's also a big presence on the social scene. Kind of a major celebrity around town. Shows up at parties, exhibits, openings, and all sorts of high-profile events. Someone I talked to compared him to Donald Trump back in the '80s when Trump was first making big real estate money and big headlines. Says Bannister is the same kind of guy now. He's got a really big ego too."

"I guess it's easy to have a big ego when you're worth fifty billion dollars," I said. "Married?"

"Yes, he's married."

"How long?"

"Forever. He married his wife twenty-nine years ago when he was starting out in business. No kids. But he's still with her. Eleanor Bannister. She was with him when he had nothing, and now he's one of the richest men in the world."

"Interesting. Which means there was probably no prenup between them when they got married."

"Who knows?" Maggie shrugged. "But it makes sense neither of them would have been thinking about a prenup back then when they were so young and before there was much money involved."

"Except now," I said, "if she catches him cheating on her, she could probably use that to get a big divorce settlement and walk away with more of his billions. So she hires someone like Wendy

Kyle to spy on him, Kyle finds out evidence of his infidelity, and then to keep her quiet . . ."

"That part is all speculation," Maggie pointed out.

"We need to find out more about Ronald Bannister and his possible involvement with Wendy Kyle," I said.

"What are you going to do next, Clare?"

"Talk to Susan Endicott."

*   *   *

I told Susan Endicott about it all. The diary page police had found in Wendy Kyle's office. The name of Ronald Bannister that was mentioned it. Kyle's premonition—or whatever it was—that she might be murdered. And everything Maggie and I had found out about Bannister so far. I wished I could have talked about this with Jack Faron, my old boss—instead of Endicott. But he was gone, and all I had left was her. We sometimes have to play the cards that we've been dealt in a hand.

For once, Endicott seemed happy with me.

"That's great stuff!" she said. "And all exclusive! We'll break it on the news tonight. The diary. The link to Ronald Bannister. All of it."

"I want to hold off on publicly naming Bannister," I said.

"Why?"

"Because we don't really know anything about how he's involved in this yet. We could just run the exclusive about her keeping a diary without mentioning Bannister specifically. That's enough— Wendy Kyle's secret diary that's been discovered—to make big news. Meanwhile, I'll keep trying to uncover more about Bannister and what was going on with him and Wendy Kyle.

Presumably, she was investigating him for infidelity, but we don't know that for sure. That's what I need to find out."

"We could confront him with the diary entry and ask him about his name being there," Endicott said.

"He almost certainly won't respond to us. And, even if he does, it most likely would be nothing more than a perfunctory 'no comment.' But if we can confirm that he's cheating on his wife and Wendy Kyle found out about it before she was murdered, well . . . that's a blockbuster story."

"How do you figure to do that?"

"Old-fashioned journalism techniques."

"Meaning?"

"A stakeout."

"You're going to stake out Ronald Bannister and hope to catch him in the act with another woman?"

"That's the goal."

"You really think you can pull that off with a stakeout of Bannister?'

"That's the beauty of the stakeout," I said. "You never know what you're going to find out until you try it."

CHAPTER 7

IF RONALD BANNISTER was worried that anyone would find out he might be cheating on his wife, he sure didn't act like it.

I waited outside Bannister's Manhattan office building at 53rd and Madison with a picture of the guy, saw him come out an hour or so later, and then followed him as he walked to a hotel called the Stratton a few blocks away.

Ronald Bannister was a good enough looking guy for his age, which was early fifties, but I had a feeling right off he was the kind of guy who thought he was even better looking than he was. He had thick brown hair, graying a bit at the temples and on the sides; no excess body weight, so it looked to me as if he worked out regularly; he was wearing a suit and tie, but he'd loosened the tie and left the collar open once he hit the street; and he walked with a purposeful stride through the crowds of people on Madison Avenue that almost shouted to the world: "I'm Ronald Bannister, and you're not!" I guess you could act like that when you were worth $50 billion.

Bannister went straight to the hotel bar, sat down, and ordered a drink. A few minutes later, an attractive red-haired woman came into the bar, looked around until she spotted Bannister, and then sat down next to him.

She leaned over and kissed him.

He kissed her back.

Then they both kissed each other for a very long time.

Wow! This must have been an easy gig for Wendy Kyle if she was trying to catch Bannister with another woman. I mean I'd accomplished that in barely an hour, including the time I spent waiting for him to emerge from his office.

I took out my cell phone—pretending I was using it to text someone—and took several pictures of Bannister and the red-headed woman in these passionate embraces. Then I switched to video and captured them that way for a while. Neither of them seemed to notice what I was doing, presumably because of my phony texting ploy. Furtive. Stealthy. Clare Carlson, Master of Deception.

It was a circular bar. I sat across from Bannister and the woman at the Stratton bar, nursing a drink. Close enough to see what was happening, but far enough away to avoid drawing Bannister's attention. Even though we'd never met, he or the woman might recognize me from TV and get suspicious. But that never happened. Neither of them was paying much attention to anyone else in the room. They were still canoodling. I sipped on my drink and kept watching them as surreptitiously as I could.

Still, no matter how careful and low-key I was, a lone woman sitting in a bar like me always attracted some notice.

"Hi," a guy said, slipping quietly into the chair next to me.

"Bye," I said."

"Excuse me?"

"Just go away and leave me alone, okay? This bar is pretty empty now. At least half the seats are free. Go sit in one of them, not next to me. I'm not interested in talking with you. I'm busy."

"Busy working."

That stopped me.

How did he know I was working?

"Yes, I'm working," I said.

"Well, you can't work your business here. Just put down your drink, get up from the bar, and walk out of here quietly."

I turned and looked at him now. He was big, maybe 6 foot 5, and muscular. Dressed in a dark blue suit. He was watching me carefully. Not ogling or anything. Just watching. All very business-like. He leaned close, put his hand on my arm, and squeezed. It was a very tight grip. Then he said in a low voice: "Get up from the bar and walk out quietly. Take it back to the street to sell, honey. No hookers allowed."

"Wait a minute—you think that's what I'm doing here?"

That's actually happened to me a few times before while I was waiting for people or staking them out alone in bars.

It didn't make it easier to stomach.

"So—even in this enlightened day and age of #metoo and all the rest of the advances we women have accomplished in recent times—I can't sit down in a bar for a drink without being mistaken for a sex worker?"

"You're not a hooker?"

"No, I'm not."

"But you said you were working..."

"I know you might find this hard to believe, but women do a lot of different types of work. Meaningful work. Welcome to the 21st Century."

He shook his head in exasperation.

"Who the hell are you then?"

I took out my business card and handed it to him.

"A damned TV reporter," he muttered.

"What gave me up? Was it the Channel 10 logo? Or the word 'journalist?'"

"What do you want here?"

"I'm working on a story."

"Here at this hotel?"

"Yes."

"What kind of story?"

"I can't tell you that."

"Why not?"

"It's confidential. Top secret. If I told you, I'd have to kill you."

He sighed.

"Well, you better not bother, harass, or interfere with the activities of any of our guests at the hotel."

"Heaven forbid, no," I said.

"Do I have your word on that?"

"Cross my heart and hope to die."

The guy looked down at my card again for a second, then slipped it into the pocket of his jacket. He got up from his seat at the bar.

"Have a nice evening," he said, "and stay out of trouble."

"Trouble is my business," I said, invoking the classic Philip Marlowe line from Raymond Chandler.

He shook his head and walked away.

I looked back across the bar at Bannister and the redheaded woman he was with. They were still kissing and hugging, apparently oblivious to the little drama that had just played out between me and the hotel security guard. I sipped on my drink some more and kept watching them.

After another ten minutes or so of nibbling on each other's faces and a few other body parts, they both stood up and left the bar. I did too. I followed them through the hotel lobby to a bank of elevators that took you up to the rooms in the hotel.

They got on one of the elevators. I watched the elevator lights in the lobby as it went up. The elevator stopped on the 15th floor. I took another elevator to the 15th floor and got off just in time to see them go into a room at the end of the hall. There wasn't much more I could do there. So I went back to the hotel lobby, sat down in a chair where I could monitor all of the elevators—and decided to wait for Ronald Bannister and his lady friend to come down. Even if it took all night.

But it didn't take much time at all. Barely an hour after they'd gone up in the elevator, Bannister and the redhead came down together, walked through the lobby right past me, and headed for the street.

Given the time it must have taken them to get settled into the room, get undressed, and indulge in whatever foreplay might have been involved, the actual lovemaking didn't take a very long time.

Maybe when you had as much money as Ronald Bannister, you didn't have to worry about wasting much time with the foreplay— it was just "wham, bam, thank you, ma'am" and then on to making your next big multimillion-dollar deal.

I followed them out onto the street. As I did so, I looked around to see if the hotel security guard was still around. But there was no sign of him anywhere.

Outside, Bannister put the woman into a waiting cab. They didn't kiss this time. The passion between them seemed to have disappeared after the trip to the hotel room. The cab pulled away into traffic, and Bannister began walking back toward his office.

I had to make a quick decision.

Follow him or follow the woman.

I knew where Bannister was and could find him again.

I knew nothing about the woman.

So I hailed a cab, pointed to the cab the woman was in that was pulling out into midtown traffic, and said to the driver: "Follow that car."

"You're kidding, right?" my driver said.

"I've always wanted to say that," I told him.

CHAPTER 8

THE TAXI CARRYING the woman from the hotel made its way to Fifth Avenue, headed south on Fifth, then west on 34th, and eventually stopped in front of a building on West 31st Street.

The woman got out of the taxi and walked inside the building.

I got out of the cab and waited a few minutes to see if the woman came back out. She didn't. I walked to the entrance of the lobby. It turned out to be a large office building with a lobby that included a security guard. There was a long list of companies and offices on a wall. I took a quick look through the names, hoping something might jump out at me as being significant. It was after 5:00 p.m., so most of them would be closed. Except, it seemed that the office the woman was headed for was still in operation at this time.

"Can I help you with something?" the security guard said. It was a woman. A heavyset woman who looked bored with her job and had no interest in talking to anyone, and that included me.

I looked back quickly at the names on the list, and I saw an insurance company called Hitchcock Life. Along with an office number for the president, Joseph Hitchcock.

"I'm here to see Mr. Hitchcock," I said. "At Hitchcock Life Insurance."

"They're not open this late."

"Damn, I was hoping to talk to him about a life insurance policy. He asked me to stop by. But I got held up until now."

"They're open from nine to five, Monday through Friday," the guard said in a voice that sounded as bored as she looked.

"Any possibility I could go up and knock on his door? He told me sometimes he works late. That's why I thought I might catch him still in his office at this hour."

"Nine to five, Monday through Friday," she repeated in the same monotone.

"Right. Nine to five. Maybe I'll come back tomorrow then."

"That sounds like a good idea," the guard said, with a sigh of exasperation that made it clear she felt this conversation had run its course.

I walked back outside and waited.

The woman I had followed here from the hotel had to come out sooner or later, I told myself. Sure enough, eventually she emerged from the building. She hailed another cab. So did I—and kept following her. This cab took her downtown, all the way into Little Italy, until it stopped in front of a six-story building on Mulberry Street. The woman got out of the cab and went into the building.

The building housed a bar and restaurant on the first floor, then what appeared to be several apartments on the floors above. She hadn't gone into the restaurant or bar, so it seemed like she was in one of the apartments.

Sure enough, a light went on in a window on the third floor. I could see a figure moving around inside.

I opened the front door and saw a list of names and apartment numbers on the wall. It said there were two apartments on the third floor. The tenants were Joseph Daniels and Jessica Geiger. I wrote both names down in a notebook I carried with me. Jessica

Geiger, of course, was the more likely of the names—but maybe the woman was staying in the Daniels guy's apartment. I sat in front of the building until the light on the third floor went out— and I was reasonably certain the woman was in for the night.

I went back to the Stratton Hotel after that, the place where she and Bannister had been having drinks, playing kissy-face at the bar, and then presumably having sex in one of the rooms afterward.

When I got there, I took the elevator to the 15th floor again. I walked to the room at the end of the hall—the one where Bannister and the woman had gone into earlier. The door was open. Either because Bannister hadn't bothered to lock it when he and the woman departed in a hurry earlier, or because a maid was working on cleaning it. If she caught me, I might wind up having another unpleasant encounter with my large security friend. But I took a chance, pushed the door open, and went in.

The room looked like it was one of the best in the hotel. It was a suite actually. With a living room, two bedrooms, and a dining area. There was a big window in the living room with a view overlooking the streets of midtown Manhattan. I stood for a second at the window, looking down at the people below—wondering if Ronald Bannister was one of them, or if not, where he was now. Maybe I should have followed him instead of the woman.

I turned back to the hotel room. In the living room, a bottle of champagne sat in a basket along with two glasses. The glasses were both still half full, and there was champagne left in the bottle too. Obviously, the maid had not done any cleaning yet. She might be back any second, but I kept looking around.

In one of the bedrooms, the bed was unmade and the sheets rumpled. Bannister and the woman had presumably had sex in this bed. But there was no sign of real disarray. Whatever happened between them must have happened very quickly. It was the same in the bathroom. Someone had used it, but it was almost as pristine clean as the housekeeping crew would have left it earlier in the day for the next guest.

Still, Bannister and the woman had been here.

That was all that really mattered at this point.

I took out my phone and took pictures of the crumpled bed, the open champagne bottle, and the rest of it to go along with the pictures I had of them kissing.

Then I let myself out and went back down to the hotel lobby— and eventually to the hotel bar.

Ronald Bannister wasn't there again.

Or the woman.

Not even any sign of my new pal the beefy security guard.

It seemed like everyone was done doing whatever they were doing for the night.

So I called it a night too, and I went home.

CHAPTER 9

I DECIDED TO stop off at a diner near the Channel 10 News offices for coffee on my way to work the next morning. Since I was there, I figured I might as well go for a couple of eggs over easy too. I threw in some bacon on the side. And why not have hashed brown potatoes too? That ought to complete all my basic food groups for the day.

As I ate, I took out my iPad and scrolled through all the stories about the Wendy Kyle murder from NYC newspapers, TV stations, and other internet/media outlets that I could find. No one had anything we didn't have at Channel 10. And I was still ahead of everyone else with my exclusive on the search for Wendy Kyle's secret diary. Plus, all the rest of the media had to quote me and Channel 10 about the contents of that first page that was found. Loved it!

By the time I left the diner and headed for the office, I was feeling great. I was well-fed, well-read, and ready to take on whatever was ahead of me for the day, even Susan Endicott.

Or so I thought.

But, as I approached the Channel 10 building, I noticed something that seemed odd. A man was sitting in a dark blue Lincoln in front of the building entrance and watching whoever went in or came out.

I couldn't see his face. Of course, it might mean nothing. He could be waiting to meet someone else who worked there. But I had done enough stakeouts as a reporter—trailed enough people, including the woman with Bannister the previous night—to pick up pretty quickly on someone who might be watching for me.

Okay, I'll play along, I thought.

Only they were going to play this game by my rules.

First, I got closer and looked at the license plate of the Lincoln. I wrote down the license number.

Then I began walking toward the front door of the Channel 10 building. Acting as if I had no idea of the man in the car watching. Just before I got to the front door of the building, I made a big show of looking in my handbag as if I'd forgotten something. It was a pretty good acting job, if I do say so myself. Then I turned around and began walking back the way I had come, toward a nearby subway station.

Sure enough, I spotted the Lincoln moving too. He was definitely looking for me. But who was he? And why was he so interested in me? Well, it was time to find out some more information about my new admirer, whoever he was.

I took out my cell phone and dialed police emergency at 911. When the operator answered, I screamed into the phone: "Someone just stole my car! Please help me! I've been carjacked!"

"Stay calm, ma'am," the operator said. "Are you hurt?"

"No, but they have my car."

"Can you give me your location?"

I gave her the location.

"How about a description of your car?"

I gave her as detailed a description as I could of the dark blue Lincoln.

"And a license plate number."

"It's FX-389," I said, reading from the license plate number I'd written down in my notebook. "Please get my car back! Please..."

I hung up the phone then and pretended to be window-shopping at a women's clothing store. The dark blue Lincoln was still behind me. I could see the car's reflection in the window of the store. I waited for the police to arrive.

Sure enough, a few minutes later, I heard a siren and saw flashing red lights on the street behind me. Police officers quickly pulled up and surrounded the Lincoln. They ordered the driver out of the car and had him lined up against the hood for a while. Finally, they let him reach into his pocket, take out a wallet, and hand over a piece of paper to the cops. Presumably the car's registration. At that point, I assumed I didn't have much longer for this little drama to play out, so I decided to make the most of the moment with the guy while I could.

I walked over as close as I could—the area was packed with other people on the street trying to see what was going on—and yelled out to the man still being interrogated by police: "Hey, buddy!"

When he turned and looked in my direction, I held my hand up and gave him the middle finger salute.

The man looked at me with surprise on his face.

But I was surprised too.

Because I recognized him now.

It was the security guy I'd run into at the Stratton Hotel while staking out Ronald Bannister and his girlfriend the night before.

Why was he still interested in me??

Did I make that big an impression on this guy?

Or was there something else going on here?

And how did he track me down here—and why?

Well, the how was easy. I'd given him my business card at the bar the night before. The card that said I worked for Channel 10 News. So that's why he showed up outside my building. No mystery on that front.

But the "why" was tougher.

All the security guard knew about me was that I was working on a story at the hotel. Nothing more. No idea what the story was.

Of course, he could have figured out it was about Ronald Bannister afterward—since Bannister was the most recognizable person in the bar while I was there.

But, even if he did, so what?

What would make a hotel security guard so interested in me that he came looking for me at my office the next day?

Unless he wasn't a hotel security guard.

But then what was he?

CHAPTER 10

When I finally got upstairs to my office at Channel 10, I decided to take stock of everything I knew so far about this story. I figured it shouldn't take me too long since I didn't know very much. But it sometimes helps me on a complex and confusing story to look over all the main parts I want to cover.

I shut my door, took out a yellow legal pad, and began to write down the people and things that I wanted to find out more about and that had been connected with Wendy Kyle. Even if I wasn't exactly sure how they all fit into the story.

By the time I was finished, my list looked like this:

Ronald Bannister

Ronald Bannister's wife

The woman he was with at the hotel—whose name might or might not be Jessica Geiger

Wendy Kyle's two ex-husbands

Any recent boyfriends

The NYPD commanding officer Kyle attacked in the act of violence that got her fired from the force

Any of her clients that I could find out from the list authorities had discovered in Kyle's office

Plus, the security guard at the hotel who seemed so interested in me, even though I wasn't sure if that had anything to do with this story or not

And last, but certainly not least, there was Wendy Kyle's diary. Why was she keeping a diary before she was killed? What was in the diary? And where was it now? I knew the police hadn't been able to find any more of it except for that first page in Kyle's office. But that didn't mean I couldn't keep looking.

I took out my iPhone and scrolled through all the pictures and video I'd taken the night before of Bannister with the girl at the hotel. Then I transferred them to my computer.

The images and video were all pretty good stuff, no question about it.

They showed Bannister greeting the woman when she arrived at the bar, kissing and canoodling with her while they drank and then going off arm and arm together toward the elevator that took them upstairs to a hotel room. There was also a picture of the two of them coming back down through the lobby later and him putting her in a cab. Plus, there were the ones I'd taken of the unmade bed, the champagne glasses, and the rest inside the hotel room where they'd gone.

I hadn't told anyone—particularly Susan Endicott—that I had this yet.

Because I knew she'd want me to get it on the air right away.

And I had a couple of problems with that.

First, if Bannister's sexcapades with this woman were unrelated to Wendy Kyle's murder, then it would be just a cheap ploy by us to get ratings—not real journalism.

Second, if I went public with this, I wasn't going to be able to get to either Bannister or his wife. I wanted to interview both of them, and I was going to try. But they weren't going to talk with me if I embarrassed them on TV like this. As long as they didn't know I knew what I knew about Bannister, I might have a chance for an interview with one of them—or even both.

On the other hand, it would be a big ratings bonanza for Channel 10 News if we used these pictures and video.

Decisions, decisions.

Ratings vs. responsible journalism.

It was quite a conundrum.

I looked back at the list I'd made on my legal pad again. It was quite a daunting list of things to do on the Wendy Kyle story. I could ask some of the reporters at Channel 10 to help me chase after some of this, of course.

But I needed to get someone in authority—someone in law enforcement—on my side too.

Sam Markham, my ex-husband, didn't seem to be directly involved in the investigation even though he was a homicide cop. So I decided to reach out to another of my former love interests.

Scott Manning.

Manning was the ex-cop and now FBI agent I'd been talking with Janet about. We'd had an off-and-on-again affair a few years ago. He eventually went back to his wife. But we'd rekindled the sexual chemistry between us by going to bed together a few times since then, although not recently. Maybe he still had fond memories of me. Maybe he and his wife had broken up. Maybe he was daydreaming right now about sweeping me off my feet with wine, flowers, and sex so that we could live happily ever after together.

I found his number in my phone contact list and punched it in.

"Did J. Edgar Hoover really like to wear dresses when he was FBI director?" I said when he came on the line.

"Who is this?"

"He was a short, fat man—he must have had a lot of trouble finding an ensemble in his size."

"My God, Clare Carlson!"

"The one and only."

"What's going on?"

"I have a question to ask."

"About?"

"The Wendy Kyle murder."

"That's a local police matter."

"But it could involve you, right? I mean, it was a bomb. That could be an act of terrorism. It would not be totally inappropriate for you in your duties as an FBI agent to have some discussions about the progress of the case with the NYPD."

"Then give whatever I find out to you?"

"That would be the plan, yes."

"Why are you so interested in evidence about Wendy Kyle?"

"I have an inexhaustible thirst for knowledge."

He laughed.

That was nice.

Always a good sign.

"Actually, what I'm trying to get is a list of Kyle's clients," I said. "Apparently the police found that list in her office. If I have her clients, I could figure out who she was investigating for them. They all might have a motive for killing her to keep her quiet. Ergo, one

of them could be the best suspect. Could you check out that list—
and maybe find out some of the names on that list—for me?"

Manning didn't say yes, and he didn't say no. But we talked a
while more, and I had a feeling he'd at least make some effort to
get what I wanted.

"How's everything with your kids?" I asked him before I
hung up.

"Good."

"And your wife, how is she?"

"Good."

"Uh, in other words, you're still with her?"

"I'll let you know if I find out anything about Wendy Kyle's
client list."

I took that as a yes on him still being with his wife.

CHAPTER 11

I NEEDED A place to start. A story journey of one thousand miles begins with a single step. Or something like that. Looking back at the list of people I wanted to talk to about Wendy Kyle, I decided I'd try first her former commanding officer first—the one she'd gotten for attacking. I figured he might be the most likely to dish dirt on her to me. Besides that, he was the only person on my list that I knew exactly where to find.

His name was Warren Magnuson, and he was a twenty-five-year veteran of the force. Magnuson wasn't just a precinct commander anymore though; his title now was Chief of Department, which made him one of a handful of top officers right below the police commissioner.

He had a big office at police headquarters, with a picture window behind him looking out over downtown Manhattan. There were lots of awards on his walls and plaques on his desk, some for his time as a precinct commander and others for his work now at 1 Police Plaza. Magnuson had sure done very well for himself after his encounter with Wendy Kyle.

She, on the other hand, had lost her job afterward. Not surprising, I suppose—but still interesting.

"Tell me about Wendy Kyle," I said to Magnuson.

"Why ask me?"

"I'm trying to put together a profile picture of her time on the force for our coverage of her murder."

"She was only in my precinct for a few months. I didn't have that much time working with her."

"Enough time for her to put you in the hospital."

Magnuson scowled at me. He was a short, squat man with balding hair. Had he really tried to force himself on her sexually—so forcefully that she had to fight back violently to get away from him, like she claimed? It was her word against him at the time, and the police brass believed him.

"That's history," Magnuson said to me now.

"But still relevant to my story."

"Why?"

"Because it cost Kyle her job and forced her to become a private investigator for divorce cases, and very likely that's what led to her being killed. So let's talk about what happened between the two of you that ended her police career."

"I don't want to talk about it."

"Look, all this about her and you is going to come out, one way or another. But you can control the messaging on this story. I'm sure the altercation with Wendy Kyle was very traumatic for you. And I'm sure you took a lot of heat for it—both officially and around the department from people who laughed about you getting beat up and put in the hospital by a young woman. We can spin this by having you take the high road. Talking about her death being a tragedy and letting bygones be bygones or whatever else you want to say. I'll bring some video people in here; we'll shoot you saying that and put it on the air as part of our story. Okay?"

Magnuson nodded.

"But before we go on camera, I want to ask you—between you and me, off the record—what really happened between you two?"

"She attacked me, that's what happened."

"Why did she attack you?"

"You'd have to ask her the reason why she did what she did."

"Well, she's dead. She can't tell me."

"What do you want me to say?"

"Did you attempt to sexually attack her the way she claimed you did?"

"No, of course not!"

"So, she was lying?"

"Yes, she was lying. I would never do something like that."

"Why do you think she would lie and make up a story like that about what happened between you two?"

"Because she was a crazy broad. A goddamned crazy broad. She seemed pissed off at people all the time. When she was on the force, and—from what I understand—after she became a private investigator too. Well, it seems like she finally got someone else so pissed off at her that they killed her."

"Do you have any idea or suspicion of who that might have been?"

"That investigation is ongoing."

"I understand the department has obtained a list of her clients—and people she was investigating for them."

"Yes, that's part of the investigation."

"I've been trying to obtain that list. Can you help me?"

"You'd have to get that information from someone else."

"Such as?"

"Public Affairs. They deal with you media people."

"They told me her client list was confidential information."

"Okay, then."

"Why do you think it's confidential?"

"So people like you can't see it." He smiled.

"And maybe because they're trying to cover up the name or names of some important or sensitive people who are on that list from Wendy Kyle's office."

"I imagine the list of people who might have wanted to see Wendy Kyle dead would be quite a long one. Clients, ex-clients, people she victimized with that sleazy private investigator operation of hers." He smiled. "That last quote is off the record, of course."

I didn't like Magnuson. I hadn't liked him since I walked into his office. And especially after he made the crack about Wendy Kyle being a "crazy broad." I didn't want to get into the semantics of what was *appropriate* and *inappropriate* when referring to a female in these enlightened times. But it made me believe Wendy Kyle's version of the events even more. When it came down to deciding between her word versus his, I was on Team Wendy all the way.

But I wanted to get him on air. So I kept my promise and let him deliver a nice, prepared spiel about her when we started shooting video of the interview.

"This is shocking news," he told the camera. "Wendy Kyle was a member of the New York City police force for five years, and she achieved much success as a police officer. Unfortunately, she had a problem dealing with NYPD policies and authority, which cut short her career as an officer. But once a member of the NYPD, always a member in our memories and in our hearts. We mourn her tragic passing and will work diligently until we find the person or persons who caused her death."

It was all BS, of course. But that's the way a lot of television news is. We're not the *New York Times* with "all the news fit to print." We air the news the way we want our audience to get it, even if it's not the whole, complete truth. This would make a good sound bite as part of our package on Wendy Kyle for the 6:00 and 11:00 p.m. newscasts.

That was my job, and I did it.

Even if I didn't like that job sometimes.

CHAPTER 12

ALTHOUGH I COULDN'T convince Magnuson or anyone else to get me Wendy Kyle's client list, I did find someone at police headquarters who was willing to show me Kyle's NYPD personnel file. I wasn't sure exactly what I was hoping to find in it. But I wanted to know more about this woman.

The official file on her read almost like two different documents, even though it was only one. There was heroic police officer Wendy Kyle who won all sorts of awards and acclaim, and then the pain-in-the-ass Wendy who got herself fired from the force.

She certainly was a paradox. A talented woman who couldn't keep her mouth shut and walk away from trouble when she should. I suppose I identified with her a bit because I knew I had some of those same qualities, good and bad.

Oh, I'd never attacked my boss the way she did. I thought about doing something like that a few times. Except, I'd always realized before it was too late there was a line I couldn't cross when it came to this kind of thing. Wendy Kyle apparently had never learned that lesson.

I started by reading the positive stuff about her.

Wendy Kyle sure was a rising star in the beginning, according to the information in the file and that I'd accumulated elsewhere. Top of her graduating class at the police academy. Lots of praise for her police work from those early days when she was working on the streets as a young cop.

Maybe the most dramatic incident came when she saved a fellow officer's life. Her partner had been wounded by a gunman holed up in an apartment building. The two of them were getting out of their squad car at the location when her partner was hit with a shot in the chest and lay on the ground in front of the building.

Kyle called in quickly for medical help and backup. Then she got back in the squad car and maneuvered it into a position to protect her fallen partner and keep him out of the line of more gunfire. She soon got him to safety. Then she volunteered to be part of the team that stormed the building and captured the shooter.

There were more heroic moments like that.

During a bank robbery in Manhattan, with the armed robber holding a half dozen bank employees and customers hostage inside, Wendy Kyle managed to slip inside from a rear door and get behind the gunman. She hid herself behind a counter until she was sure the time was right—e.g., the hostages weren't in imminent danger—and then came up from behind and smashed the gun out of his hand. She cuffed him, read him his rights, and had the situation completely under control before the rest of the police got inside. All six of the hostages cheered for her when it was over, according to witnesses.

Another time she dove into the East River to rescue a ten-year-old boy who had fallen into the water while trying to fish from the edge of the East River Drive highway. Passing motorists called 911, and Wendy Kyle was the first member of law enforcement on the scene. She dove into the water and pulled the struggling boy to shore. She then gave him artificial respiration until the first ambulance arrived. The boy's parents praised her and the NYPD for saving their son's life.

"Everyone said she was tough with criminals, but kind and compassionate in dealing with victims," said one NYPD job evaluation of her performance on the force at this time. "She was especially compassionate with women victims of crimes. She showed an extraordinary amount of concern for women who had been violated in some way, usually sexually."

Interesting.

Which is probably why she went on to do the kind of work she did as a private investigator.

Trying to right wrongs that had been done to women by men.

The first negative thing in her NYPD record involved the death of a woman at a midtown apartment building.

The woman had been found dead in her apartment with a liquor bottle and barbiturate pills next to her. Wendy Kyle and her partner were the first officers to get the 911 call and show up at the scene. When detectives arrived, she refused to leave—even though it was now their job to carry out the rest of the investigation into the case, not hers. According to police records, when the detectives began treating it as a suicide, she began to argue with them that it was a murder. At some point, she got physical—pushing one of them and taking a swing with her fist at another.

She was eventually subdued by other cops and removed from the scene. Afterward, there was an official police investigation into her actions: she was then suspended and a personal reprimand was put in her file.

After that, she seemed to be increasingly at war with the police department that she'd once been so dedicated to serving, making numerous complaints of police corruption and malfeasance, sexual harassment against her, and all sorts of other allegations of wrongdoing. Her clashes with other cops—particularly superior officers in the department—resulted in more suspensions and reprimands.

There were also allegations of excessive force and police brutality against suspects she arrested—specifically against men.

She smashed one guy's head on the roof of a squad car so badly that he needed twenty-five stitches after arresting him for exposing himself to a woman on the street. Another time a rape suspect claimed she used her nightstick to beat a confession out of him. And a video of her going off in a tirade of abuse on someone she arrested for grabbing a woman's buttocks went viral on the internet. A lot of people loved it, but not the police brass. That turned out to be just the latest of black marks against her in the file, culminating later with her infamous encounter with Magnuson.

Along the way, she'd also made lots of enemies in the department by complaining—and filling formal charges—about her allegations of corruption and sexual discrimination in the NYPD.

Much of the sexual discrimination stuff was common in the department for a long time in its treatment of women officers.

She talked about derogatory remarks of how she should go back to the kitchen and not try to do a man's work. About finding tampons and sex toys and the like that had been left for her at her locker. And she said that numerous men—Magnuson and others—had exhibited inappropriate sexual behavior and actions with her on multiple occasions.

But she also made serious allegations about police corruption that she said she'd brought to police officials—but claimed no one had ever acted on them. There were no specifics about what the charges were or which police officials were involved in the NYPD file. I didn't figure there would be. Someone would have edited those names out.

Along with the personnel file, there was a separate biographical file on Wendy Kyle. I wondered if this had been added before or after her dismissal from the force.

She was thirty-two years old—born on April 20, 1992, in Indianapolis. Her parents were George and Betty Kyle. He was a schoolteacher and she worked as a nurse at a local hospital. Wendy was their only child. By all accounts, the Kyles seemed to be a happy, All-American family.

Until tragedy struck when Wendy was twelve years old.

George and Betty Kyle were driving home when a drunk driver lost control of his car, crashed through a median barrier, and collided head-on with their car. They were killed instantly, leaving little Wendy without any family.

For twelve-year-old Wendy, the lack of any other family—or at least any family willing to take her in after the loss of her parents—meant foster care. And, for the next few years, she lived in different foster homes. Each one seemed to be worse than the others, and she was always unhappy.

Her grades suffered, she was constantly in trouble at school, and she was suspended from classes several times as a young teen. For school misconduct—but also for underage drinking and taking drugs and a bunch of other violations. Only her age saved her from being arrested for some of it. There was even a period when she was living on the street in Indianapolis.

But then her life dramatically changed once again. This time for the better.

A police officer who encountered her one night on the street took pity on her after he learned about everything she'd been through since her parents died. He decided to try and help her.

He and his wife had lost their own daughter a few years earlier to leukemia, and they were childless now. They agreed to be foster parents to the troubled teenaged girl.

The transformation was amazing. Living in a loving, stable home again, Wendy responded by staying out of trouble for the rest of her teen years and graduating high school with top honors. Moreover, she embraced her new family wholeheartedly, allowing them to take the place of the family she had lost.

The fact that her new father was a policeman was particularly important to her. She began to tell people that she wanted to be a police officer too, just like him. She wound up studying criminal justice at Ohio State and then later she moved to New York City to sign up with the NYPD.

It was a real uplifting success story.

At least until it all went bad for her in the NYPD.

I was very interested in talking to the adoptive parents. Their names were Tom and Rita Coletti. Even if only one of them was still alive, it would be a terrific interview to go with all the rest of our Wendy Kyle coverage.

But I discovered they were both dead. Tom Coletti of a heart attack in 2013; his wife, Rita, from ovarian cancer in 2017. Damn. That's what happens in stories like this when you try to reach out to people from the past to get them to talk. They die. They disappear. And they are of no help whatsoever.

CHAPTER 13

THE NO. 4 TRAIN taking me back uptown after my visit to Police Headquarters was packed. The only place I could find to sit was wedged in between a teenaged girl singing along with a Justin Bieber song she was listening to on her iPhone and a middle-aged man reading a Jehovah's Witness pamphlet. Listening to Justin Bieber or a diatribe from a Jehovah's Witness follower—I tried to imagine which one would be the worst torture.

As we began moving, I tried to ignore them both and concentrate on Wendy Kyle. Did she really make up the story about Magnuson trying to sexually assault her? It hardly seemed likely to me. Still, her records showed she had had a number of run-ins with the people she worked for like Magnuson.

There were all those reprimands and suspensions that she racked up before him. Maybe she had been out to get Magnuson as some sort of payback, and it backfired on her. People do things for a lot of strange reasons. But she just didn't seem the type of person to do something like that. It didn't fit what I knew about her. She was more in your face and confrontational when she was mad at someone. That's how she handled things. Not making up a phony story or accusation about them.

After a five-minute ride, we pulled into the Union Square sub-way station and the guy with Jehovah's Witness reading material got off. His seat was filled by a guy listening to rap music. He was wearing headphones, but the sound was turned up so high I could still hear the beat of the music. It went nice with Justin Bieber coming from the girl on the other side. Sort of a stereo effect to help me with my thinking.

Anyway, I was still operating on the premise that Wendy Kyle's murder was connected to her private investigation work spying on cheating husbands, not to her police career beforehand.

I'd gone through her police record because it was available and the easiest and most direct source of information to check out.

But that all happened a while ago—several years earlier—and she was involved in so many more sensational, controversial, and potentially dangerous jobs with her Heartbreaker Investigations business.

There were a lot of potential suspects there, men who didn't want their sexual secrets exposed.

I still wanted to see Wendy Kyle's client list.

But I already had a prime target to go after in Ronald Bannister. She specifically mentioned him in the diary entry page found in her office as being relevant to whatever might happen to her. So was Wendy Kyle's murder somehow connected to an investigation of Ronald Bannister's sex life? Was it possible that's what got her killed? Maybe. But, even if she was investigating Bannister's extra-curricular sexual activities, was that important enough for him to have her killed?

I mean, he had shown no effort to hide whatever he was doing with the redheaded woman in the hotel when I saw that. And he and his wife had been married so long, she was very likely going to get a huge cash payout in any divorce settlement, whether or not he was playing around on the side.

Then what was the motive? Okay, maybe Wendy Kyle had uncovered some other piece of scandal or incriminating information about Bannister in her investigation. But what could that be? I rolled that around in my mind for a while, but I got nowhere.

So where should I go and what should I do next? Well, I'd gone to see Magnuson because I figured he was the one person on my list of people to talk to that I knew how to find. Except that wasn't totally true. I knew how to find someone else on that list too. The security guard at the hotel. The one who'd come looking for me and followed me the next day. How did he fit into all this? I had absolutely no idea. Maybe I should go ask him.

We were pulling into Grand Central Station at 42nd Street now. I got off the train and said goodbye to Justin Bieber and the rap music. Then I started walking back to the Stratton Hotel where I had seen Bannister and the woman at the bar. Yep, maybe my pal the security guard there could fill in some of the blanks.

It was still early in the day, and the hotel bar was pretty empty. I didn't recognize the bartender as the one I'd seen the other night. I sat down, waited for him to come over, and then asked him about the security guard I'd met there.

"Are you ordering something?" he asked when I was finished.

"I'm looking for information."

"I don't get paid to give out information. I get paid to serve drinks."

"Do you mean I have to order a drink to sit here and talk with you?"

"This is a bar, lady. That's the usual arrangement."

"Alright. Get me a . . . a . . . seltzer water."

"Gee, big spender, huh?"

"I'm working."

"So am I," he said, looking around at the practically bare bar around us. "Barely."

"Well, I'm sure your sparkling personality will pull in some big tips for you before the shift is over."

He scowled at me.

Then he slowly began walking away to get my order.

Just no charming this guy.

When he came back with the seltzer water, I asked him again about the security guard.

"Go ask the concierge in the front lobby," he said.

"That's all I get from you for buying this drink?"

"Take it or leave it."

The concierge wasn't much more help than the bartender.

"Why do you want to see this person?" he asked me.

"I'd rather not say."

"Does it involve a problem with the hotel?"

"No, it's personal."

"What is the man's name?"

"I—I don't know."

"You have a personal reason to see someone whose name you don't know?"

"Just let me know how I might find a security guard here."

He eventually directed me to a location he said was the security office in the basement of the hotel.

I thanked him, but he had already turned away and was talking with someone else.

I was pretty sure the concierge didn't like me any better than the bartender.

The guy I found in the security office was better. He turned out to be an ex-NY cop who recognized me from TV news. That always helps. He said his name was Jake Sloan, and that he was the head of the hotel's security. Sloan looked like an ex-cop turned hotel security chief—about sixty, gray hair, a bit overweight, but you could tell he still had that cop look about him.

I explained to him how I was looking for one of his security guards.

"I've got two people who work for me here: Ed Whalen and Betsy Grantham. We split up the shifts between us. Which one do you want to talk to?"

"It must be Ed Whalen," I said. "This was a man."

I described the security guard I'd met at the bar to him.

"That ain't Ed Whalen," he said when I was done.

"Are you sure?"

"Absolutely."

"Why?"

"Because Ed Whalen is Black."

"And the only other person that works for you is a woman?"

"Right."

"Then who did I meet here the other night?"

"I have no idea."

If he wasn't a security guard, that meant he was at the bar for some other reason. That's why he noticed me. And I could think of only one other reason that this guy was there that night at the same time as me.

He was watching someone too.

He was watching Ronald Bannister.

Just like me.

CHAPTER 14

THERE WAS A message saying Susan Endicott wanted to see me as soon as I got into the office. That was not good. A meeting with Susan Endicott was never good. I was pretty sure what she wanted to talk to me about. She wanted a Wendy Kyle exclusive story from me that we could break on the newscast. And she wanted it in a hurry.

Much as I hated to admit it, she was right.

I mean, I'd been chasing around after leads and people to interview and all that for a few days now. But—except for the evidence of a diary page in Kyle's office—our coverage of the murder had been the same breaking news that every other TV station, newspaper, and website in town covered.

I'd held back the name of Ronald Bannister when I talked about the diary entry on the Channel 10 newscast.

I'd held back the pictures and video of Bannister kissing the woman at the hotel from everyone, even Endicott.

Sooner or later, I was going to have to deal with all this.

And this might well be the "sooner" moment.

*   *   *

Except Susan Endicott threw me a curveball when I showed up in her office. For one thing, she smiled at me. Endicott never smiled at me or pretty much anyone else. I should have figured out right then that something was up with her.

"It looks like the sale of the station is going through in the next few days," she said as soon as I sat down in front of her desk. "Brendan Kaiser—and Kaiser Media—are selling it to Kellogg and Klein. That's a consortium which has been buying up a lot of media companies around the country."

"I don't like the sound of that. Who will we be dealing with?"

"Hard to say. There's not one person like Brendan Kaiser. There's a CEO, and a head of operations, and a few others at the top. It's going to be a lot more corporate. Neither of us will be able to go to someone we know like Brendan Kaiser like we have in the past."

That was a problem. I'd built up a relationship with Kaiser over the past few years. He' been impressed by the big exclusives I'd broken for the station. I think he liked me personally too. Whenever I had major problems in the past, I went to Kaiser for help and advice. So did Endicott, I knew from past experience. This new way of operating was going to be difficult for both of us.

"I have an idea about something we can do about this," Endicott said.

"Pool all the money from our expense accounts and buy the station from Kaiser ourselves?"

She smiled. She actually smiled again. What the hell was going on with this woman today?

"We get together and put up a united front."

"Who?"

"You and me."

"You're kidding."

"No, I'm serious. Think about it. The new owners will want to make changes. They might decide they like you as news director and on the air, but want to get rid of me. Or they might like the results I've gotten here in the past year, but not want you as the face of the news here like Kaiser did. Anything can happen in a new situation like this, to you or me. I don't want this to be a 'you or me' situation where we're divided in front of the new bosses. I think we should put up a united front, put our differences aside, and try to work together."

"Are you suggesting an alliance?"

"Yes."

"We don't have to be friends or anything, though, right? Hang out together after work? Swap stories about our love lives? Throw pajama parties together?"

"Look, Carlson, I don't like you. I think you've got a smart, obnoxious mouth and no respect for authority, and you're not as good at your job as you think you are. To be honest, I can't stand you or anything you do or say around me. If it was up to me, I would have fired your ass out of here months ago."

"Is this the part where we're putting our differences aside?" I asked.

"But—and this is a big *but*—I think we can help each other here. What do you say?"

I wanted to say something witty and snappy back to her, but I didn't. Because everything she'd said did make sense.

"What do you want me to do?" I asked.

"Just work with me, not against me, in the newsroom for a while."

"Okay."

"Don't argue with me in public where the new bosses can see it, only behind closed doors."

"Uh, okay."

"And finally, stop making fun of me in front of the staff."

"That one might be a bit difficult for me to pull off."

"I'm serious. No laughing or making faces or stuff like that when I say something you don't like. Agreed?"

I sighed. "Not even a smile or a small chuckle?"

In the end, I agreed to do what she wanted. I formed an alliance with Susan Endicott. Hey, Hitler and Stalin once formed an alliance before they went to war. That alliance didn't last long, and I didn't figure my alliance with Susan Endicott would either. But I decided to try and get along with her as best I could until we knew more about the new owners.

We talked then about the Wendy Kyle story. She wanted to know everything I had. And so I told her. Everything. Including finally showing her the pictures and video of Ronald Bannister from the bar.

"Holy crap, this is sensational stuff!" she said. "This could be a ratings bonanza for us. But I don't think we can put it on the air. Not yet. Not without more information."

"I agree. I wasn't sure you would."

"The implication, of course, is that Kyle could have caught Bannister cheating on his wife like this. Bannister's wife hires her, he finds out she has this kind of evidence and kills her—or has her killed by someone—to make sure the wife doesn't get it to use in a divorce. Makes sense. But a lot of that is still speculation."

"Interesting speculation though. Maybe we could run some of it in a story about how we're not sure this is linked to the Wendy Kyle murder, but Bannister's name had been found on a document in Kyle's office so we're turning this material over to the police for their investigation. Something like that."

Endicott thought about that for a few seconds.

"We'll have to reach out to Bannister first. His wife too. Tell him we have these pictures and video of him and what they show."

"Do you think he'll respond?"

"We have to make the effort for legal reasons."

I nodded. "I'll reach out to both Bannister and his wife now."

It didn't take long to get a response from Bannister. Actually, the response came from his lawyers. A very large law firm. They warned us that the pictures were an invasion of privacy against Bannister and potentially defamatory for us to suggest he had anything to do with the death of Wendy Kyle.

That was pretty much what I expected.

What I didn't expect was the response from Mrs. Bannister.

"I'd like to speak to you in person, Ms. Carlson," she said in a phone call that shocked the hell out of me. "No cameras, no recording devices. Only you and me. Will you do that for me?"

"Yes, I will."

"Then let's meet this afternoon."

"Where?"

"Come to my home. I live at the Brantley House." She gave me the address. "It's right across from Central Park."

"Mrs. Bannister, I really appreciate this . . ." I started to say.

But she'd already hung up.

CHAPTER 15

THE BRANTLEY HOUSE is one of those grandiose buildings you see in New York City that look like they've been transported here directly from the 19th Century.

It was big and it was impressive. Old-world architecture and made with expensive-looking gray brick; two big columns at the front door; a chandelier adorned the lobby inside. There was a huge fountain too. A sign with the words "Brantley House" was by the door. It might as well have said "money." Because that's what the place reeked of . . . lots and lots of money.

Exactly the kind of place where you'd expect Ronald Bannister and his wife to live.

A doorman was there when I walked into the lobby. This guy looked like he meant business. He was wearing a tan uniform with dark brown lines on the pleats of his pants, brown gloves, and a white hat with a brown peak. There were even gold braids hanging from his shoulder, giving him a real military look. Finally, he had a badge on his chest that said "Brantley House" in case you forgot where you were.

The doorman did not give me a cheerful hello. He did not ask to hold the front door open for me. He did not offer me a tour of the Brantley House. He stood there stiffly at attention while I approached him. I wondered if maybe I was supposed to salute him or something.

I told him I was here to see Mrs. Eleanor Bannister. He checked with her by phone, then directed me to one of the elevators that would take me up to Mrs. Bannister on the top floor.

"It's the penthouse," he said.

"Of course it is," I told him.

Penthouse didn't even come close to describing the place once I got inside. The living room was the size of a football field; the dining room was bigger than my whole apartment; and there were so many bedrooms and bathrooms that a person could get lost trying to brush their teeth before bed.

Eleanor Bannister looked about the way I expected her to look, but more glamorous. She was about fifty, I guess—the same age as me. But she was trying hard to look forty. Or maybe thirty-five. She had long brunette hair, with bangs over her forehead. I figured she'd had at least a few face lifts along the way. Expensive-looking jewelry—earrings, rings, bracelet, and necklace—and wearing a purple pants suit with a crisply starched white blouse.

She was pretty, but not as sexy as the redhead I'd seen making out with Ronald Bannister at the bar. Which is probably why he went looking elsewhere for sex.

There were brief introductions, and then we sat down together on a plush velvet couch with a panoramic view from a picture window of Central Park.

"I agreed to see you for one reason, Ms. Carlson," she said to me now. "I know who you are, I've seen you on TV, and I know how relentless you can be as a journalist. I do not wish to be hounded or stalked for an interview every moment I step outside my front door. So I decided it made more sense to simply confront you directly and get this out of the way so you don't become a nuisance. What is it you want to ask me?"

Practical. No-nonsense. I kind of liked that in this woman.

I took out the pictures and video screen grabs of her husband with the woman in the bar. Plus the pictures of the inside of the hotel room they'd used later. I placed them down on a coffee table in front of her. I expected her to be shocked. But she was not. She looked at the pictures, then back at me, and shrugged.

'Why are you showing me these?" I asked.

"It's your husband."

"I'm aware of that."

"He's kissing another woman."

"Okay."

"A woman who is not you."

"Is this the news 'story' you want to ask me about? Does this qualify as news these days in the journalism you practice? Taking sensational—what you imagine are scandalous—pictures of two people in a bar? What is the story you're after here, Ms. Carlson?"

"It's about Wendy Kyle."

She didn't say anything.

"You do know who Wendy Kyle is, don't you, Mrs. Bannister?"

"She's a woman—a private investigator—who was killed in a car explosion."

"How do you know that?"

"I saw it on TV. It was on the news. Maybe even your news."

"Did you know Wendy Kyle?"

"No. Of course not. Why would you ask something like that?"

"Because she left a piece of writing behind in her office mentioning your husband as one of her cases."

I waited to see what she would say. I thought that might be the question that would set her off. But she looked more bemused by it than shocked or angry or scared.

"Ah, I believe I understand where you're going with this now. You think I hired this Wendy Kyle to spy on my husband and see if he was being unfaithful to me. Well, as you've shown here, he certainly is unfaithful. I'm sure the Kyle woman could have found that out very quickly too. You speculate that my husband may have found she had somehow gotten evidence to expose him—and that this could cost him an extremely large amount of money in a divorce settlement with him and me. Thus, it could have been the motive for Ronald—or someone he employed—to kill her before she got a chance to show this kind of material to me. Is that the scenario you've come up with for the Wendy Kyle murder?"

"Well, it is a logical hypothesis."

"No, it is not."

"Why?"

"Because I never hired Wendy Kyle. I never had any communication of any kind with Wendy Kyle. And I could care less about what my husband is doing with some other woman."

Now it was my turn to look shocked.

"You have an open marriage?"

"Ronald and I were married twenty-nine years ago when we were very young and had very little money. Over the years, that has obviously changed. There is now a great deal of money. Ronald is not the same man he was back at the beginning of our relationship, and I'm not the same woman. We lead separate lives. But we remain together as husband and wife for a variety of reasons, some of them financial. There's plenty of money for both of us. I have no desire to divorce Ronald. I have no desire to split his fortune with him. I'm very happy living the life we lead now. And, if that involves him amusing himself with a woman like that redhead in the picture—I really don't care."

She picked the pictures up again, handed them to me, and smiled.

Yep, this woman was practical, no-nonsense, and damned tough.

And—for whatever it was worth—I believed her.

"So then what's all this nonsense about Ronald—or me—having some involvement in the murder of this Wendy Kyle woman?"

"Well, now that I've talked with you I believe that's what it is, Mrs. Bannister."

"What?"

"Nonsense. All nonsense."

CHAPTER 16

EVEN IF CHANNEL 10 wasn't going to use any of the Ronald Bannister stuff on air—at least for now—we still needed some Wendy Kyle stuff to make a splash on the evening news. So we put together a special report with all the people I'd been able to talk to and also other reporters I'd sent out to gather more information about her life—and her death.

Just like with everything else we'd found out with Wendy Kyle, most of it turned out to be not what we expected.

Nothing about Wendy Kyle was what it seemed.

And everything we thought we knew about her hadn't always been true either.

Both with the NYPD and as a private investigator, she was an incredibly complex person. A paradox of vice and virtue, depending on who you talked to.

"The big surprise was her ex-partner—or one of them anyway, she had a lot—Bernie Grayson," said Cassie O'Neal, one of the Channel 10 reporters. "Grayson was the guy whose life she saved on the street early in her career. Maneuvering her patrol car—at great risk to herself—to get him out of the line of fire from the sniper who had wounded him. She got awards for bravery. You'd think that Grayson, of all people, would be grateful. And broken up about her death. But he wasn't like that at all.

"I've got him on video going on about what an ingrate and backstabber and disgrace to law enforcement she was. He said she tried to bring charges against him after the heroic stuff— accusing him of corruption, sex harassment, and police brutality on the street. He's still on the force. I figured he might not want to go on the air with all this. Instead, go with some sort of more traditional condolences for a dead former NYPD partner. But he said he wanted the world to know what kind of person she really was."

Very similar sentiments to what I got from Magnuson, her former commanding officer. Although he had a lot more reason to be upset with her than Grayson, you would have thought. But the reaction of both men to Wendy Kyle's brutal murder was the same. No sympathy, no compassion—almost gleeful at her tragic demise. Even though she had saved the life of one of them.

Things got even stranger when Cassie reported back on her conversation with Bert Moyer, one of Wendy Kyle's ex-husbands. You would think an ex-husband would have mostly bad things to say about the ex he divorced. Believe me, I've been there—and I know divorce can get pretty nasty with a lot of bad feelings on both sides. But Moyer was very broken up about Kyle's death, and he talked glowingly of her and their time together.

"Moyer's a lawyer," Cassie said. "They met on a court case of someone she arrested early in her career. He said they were married for a year and a half. They knew they weren't right for each other, but still liked and respected each other. Weird, huh?"

"Not like any divorce I ever heard of," I said.

"Well, you should know, you've had a lot of experience at it."

My checkered marital history was always a great amusement among the staff here at Channel 10. I usually played along with the jokes too. But the truth is I did sort of understand what Moyer was saying. Yes, all of my marriages had ended up unsuccessfully. But, like Moyer and Kyle seemed to have done, I managed to maintain good relationships with my exes without a lot of anger and bad feelings.

"And you got him to say all this stuff for air?"

"Plenty of quotes we can use on video tonight."

"What about the other ex-husband? She was married twice."

"His name is Ted Lansmore. Haven't tracked him down yet. He was on the NYPD too, but Lansmore left the force around the same time she did. Not sure where he is now. I'm still checking on him."

There was a lot of varied reaction, too, from people we spoke to in the neighborhoods around her office in Times Square and her apartment on the Upper East Side.

The manager of the office building said she'd once threatened him with a gun during an argument. A superintendent in her apartment house remembered a violent altercation when she pushed a doorman. But others said she was always very kind and friendly to them. Also, that she had done volunteer work at a homeless shelter for women in the neighborhood. She helped to feed and find shelter for needy people on the street too, they said. And that she had specifically befriended one of the women, even allowing her to come up to her apartment at times to shower and clean up. No one knew this woman's name for sure, but they said she called herself *Reby*.

Hmm.

Reby.

Along with Ted Lansmore, the ex-husband.

Two more names of people I needed to track down.

To try to find out who in the hell the real Wendy Kyle was.

*   *   *

"Any idea what made her change so much?" I asked at the news meeting where Maggie and the rest of the staff went through all of this with me. "What made her change from model police officer to crazy woman? First as an NYPD officer, then as a woman PI dedicated to exposing cheating spouses to their wives or girlfriends?"

"All we know is that people said it seemed to begin after the death of a woman," Maggie said. "Wendy Kyle was one of the first officers on the scene after a body was found in an apartment in Murray Hill. There was alcohol and pills there, and it was ruled a suicide. Police said the victim had been a troubled addict. But Kyle kept insisting it was murder, and the police were covering up something."

I remembered reading about the same case now in her NYPD personnel file. According to the records of her job performance, it was the beginning of her long slide from NYPD hero to eventually being booted off the force after the altercation with Magnuson.

"Why did she think the police would want to cover up the murder of this woman?" I wondered out loud.

"I have no idea."

"Do we know any more about the identity of the dead woman?"

"Troy Spencer. Died April 8th, 2016, at the Prescott Building on East 33rd Street. Official ruling: suicide from alcohol and barbiturate overdose."

All of this left us with a lot of questions.

But we still had plenty of material to go with for the evening newscast.

*   *   *

And so, a few hours later, Brett and Dani opened the 6:00 p.m. show by introducing me with the lead story:

> ME: *Channel 10 News has been conducting an exclusive investigation into the murder of Wendy Kyle, the ex-NYPD officer and controversial private investigator killed by a bomb blast as she sat in her car in Times Square several days ago.*
>
> *We've discovered that plenty of people had motives for wanting her dead.*

*   *   *

It should have been a moment of triumph for me, and it was. I mean, I hadn't broken the whole story yet, but we were way ahead of anyone else in the media now with this on Channel 10. I was pretty happy about that.

Except that—when I got off the air—I got a phone call.

It was from my daughter, Lucy.

And what she told me made me forget about Wendy Kyle, and Susan Endicott, and the new owners at Channel 10, and even about me turning fifty soon.

At least for a while.

CHAPTER 17

"I NEED SOME legal advice," I said to Janet.

"What kind of legal advice?"

"About marital problems."

"Un, you're not married, Clare."

"It's for someone else who asked me for my help."

"Who in the world would ever ask Clare Carlson for help about their marital problems?"

It was the kind of joke I usually made about my disastrous marriage history. Three marriages—three divorces. Sometimes people like Janet made the jokes too, and I always laughed. But not this time. I guess that's what made Janet realize how serious I was, even before I answered her question.

"It's my daughter," I said. "I'm talking about Lucy."

"This is about your daughter's marriage?"

"It's over. She just told me. Her husband, Greg, moved out on her and my granddaughter, Emily, a few days ago. He's living with another woman."

We were sitting in Janet's office. It was a terrific law office on Park Avenue in the 40s, with views of Manhattan skyscrapers outside the windows. I never was sure exactly how much money Janet made as a lawyer, but—looking around at her office—I figured it had to be a lot. More money than me.

Janet looked stunned at the news.

"From everything you said, I thought that was a pretty good marriage," she said.

"So did I."

"I guess there really aren't that many good marriages."

I'd always thought that because of my own divorces. And the breakups of other women I knew with their husbands. And even now, learning of the sordid details of marriages gone bad by covering the Wendy Kyle murder and seeing the things she'd been investigating.

But this now—my own daughter's marriage and her family life imploding—well, this one hit me hard.

Janet talked about some specific things Lucy should do very quickly. Like making sure she had official possession of her home. Custody of Emily. Access to all the bank accounts and other financial holdings her husband had set up in the past.

"If he's already moved out and living with another woman, she should be able to get this all accomplished relatively easily. Any good lawyer can do that for her."

"Is there any way you could represent her, Janet?"

"No. I'm here in New York, and she's in Virginia. That doesn't work. But I'll reach out to contacts and see if I can find someone good to represent her in Virginia."

"Thanks. It's all very confusing. This comes out of the blue for me, totally unexpected. It makes me realize how little I know about Lucy or anything about her life. Sometimes it feels like we're strangers."

"She is your daughter, Clare."

"Yes, but, as you know, we haven't exactly had a normal mother–daughter relationship."

I basically did not know my daughter for the first twenty-five years of her life.

I was her biological mother, but that's all in the beginning. I got pregnant during my freshman year of college at a drunken fraternity party, I gave birth to a baby girl, and then I gave her up for adoption that same day at the hospital.

Eleven years later, she was kidnapped off the streets of New York City from her adoptive family, and it became a sensational crime story in the media. I won a Pulitzer Prize reporting on it for the newspaper where I worked then, even though I never told anyone about my connection to Lucy as her biological mother. She was never found then, and everyone presumed she was dead.

But fifteen years later—with me now working for Channel 10 TV news—I broke another big story about what really happened to her and eventually discovered she was still alive. Her new name was Linda Devlin, and she lived with her husband and daughter in Winchester, Virginia. I reconnected with her again after all that time, and we had established a rewarding—albeit unique and different—mother–daughter relationship.

Until now.

Now all the failures of my own marriages had somehow surfaced in my daughter's marriage too.

Was that because of me?

Was this all somehow my fault?

Like mother, like daughter?

I talked with Janet about what else I could do to help my daughter.

"I can't go down to Virginia and stay with her and Emily," I said. "Not with everything going on here with my job. Susan Endicott. The new owner coming in. And the Wendy Kyle story."

"No, you can't."

"And I can't ask her to come to New York and stay with me either. Even if she wanted to, she'd have to pull Emily out of school and transfer to a new place here. That would be terribly traumatic for the girl, especially after everything else she has to deal with over her father suddenly being gone."

"Right. Besides, Lucy needs to stay there in Virginia to make sure she maintains all of her legal rights in the divorce proceedings."

"I can't even go down there and shoot that son of a bitch Greg in the heart for what he did to them. If I did, I'd go to jail for it. And I don't think I'd fit in well in prison. Orange is not a good color for me."

"Yeah, that's probably not an option either."

"So what should I do?"

"Just be there for her, Clare."

"How?"

"In whatever way your daughter needs."

I shook my head.

"I don't know. I've kind of been pretending to be a mother the past few years since we reunited. Talking to her and Emily a lot. Getting together on holidays. A lot of things families do. But now . . . now I'm not sure exactly what I need to do to try to help things be right for her again."

"Just be a real mother," Janet said.

"I don't know if I can do that."

"Sure, you can."

"I never have been a real mother to her."

"Speaking as a mother myself," she said, "sometimes you can surprise yourself by what you're able to do to protect and show your love for your child."

CHAPTER 18

SCOTT MANNING CALLED to say he had some information about Wendy Kyle from the NYPD. He said he was in the area of the Channel 10 building for some other business, and maybe we could meet up to discuss it. That was interesting. He could have told me whatever he found out over the phone. But he wanted to see me in person.

Maybe he made up the story about happening to be in the area. Maybe he'd gone out of his way to be here because of me. Or maybe he did have some business in the same part of Manhattan as Channel 10 and he was telling the truth about that. Sometimes I overthink things too much.

I considered meeting him for coffee or a drink or lunch. But I wanted to keep things professional between us. At least for now. I told him to come up and meet me in my office.

A few minutes later, Maggie brought Scott Manning in to see me. She gave me a WTF look as she did so. Maggie knew all about my previous relationship with Manning, and I don't think she approved. I ignored her, smiled at Manning, and then Maggie left us alone in my office.

For whatever it was worth, he was still as attractive a guy as I remembered from the last time we'd met a few years ago. Curly brown hair; slightly unshaven, but in a sexy way; wearing an open-collared white shirt, jeans, and a blue sports jacket. Casual. Cool. He looked damn good.

"I've never been to your office before," he said after he sat down.

"What do you think?"

He looked around. There wasn't much to see. My office is a small cubicle of the Channel 10 main newsroom.

"I thought it would be bigger," Manning said.

"Be it ever so humble . . ."

"There's no windows either."

"I have to wait until I take over Katie Couric's old office at either CBS or NBC before I get windows."

Manning looked around some more. His eyes stopped on a calendar posted to a bulletin board next to my desk. I had a date on the calendar that I had circled prominently in bright red magic marker.

"Important day coming up?" he asked.

"My birthday."

"Is it a big one?"

"Yes, one of the milestones."

"Which one?"

"I turn thirty-nine."

He laughed at that.

"Well, don't worry, Clare, you look a lot younger than thirty-nine."

"Thank you."

"Actually, you look younger than the age of twenty-nine."

"Oh, c'mon."

"Okay, I'll stop.'

"No, don't stop. I love this. Keep going with the compliments on how young I look!"

Okay, I was flirting with him a bit now. But nothing serious. I mean, it wasn't like I was going to rip off his clothes and have sex with him right here on my desk or anything. Although, since my office had no windows, that wasn't completely out of the question as one of my options.

"Ronald Bannister's name isn't on the client list they found in Wendy Kyle's office," Manning said now, bringing me out of my fantasy world and back to reality. "Neither was his wife's name. So the idea that Kyle was investigating Bannister for cheating on her seems to be a dead end."

That wasn't a total surprise to me after my conversation with Mrs. Bannister.

"But Bannister is mentioned in the diary page they found. Like your source told you. I was able to get a copy of that."

He showed it to me now. It said:

If you're reading this, I'm already dead.

How's that for an attention-grabbing opening line?

I know, I know . . . it's a bit melodramatic. And I'm not normally the melodramatic type. Really. No, Wendy Kyle is the kind of woman who deals in facts for a living, the kind of woman who doesn't let emotion cloud her judgment and— maybe most importantly of all—the kind of woman who never blindly puts her trust in anyone.

Especially a man.

Hey, I'm not some man-hating bitch or anything like that, no matter what you may have heard or thought about me. I like men. I love men, or at least I've loved a few men in my life. It's just that I don't trust them anymore.

So wouldn't it be ironic—or maybe a little bit fitting, to look at it completely objectively—if trusting a man this one time was what wound up costing me my own life in the end?

Here's the bottom line for me: If I don't succeed in what I'm about to do in the Ronald Bannister case, well . . . then it is important someone knows the truth about what happened to me.

And that it was the lies—all of the damn lies men have told—that were the death of me.

"So Bannister must have been connected somehow to Kyle in the final days of her life," Manning said. "The police were able to ask Bannister about why his name would have been mentioned by her like that. He said he had no idea."

He told me something else his NYPD source had said to him.

"The client list wasn't hard to find. There was a hard copy of it in her files, and it was also pretty easy to download off her computer. On the other hand, the diary page was not on the computer or anywhere in her office. Except for this one page. It had slipped behind a filing cabinet and couldn't be seen easily. Which suggests . . ."

"Someone went through her office and deleted the diary from her computer and took the printed copy too, except for the one page they accidentally missed. They didn't care about the client files. Which means whoever killed her very likely wasn't a client or someone she was investigating. It was someone she talked about in that diary."

"Bannister? He's the one name we saw."

"Why do you think she was keeping a diary? That would have some pretty explosive stuff in it."

"And, if there is more to the diary, where is it now?" Manning asked.

I shrugged. "Here's another question. Whoever did this must have been there after she left the office and went to start her car. But it wouldn't have taken the police long to be up there searching the place too. As soon as they identified who the victim of the bomb blast was, that would have been their next stop. But presumably all the rest of this was gone by then. How could anyone else have gotten up to her office so fast? Unless they were already at the crime scene."

"You mean the killer?"

"Or someone from the police."

"You think a cop may have taken the evidence from the diary?"

"I'm looking at all the possibilities."

I thought about everything Manning had told me.

"I'd still like to see that entire client list," I said. "What are the chances I could get a copy of all the names?"

"Zero."

"But you saw it. And you got the diary page."

"Look, I had to call in a lot of favors from old friends on the force to get this much. I'm not exactly the most popular guy with the NYPD after the way I left for the FBI. But I have friends—one friend, in particular—who helped me by getting me the diary page and showing me the client list. That's all he could do. I don't even have a copy of the client list myself."

"Any surprising names on that client list jump out at you when you read it?"

"You mean like the police chief, or the mayor, or some other VIP Kyle was investigating for cheating on their wives?"

"Hey, a girl can hope . . ."

"But . . ."

"But what?"

"Well, there is something I saw on the list. A name you might know."

"Who?"

"Deborah Harkness."

I thought about the name. I had no idea who Deborah Harkness was. I told that to Scott Manning.

"You probably know her by her married name."

"Which is?"

"Deborah Markham."

The wife of my ex-husband Sam Markham.

Suddenly, a lot of things made sense.

Like why Sam wasn't assigned to investigate this case.

"Deborah Markham, aka Deborah Harkness, hired Wendy Kyle to see if her husband Detective Sgt. Sam Markham was cheating on her with another woman," Manning told me.

CHAPTER 19

I WASN'T SURE who to talk to about this.

I wasn't ready to confront Sam with questions. Not yet anyway. He'd blow up at me. Or lie about it, then blow up at me. Either way, it would torpedo our current relationship—whatever that was.

I couldn't go to Sam's wife and ask her if she hired Wendy Kyle to spy on him. She would tell Sam and that would make him even madder. Besides, she knew who I was—I was Sam's ex-wife before her and she didn't like me very much simply because of that. There was no way she was going to open up to me.

I couldn't go to Sam's partner, Kate Gallison—who I suspected might have been the target of Kyle's investigation with Sam, the woman he most likely was having an affair with. She didn't like me either. Besides, she carried a gun. She might not just get mad at me; she might even shoot me.

I didn't want to talk about it with Susan Endicott, even though I knew I should. I still didn't trust Endicott or her judgment, despite our current nonaggression pact.

I didn't even want to confide in Maggie about it, even though I trusted her more than anyone else at the station.

The situation seemed pretty clear to me though. Or at least I had a working hypothesis about it. Sam's wife suspected he'd been cheating on her. Whether he was or not, I knew Sam had a wandering eye because he'd propositioned me a few times while he was married to his new wife.

I had to figure there was a very good chance he was playing around with another woman, and Kyle had found out about it. But what *other* woman? The most likely candidate was his new NYPD partner, Gallison. I'd seen the dynamics between them that day at the station house. If I'd picked up on that in a few minutes, Sam's wife likely sensed something was going on too— and that's how she wound up on Wendy Kyle's client list.

This certainly explained why Sam wasn't involved in the murder investigation. The police had discovered Deborah Harkness was Sam's wife—and that made him a potential suspect. Not a prime suspect—there were likely many names of clients Kyle had done investigations for. But still a possible suspect. In any case, he couldn't be impartial on the case, so they made sure he wasn't involved.

Did Sam know any of this? Did they confront him and question him? It didn't seem like he knew anything when we talked at the precinct. He simply said the case was being handled by top police brass, not him. He seemed more bemused and curious about it than defensive. But did he find out more later?

Questions, questions, questions.

But the biggest question was what I did next.

I could only think of one person I was comfortable discussing this with. Jack Faron. My old boss at Channel 10. The executive producer Endicott replaced. Jack had always been there for me to go to for advice about tricky situations like this. Maybe he could still do the same thing.

*   *   *

I met Jack Faron at a bar near the location of the newspaper where we both once worked. The newspaper was long gone now, but the bar was still there. Jack had actually hired me as a young reporter at the paper in this bar a lifetime ago, so it always used to hold a special meaning for me. I suppose it still did.

"You look good, Clare," he said when I slipped onto the stool next to where he was sitting at the bar, sipping from a glass of lager beer.

"So do you," I said, ordering a Corona—my beer of choice—from the bartender.

"No, I don't." He laughed.

Faron was right. He didn't look good. It had been a year since his forced "retirement" at Channel 10 to make room for Susan Endicott. And it looked like he'd spent much of that year eating his way through every buffet table in town. He always had a bit of a weight problem, but now it looked like he'd put on at least twenty-five pounds.

"At least I don't have to fit into a suit anymore," he said.

He was wearing a baggy pair of khaki pants, a loose nylon sports shirt, and sandals. He looked a lot different than the buttoned-down guy I worked for at Channel 10. Still, I wasn't here to critique his grooming or healthy eating choices. I wanted to pick his brain.

I took a drink of my Corona and asked him what he'd been up to. I'd been meaning to reach out to him more since he left, but never got around to it. That's what happens when people aren't working together anymore. You say that you'll stay in touch, but you never do.

He said he'd been doing some traveling, a bit of consulting work for a PR agency friend of his, and hoped to teach some courses at the CUNY Graduate School of Journalism soon.

"But you didn't ask to meet me here to hear all this, did you?"

"No, Jack. I need your help on something."

"Something you can't get from Susan Endicott?" He smiled. "How are you and Endicott getting along?"

I told him about the agreement we'd made about acting as a united front for when the new owners took over.

"That's smart," he said. "For both of you. I'm glad you did that. Maybe you'll both survive."

I drank some more beer.

"So are you going to tell me why you wanted to see me, Clare?"

"It's about Sam Markham."

"Your ex?"

"Yes. I think he could be deeply involved in the Wendy Kyle investigation."

"As a homicide detective?"

"As a potential suspect."

I told him everything I knew about Sam's wife being on Wendy Kyle's client list and all the rest.

"I can't go on the air with any of this. I don't even know for sure what it means. But if I go public, it makes Sam look like a potential suspect. I need more facts, but I can't ask anyone questions without turning this into a big mess. I want to do something, but what do I do, Jack?"

He asked me more questions—a lot more questions—about Sam and his wife and the partner and the client list and the diary page.

I answered them as best I could.

"So the police know about Markham's wife hiring Kyle?" he asked when I finished.

"Yes. I got her name from the client list that the police have."

"Then they must know everything else you do too."

"I suppose."

"Which means they're investigating Markham."

"They have to be."

"Even though he hasn't been suspended or anything."

"Not yet."

"Only taken off the case."

"Right."

"Uh-huh. Then here's my suggestion on what you should do. Are you ready?"

"Okay, tell me."

"Nothing."

"Nothing?"

"Sit on this. Let it play out. If your ex-husband is not involved, you'll be glad you did that. If it turns out—God forbid—that he somehow was, you'll still be ahead of the story. You can worry about reporting it then."

"Do nothing, huh?" I said.

"Do nothing—at least for now."

"Keep this all to myself?"

"Right. Don't talk about it with anyone else."

"So I need to just keep my mouth shut for now, huh?"

"Can you do that?"

"Keep my mouth shut? I think so."

He smiled. "Well, that will be a Clare Carlson first."

CHAPTER 20

"How do you make a car bomb to kill someone?" I asked.

"Susan Endicott is driving you that nuts?" Dani Blaine asked.

"Nah, Clare wouldn't blow up Endicott in her car," said Brett Wolff. "She'd want to kill her with her bare hands. Face-to-face."

As you can see, the disconnect between me and Endicott was pretty visible to the rest of the newsroom. But the truth is Endicott had irritated a lot of other people here too. She was rude, abusive, and at times, bullying. She was definitely not at the top of everybody's popularity list.

"Maybe we should all get together and do it together on Endicott," Maggie said. "Like they did in *Murder on the Orient Express*. Everybody stabs her individually so we can all take responsibility—and credit—for her death. Nobody's totally guilty, nobody's totally innocent either. It will be the crime of the century."

I'd brought a lot of this on myself since I frequently did a lot of jokes in the news meeting. So now everyone felt comfortable doing the same. The result was some pretty colorful and wild and joke-filled meetings. I liked it that way. Most of the time. But right now, I was serious.

"We're talking about Wendy Kyle here, people," I said. "She was not shot to death. She was not stabbed to death. She was not beaten to death or strangled. Someone rigged an explosive to her car and blew her up. That is not a common way to murder someone. I want to find out more about how a person can build a bomb—and then rig it for murder like that. Anyone have some ideas?"

Maggie spoke first.

"I went back and read the police report again," she said. "One thing I found out is that bomb experts don't believe it was starting the ignition of the car that caused the blast; they believe it was simply opening the door on the car that set it off. They say that's very significant."

"Why?" I asked. "She's still dead either way, isn't she?"

"It's significant because it takes a fairly sophisticated knowledge of bombs and explosives and ignition techniques to rig a bomb to the ignition system of the car. On the other hand, planting it on the car so the opening of the door sets it off is much simpler. You don't need to be a bomb expert to do that. Only learn a few things."

"So the fact that the explosives were set for the door opening suggests it didn't have to be anyone extremely expert in bombs and explosives?"

"That's what the police say."

"Which expands the list of possible suspects who might have done it."

"I'm afraid so."

That complicated the police efforts—and my own—to solve Wendy Kyle's murder. If the suspect had been thoroughly proficient in bomb techniques, that would have made it simpler to locate suspects. Now everyone had to work through a much wider list. Many more people who had reasons to want Wendy Kyle dead now could very easily have been who set that bomb.

"Here's what I want to do," I said. "I want everyone to ask around and find out everything you can about what it takes to build a bomb like this. Reach out to military people, police sources—whoever you can think of that might know something. This is a very unusual way to commit murder. I think it would be a good element to talk about the details of a bombing on the newscast for the Wendy Kyle story."

There were nods around the room.

"Definitely agree," Dani said. "I'd love to find out more about how to build a bomb myself. I'd like to put one together for a certain anchorman I know the next time he causes a problem."

"The only problem we have is you," Brett snapped.

Here we go again, I thought to myself.

Brett and Dani going at it.

I had a feeling—call it a crazy hunch—that things weren't going so well in their marriage at the moment.

*　　*　　*

"We've had people out talking to everyone we can about it. Bomb experts, police sources, federal terrorist officials," Maggie said to me later in my office. "Lots of stuff we already knew. But it is interesting.

"A car bomb, also known as a Vehicle Borne Improvised Explosive Device—VBIED—can be set off in a variety of ways: starting the engine, opening the vehicle door, hitting bumps in the road once the vehicle is moving. As we now know, it appears the door was the means of ignition in this case. The most common way of attaching the bomb is to the bottom of the car."

"What exactly sets the bomb off?"

"Can be a lot of things. A timer fuse. A cell phone. But the simplest way—and the way we assume was used by the bomber here—is to have the opening of the vehicle door connect with some kind of charge to the explosive in the bomb and then—boom!"

"How close does the bomber have to be to the blast?"

"With this kind of bomb, they don't need to be there at all."

Maggie went on for a while more. It was all helpful, if not groundbreaking. Enough to put on the air tonight to fill more air space on the Wendy Kyle story that was getting us big ratings. More good ratings numbers would make Susan Endicott happy. And hopefully the prospective new owners too.

Maggie was almost finished when her cell phone buzzed. She looked down and checked it.

"Jesus!" she said.

"What?"

"This is from Janelle Wright. She just got this from a police source. They found pieces of Wendy Kyle's clothing in the debris. They're going over it to see if there's any DNA from the killer for any reason—anything not from Kyle. And they've got something. Not from Kyle's clothing remains. But a small piece of clothing—a shirt or a blouse, they think—that appears to have come from someone else."

"From two different people?" I asked.

"Maybe she had an extra blouse or other piece of clothing in the car just in case she wanted to change."

"Or . . ."

"Or someone else was there," Maggie said. "Like we talked about before, if the bomber wasn't experienced at this, they might have been too close at the end. Wanted to make sure everything worked right, so they were at the scene. But they didn't get away from the force of the bomb blast fast enough. So maybe it was someone that was close to the car with Kyle before the blast. Someone who lured her there to make sure she opened that door to set it off. But he got too close. And suffered some kind of damage himself."

"But not enough damage to get out of there before the police and bomb squad arrived."

"Apparently."

"Which means we might well be looking for someone who has suffered some kind of an injury that could have come from a bomb blast."

"Yep. That could really narrow down the last of potential suspects," Maggie said.

I thought about Sam Markham. No sign of anything wrong with him that day I went to the precinct to ask him about the Wendy Kyle murder.

Same with Ronald Bannister. He didn't seem impaired or injured in any way that night I saw him at the hotel bar putting the moves on the redhead.

"Let's get this on the air for the 6:00 p.m. show tonight."

"Are you going to do it yourself?"

"Let Janelle do it. She did a helluva job coming up with this."

CHAPTER 21

"I NEVER SAW it coming," my daughter said to me. "Oh, now looking back, I guess I should have been aware of the signs my marriage was falling apart. That my husband was interested in another woman. But I thought right up until the end that we had a happy, normal marriage. Of course, I'm not too familiar with happy, normal marriages, am I? Not with my family history."

She was right about that. Most people know the story about me and Lucy by now. I gave birth to her as a single college freshman who had a one-night stand with a guy who never even knew she existed. I gave her up for adoption right away, and her adoptive parents later divorced after her sensational kidnapping, which made her a national news story.

She was named Lucy Devlin then, but later became Linda Nesbitt after she married Gregory. With a husband and a nine-year-old daughter of her own, it seemed like she had finally found some stability in her life. But we never know what life has waiting for us around the next corner. I'd learned that lesson a long time ago. Now my daughter was finding it out too.

I was at my desk in the Channel 10 newsroom working on the Wendy Kyle story, but I wanted to spend a few minutes on the phone with my daughter to make sure she was okay.

"Did you speak to that lawyer Janet reached out to for you?" I asked.

"I did. He seems very good. But I have a lawyer here now. A woman lawyer, which I kind of like. She was recommended to me by some friends in a divorce counseling group I've been attending. I think I'll stay with her. I gave her name to Janet, who checked her out—and said she had a good reputation."

"The right lawyer is very important in this kind of thing," I said.

"I know. Actually, I don't think the divorce will be too complicated or messy. Greg has been very reasonable so far. I think he feels guilty about what he's done, and he'll do the right thing by me and Emily."

"What about custody?"

"I worry about that the most. I would love to have complete custody of Emily, and we could live together all the time without her father."

"Doesn't seem likely."

"No, the lawyer says I'll have to agree to some kind of joint custody."

"So they'll split up Emily's time between Greg and you?"

"Right. I'll get Emily three or four days a week; then she'll be with Greg and his new girlfriend the other days. I worry about the effect that might have on Emily. Being deprived of a normal family life at her age."

"You survived that kind of thing pretty well," I pointed out.

"Yes, I did." She laughed.

"Emily will be fine," I said.

Before we hung up, she talked about something else.

"We were still having sex," she said. "Right up until the end. Until he announced he was leaving me for another woman."

"Okay," I said slowly.

"Why?"

"Why what?"

"Why did he still screw me at the same time he was screwing her? And why did he decide he wanted to screw her more than me in the end? Why couldn't I give him everything he wanted, and why could she? And why could I not see any of this happening until it was too late? I can't wrap my head around that."

I didn't say anything to that question. There really was no response. All I did finally tell her was: "Sometimes it's hard to explain why a marriage falls apart. It's hard to explain the reason for divorces. It just . . . just happens."

"I thought you might have some insight on it because of your own, well . . ."

"Extensive experience in this matter?"

"Yes."

"I have been divorced."

"Three times," she said with a laugh.

"And I still don't understand what happened in any of them."

"Did any of your husbands ever cheat on you the way Greg did with me?"

"No, they were all faithful."

"What about you? Did you sleep with anyone else during your marriages?"

"No, that was never an issue—on either side—in all three of them."

"So what went wrong for you?"

"Like I said, divorce sometimes can't be explained."

*   *   *

After I hung up, I was still thinking about our conversation as I plowed through notes and other information I'd compiled on Wendy Kyle.

And thinking about myself too.

It was true that I'd never cheated on my husbands when I was married, like Greg had done with my daughter. I wasn't like Greg. I wasn't like all the people in Wendy Kyle's life that she investigated for cheating on their husbands or their spouses or their other loved ones. No, I was a better person than that.

Or was I?

Because I had cheated.

Or at least taken part in the cheating.

I'd been the other woman in someone else's marriage. Scott Manning. The ex-cop and now FBI agent I'd made contact with again. He was married—albeit not always happily—and had a family on Staten Island. He was technically separated when we met, so I used that as an excuse for my behavior. But later, even after he and his wife got back together, we slept together again. No excuse for that one.

The worst part was I had met—and liked—his wife. Manning was wounded at one point, and I was able to save his life. She thanked me profusely for this when we met at his hospital bed. I didn't know if she had any idea about our personal relationship or not, but I still felt guilty. Especially after our recent meeting in my office where I'd been flirting with him again the way I used to.

I guess I was still hoping I had a chance with him. That he'd start cheating with me again on his wife. And then maybe one day leave her for me. And I'd jump at the chance to be with him again. I'd do whatever it took to make that happen for me and him. No matter how guilty I might feel about it.

Or at least I thought that was the way I felt.

Now, after finding out about my daughter's broken marriage and reading again about the destruction done to so many families and people because of the sex, secrets, and betrayal being investigated by Wendy Kyle . . .

Well, I wasn't so sure.

CHAPTER 22

It was Sweeps Weeks coming up for us at Channel 10 News. That's the period of the year when ratings become even more important for measuring audience size to sell advertising for the station.

For anyone who works in TV news, this is a very stressful time. Especially for me now with Susan Endicott looking over my shoulder all the time and new owners about to take over.

Of course, the TV sweeps period is a lot different now then it was back in the old days of television.

Back then, anything was fair game to do in terms of outrageous stunts to draw big ratings:

Having the weather woman do the summer forecast from the beach dressed in the skimpiest of bikinis.

Assigning an attractive female reporter to take lessons in pole dancing at a local strip club.

Hell, I remember one station had a reporter working as a dominatrix for a day in a BDSM dungeon.

These kinds of things could send ratings soaring back then. But times have changed now. Especially when it comes to sex. With #metoo and all the heightened new awareness of what is politically appropriate and what is insensitive, no station—including us here at Channel 10—could go for that kind of thing now.

There was another big change too. In the old days, sweeps were even more important than now because there were only a handful of stations for people to get their local news. Now with streaming and YouTube and Twitter and all the other options on the internet, the viewing results were much more splintered.

Still, it was a big deal for us at Channel 10—and it was my job to make sure sweeps was a success for us.

And so that's why I was talking about it with everyone at the morning news meeting.

"Ideas," I said. "Hit me up with ideas, people."

Vic Zizzo was the first to speak. "I think this might be a good time to take another look at my helicopter . . ."

There were groans around the room. From me too.

"No, wait a minute. Me being aboard a helicopter would be a good stunt for sweeps weeks. The idea of me in a helicopter in the air over the Brooklyn Bridge reporting on the traffic down below would get us a lot of attention."

"The station is not buying you a helicopter, Vic," I said.

"But, Clare, can't you at least consider it?"

"I'll tell you what I will do. I'll buy you a rowboat and you can report on Brooklyn Bridge traffic from the East River below it."

Donna Strickland, our sports reporter, had a doozy of an idea too.

"Going to the Ballpark Can Kill You," she said. "That's the title of a series I want to do on air. We go to both Yankee Stadium and Citi Field showing the food people eat there. Hot dogs, ice cream, pizza. I talk about all the calories and cholesterol and bad stuff you consume at a Yankees or Mets game. What do you think?"

"So you want to convince people not to go to baseball games?"

"I guess."

"But we like baseball games."

"I don't. It's a stupid game."

Terrific. I had the only sportscaster in the country who hated sports. Or at least hated the sports we cared about—baseball and football. I was afraid to ask her about the NBA.

"How about we tweak that idea a little bit, Donna?" I suggested. "Instead of showing how bad the food is, we show how you can eat healthy there too. All of the baseball parks have a wide variety of menus available now for fans—salads, fruits, foods from around the world. We tell people how they can go to someplace like Yankee Stadium and still eat food that's good for them and their diet. We'll called it 'The Yankee Stadium Diet.'"

The next surprise came from Brett and Dani, our married co-anchor team.

"We could do a show called 'At Home with Brett and Dani,'" Brett said. "We'd shoot it at our house remotely that night with our baby and everything."

"Yes," Dani said. "Maybe even do some of it from the kitchen. I could be cooking while I'm reporting the news. Brett too. He loves to cook. I think that would give a real homey and family feel for the show. What do you think, Clare?"

"Uh, but you two don't live together."

"Yes, we do."

"I thought you were separated and getting divorced."

"We're back together again," Brett said.

"Yes, Brett broke it off with the woman he was seeing, and we're going to try to make our marriage work."

Damn. It was tough trying to keep up with the latest on the Brett and Dani soap opera. Every time I turned around, there seemed to be another breaking news bulletin on the state of their relationship.

"That's what we decided," Brett said. "I apologized to Dani, and she took me back. I said I was sorry for ever sleeping with that other woman."

"And I'm sorry I slept with another man," Dani said.

Brett looked over at her with a shocked expression.

"You never told me you slept with another man while we were broken up?"

"You never asked."

"You should have told me that."

"You should have told me you were sleeping with your bimbo, but you didn't. I had to find out about it on my own."

"Okay, I think the 'happy at home' segment with Brett and Dani' is not a possibility at the moment," I said.

We eventually came up with some workable ideas for sweeps, then we got down to the best part of the meeting for me. The day's news. Figuring out what we were going to put on our newscast that night.

Jaime Ortiz, the former police commissioner, had widened his lead in the race for governor. "This guy could be a new political superstar," Maggie said. "People are already talking about him as a potential candidate for the White House four years or so down the road." There was also a looming strike by city doormen and apartment building workers; a massive traffic pileup on the BQE with an overturned tractor trailer that provided some good video; a hate crime in Queens when a woman threw a plate and hurled anti-Asian slurs at a worker in a Chinese takeout restaurant when her food wasn't ready on time; the Mets were on their longest winning streak since their 1986 World Series year; and our weather reporter, Monica McClain, was predicting terrific beach weather for the foreseeable future.

The real story I cared about, though, was still Wendy Kyle.

I'd decided to assign our reporters some of the names and things on my list to check out. I told Cassie O'Neal to try to get to the ex-husbands. Janelle Wright was supposed to find Kyle's old

NYPD partners and other people she'd worked with on the force. I also wanted reporters to go back to the neighborhoods around Kyle's private investigator office in Times Square to see if they could find anyone who knew anything about her that could be significant.

Me, I had my own lead I wanted to follow up on. The redhead who was at the hotel bar that night with Ronald Bannister. She'd disappeared into that downtown apartment house after she left him, and I had no idea where she was right now. Maybe I could find her.

Hopefully, we'd get enough new Wendy Kyle material for our newscast tonight.

But, even if we didn't, I still planned to lead with Wendy Kyle again—even if we just had to rehash a lot of the old stuff we'd already reported.

"Wendy Kyle: The Woman Everyone Loved to Hate—But Who Hated Her Enough to Kill Her?" Maggie said. "That's what we're looking for, right?"

"That's it."

"What does the Wicked Witch think about all this?"

"Susan Endicott?"

"She's the only Wicked Witch here I know."

"I do my best not to talk to her."

"Do you think you're going to be able to do that once the new owners take over?"

"I don't know, Maggie. I'll just keep doing my job. And that's all any of us can do."

I ended the meeting then the way I often did. "Okay, time to roll . . . and, people, let's be careful out there."

CHAPTER 23

I HEADED DOWNTOWN back to Mulberry Street. That's where I had trailed the woman Ronald Bannister had been kissing in the bar. Maybe she could tell me something more about him. Maybe she could help me figure out how he fit into all this. Maybe she could give me some tips on how to pick up a billionaire like Bannister so I could sleep with a rich guy too.

The building looked different in the daylight than it did the night I'd been here before. I realized now that the entire first floor was an Italian restaurant named Marcello's. There was a menu by the front door. It featured a dazzling array of pasta, with the specialty of the day: chicken parmigiana.

I liked the sound of that. I could forget about the redheaded woman and stuff myself with Italian food. Except it wasn't even 10:00 a.m. yet, and the restaurant wasn't open. Besides, chicken parmigiana is not exactly your ideal breakfast meal.

I made my way instead to a side door with a small lobby and names on the intercom of those who lived in apartments above the restaurant. The names on the third floor—where I'd seen the woman go the night I followed her—were just like I remembered them. Jessica Geiger and Joseph Daniels. I pushed the button to buzz Jessica Geiger.

I wasn't sure exactly how I was going to handle this. At the moment, I had the element of surprise when it came to dealing with this woman. She didn't know I had been watching her at the hotel bar, and she didn't know I'd followed her home here afterward. I could come up with some sort of clever cover story about why I wanted to see her. Or I could simply straight up tell her I was a TV newswoman.

As it turned out, I didn't have to do either because there was no answer. I tried several times. But nothing from Jessica Geiger's apartment.

Without any other viable option, I pressed the buzzer for Joseph Daniels. Who knows, she might be with the Daniels guy.

I did get an answer this time.

A woman's voice on the intercom.

Sounded like an elderly woman.

I told her who I was, said I was working on a story for Channel 10 News, and asked if I could come up to talk to her. You never know how people are going to react to something like this, but I guess she was intrigued. She buzzed me in and met me at the door of her apartment a few minutes later.

"I recognized your name," she said by way of explanation when we sat down in her living room. "I recognize your face now too. That's why I let you up. I know who you are. Although I can't imagine why a big star TV newswoman like you might be interested in talking to me."

I smiled.

"You're not Joseph Daniels?"

"No, that's my husband. He passed away."

"I'm sorry."

"I'm Naomi Daniels."

"And you leave your husband's name downstairs in the lobby on the mailbox?"

"Yes. I'm not sure why. I suppose in his memory. Or maybe for protection so people don't know there's just a woman living alone up here. Anyway, I've never bothered to change it. But what does any of this have to do with you and your reason for being here to talk to an old woman like me?"

Norma Daniels was definitely up there in years. Probably well into her seventies. But dressed impeccably in a sundress and sandals and her hair perfectly combed. I saw a picture of her and her husband on a table next to where we were sitting. They looked like a happy couple. Now he was gone, and she was alone. But she still seemed full of life.

"I'm actually looking for Jessica Geiger," I said.

"Oh, she's gone too."

The hair on the back of my neck stood up.

"Do you mean she's *dead*?"

"Oh, no. At least not as far as I know. She moved out. A few months ago."

"And no one bothered to change the name in the lobby?"

"I guess."

"What did she look like?"

Norma Daniels described a woman of about fifty with short dark hair and a stocky build.

That sure didn't sound like the redhead from the bar.

Just to be sure, I showed her the pictures on my iPhone.

"This is not Jessica Geiger, right?"

"Not even close. But I have seen that woman. She's been in the building. And I have heard someone going in and out of Jessica Geiger's old apartment. So that could be the one you're looking for."

"How would I find out who's the tenant of that apartment now?"

"Check downstairs at the restaurant. They own the building. I've lived here for a long time, and there's been several owners. But I pay my rent to them now. They would know, assuming there is someone living there again."

I thanked her and then started to leave to go downstairs to the restaurant.

"Are you going to put me on TV?"

"Well, it's possible."

"You can use my name. Of, if anything else comes out of all this, bring some cameras around and shoot video of me."

I laughed. "I just might do that."

"Never too old to become a TV celebrity," she told me with a big smile.

*   *   *

There was activity inside the restaurant now. I looked through the window and saw people milling around. There were a few who looked like waiters, and a chef too. Another guy stood by the register who I assumed must be the manager. He was the one that I needed to talk to.

I was about to push the door open and go inside when another figure came into view. He walked over to the man I thought was the manager. The two of them soon became involved in what looked like an animated discussion.

It wasn't hard for me to identify this guy.

The big man from the bar at the hotel

The one I thought was a security guard there, but really wasn't.

And here he was, showing up unexpectedly at the same address where'd I'd tracked the redheaded woman at the bar that night with Ronald Bannister.

What in the hell was going on here?

Well, I didn't have the slightest idea.

But I backed away from the door and got out of there before he spotted me.

CHAPTER 24

OKAY, I KNEW NOW—or at least I was pretty sure—that the phony security guard and Ronald Bannister were both somehow involved in all this.

I mean this guy had been at the hotel bar with Bannister that night like I was.

And now he shows up at the place where I'd followed the red-headed woman Bannister had gone upstairs to the hotel room with after leaving the bar.

Even if I believed Bannister's wife, who said that she had never hired Wendy Kyle to spy on her husband—and I did believe her—I still wanted to talk to Bannister about all this and about why his name was in that diary entry police found in Kyle's office. Except Ronald Bannister had made it very clear—in the form of a legal letter even—that he had no intention of letting me interview him.

So what should I do next?

Well, just because Ronald Bannister wouldn't talk to me, that didn't mean I couldn't try to talk to him. Maybe I should go under-cover and pull the Honey Trap maneuver on him. Dress myself up sexy like Wendy Kyle did, then hit on him and see if he reacts. If he does, I start asking him questions about things like why Wendy

Kyle might have had his name in the diary page left behind at her office.

The only problem with that was I wasn't sure I was Bannister's type. A woman pushing fifty might not be the right bait to attract him in the Honey Trap. No, his tastes ran more like the redhead in the bar, or someone like Wendy Kyle had been. If he rejected my advances, I'd never get the interview with him. Even worse, I'd have to deal with the trauma that he didn't find me hot enough to cheat with on his wife. I take rejection very badly.

I thought about some of my other options to pursue the story.

I could go back to Wendy Kyle's office. Maybe I could sneak into her old office. Maybe she left behind a piece of evidence that could turn the whole story around. Which would be nice, but unlikely. I was certain the police had combed every inch of that office after finding the client list and the opening diary page and who knows what else. So that seemed like a dead end too.

But what about the place where she lived? The police probably checked that out too, but not as painstakingly. There was a better chance of finding something there for me than in her office. Presumably her furniture and other possessions were still there until someone had a chance to move them out. That gave me an idea.

I Ubered up to her building at 96th Street and Third Avenue. It was quicker than the subway and also helped me avoid any more distractions from Justin Bieber or Jehovah's Witnesses or loud rap music. By the time my car got to 96th and Third, I had finalized my plan on what to do at Wendy Kyle's building. It was quite an excellent plan, if I do say so myself.

The building itself was a big one, with probably more than 200 units of varying sizes. Only a few of these were two-bedroom apartments, I found out from the building website. That was good. Because I knew Wendy Kyle's apartment had been a two-bedroom.

"I'm looking for a two-bedroom apartment," I told the manager of the building when I found him.

I gave him a story about how I'd just gotten transferred here from another city and needed to find a place to live in Manhattan as quickly as possible. There was always a chance, of course, that he'd recognize me from TV as a reporter. If that happened, I'd have to go to Plan B. And I didn't really have a Plan B. But my original plan worked.

"We do have a two-bedroom that will be opening up very soon," he said.

"Good. Can I see it?"

"Uh, not yet. The previous tenant's belongings are still there."

"But that tenant is leaving?"

"Well, yes. I'm sure she won't be with us much longer. That is, she's gone—and her belongings will be gone soon too."

I guess that was a way of not having to tell me straight out that the previous tenant had died in a horrific bomb blast.

"It would be a few more days, and then I'd be happy to show you the place once its empty."

"Gee, I'd like to find something right now. Couldn't I go in and take a peek? Even if the previous tenant's stuff is still in the apartment? I don't mind. I want to get a feel of the place."

"I don't know . . ."

"Look, I need to decide on something today. All I'm asking is you let me check it out. I'd like to rent in this building. I've heard good things about it. But if not, I'm going to have to look elsewhere. C'mon, give me a key so I can go in and look. It'll be no bother at all for you. I can't wait a few days. I'll have to take something else . . ."

That did it. He rummaged around in his desk, took out a set of keys, and handed them to me. Then he gave me directions to get to the apartment.

It turned out to be on the 12th floor. And it had been Wendy Kyle's apartment, as I had hoped. I confirmed that as soon as I went in and saw pictures of her in the hallway. Some of them from her police days, some from her work as a private investigator, some of her in casual shots. She looked good in all of them. Damn, she had been an attractive woman.

I did a quick check around the living room, then went through the drawer and closets in her main bedroom. The closets were filled with fashionable clothes, many of them very sexy. Tools of the trade she did for Wendy Kyle. Setting the bait for her Honey Trap. There was lots of expensive-looking jewelry in the drawers too. I wondered if the manager downstairs knew this. If he did, he probably wouldn't have let me come up here alone and maybe steal it.

The second bedroom had been turned into a kind of informal office. Except I didn't find much of interest in there. It was more of a personal office with her paid bills for electricity and cable and stuff like that. She apparently kept her professional records at the Heartbreaker Investigations office in Times Square. By the time I'd finished looking through all this, I was getting dejected.

I walked back into the living room and started looking through it more carefully this time, even though I wasn't confident I was going to do any better here than in the rest of the apartment.

I mean, the good news was my plan had worked beautifully, and I'd talked my way into Wendy Kyle's apartment.

The bad news was I hadn't found out anything significant by doing this.

I was still looking around there when I heard a key in the front door. Probably the manager coming up to see if I liked the place. I wondered if I should tell him about the jewelry in the bedroom. But then he might steal it himself.

Except when the door opened, it wasn't the manager at all.

It was a woman.

"Who are you and what are you doing here?" I asked because I couldn't think of anything else to say.

"Who are you and what are you doing here?" she answered.

"I asked first."

She walked in and stood in front of me. If this woman was afraid of me at all, she sure didn't act like it.

"I'm a potential tenant," I said. "The manager let me in to see if I wanted to rent this place. It does seem like a very interesting apartment."

"That's a load of crap," she said with a laugh.

"Excuse me?"

"You're a TV reporter. Clare Carlson. I've seen you on the air. Reporting about Wendy's murder."

I sighed.

"Guilty as charged," I said. "Okay, I'm a reporter. I tricked the manager into letting me in here. I wanted to look for something— any clue at all—that might tell me who and why someone murdered Wendy Kyle. That's what I'm doing here. Now it's your turn. Who the hell are you?"

"My name is Alex Sinclair," she said. "I was Wendy's partner."

"Partner in her investigative business?"

"No, her sexual partner."

"You mean you and she were . . ."

"That's right. We were lovers."

CHAPTER 25

"WENDY KYLE WAS bisexual," I said.

"Yes, she was."

"And you were her significant other?"

"We've been in a relationship for the past six months."

"I didn't know Wendy was, uh . . ."

"Bisexual?"

"Right."

This woman had me a bit off my game. She'd caught me off guard when she walked into the apartment while I searched it. And then, she'd hit me with the bombshell revelation that she was the female lover of Wendy Kyle.

She looked a bit older than Wendy Kyle had been—mid-forties or so. Short blonde hair, full but not fat figure, dressed in a snappy two-piece business suit that made me figure she was some kind of a professional person.

I have to admit that I was surprised Wendy Kyle's most recent lover was a woman, not a man. I mean, she'd been married to a man, she investigated men having affairs, I assumed she slept with men too. Or maybe she'd had so many bad relationships with men that she decided her romantic life would be better with a woman.

I didn't care about any of that, of course. What was important was this woman had been close to Wendy Kyle before she died. I had to try to find out from her what she knew.

"Would you talk to me about Wendy?" I asked her.

"On the air? No."

"Why not?"

"Because someone murdered her. Someone who was unhappy about what she was doing. I'm not putting myself out there as a target too. Whoever did this to Wendy might figure I knew whatever information they wanted to keep quiet. They'd want to find out what I did or didn't know. The same as you."

"What if we talked about Wendy off the record? You tell me whatever you can to help my story, and I'll keep your name out of it."

"I'll be a source?"

"Yes."

"An unidentified source."

"That's right."

"Sort of like Deep Throat."

This had happened to me before. Even though it's been more than fifty years since Watergate and Woodward and Bernstein, everyone thought being a news source was like Deep Throat.

"Yes, like Deep Throat," I said.

"I'm still not sure. Why should I do this? Why should I help you?"

"Because I want to find out the person who killed Wendy and why. I think you do too, Alex."

She told me she was a lawyer. Wendy Kyle's lawyer. They'd met when Wendy had litigious issues in her investigation business. Someone had sued her for invasion of privacy and claimed she'd used illegal surveillance tactics that cost him a lot of money in a divorce case. One thing led to another, and Wendy and Alex soon began a personal romantic relationship.

"I think she was still interested in men," Alex Sinclair said. "I mean, I'd get pissed when I saw her checking out some attractive guy in a bar or whatever, and I worried one day she might leave me to go back with a man. But I knew she loved me too. I don't think I was her first woman. But I was never sure if it was simply a passing phase with her and she'd tell me that. But I guess now we'll never know. She was a complex woman. You had to take Wendy with all her strengths and her faults. But I loved her unconditionally."

Her eyes glistened with tears as she said that, and she wiped them away with her hand. My God, this woman would have been a great interview on the air for TV if I could have gotten her to go public. But I'd made her this deal—given her my word I'd keep her out of it—so I just listened to whatever she was telling me.

"Do you have any suspicions about who murdered Wendy?" I asked.

"Wow, that's a long list of possible suspects, huh? But I'm sure you already know most of them. The people at the NYPD that got her fired. All the cheating husbands she'd exposed who lost big money because of it in divorce proceedings. Wendy pissed a lot of people off."

"But no specific name comes to mind?"

"No, I can't imagine anyone hated her enough to put a bomb in her car." She shook her head sadly. "It's still so hard to believe something like this could have happened to her."

I asked about the client list and the diary page police had found in Wendy Kyle's office, but she wasn't any help on that.

"Wendy and I tried to keep our professional life out of our relationship," she said. "Oh, yes, I was her lawyer. But she only involved me in her work when there was some legal issue or pending lawsuit. She never really talked about things like the identities of her other clients or the things she did for them. I didn't really want to know either."

"Did she ever mention Ronald Bannister's name?"

"The billionaire?"

"Yes, that's him."

"No. Why would she? Was she doing something involving him?"

"That's what I'm trying to find out."

I wasn't getting much from her, but I kept going.

"When was the last time you saw Wendy?"

"The night before she died. We spent that night together. Right here in this apartment. Then she went to work in the morning. It was the last time I ever saw her."

"Did she seem upset by anything that morning? Worried? Concerned something might happen to her? Because that's what she said in the diary entry found in her office. That she feared for her life."

"She didn't say anything to me that morning. But she had seemed very unnerved for the past few days. Very stressed out. And yes, maybe worried about her safety too. I asked her about it a couple of times, and she wouldn't talk about it. I was going to ask her more about it, but—well, she died right afterward."

"And you have no idea what she might have been stressed out and worried about?"

"Not really."

"Did you tell the police she seemed stressed out and scared about something before she died?"

"Of course, I told the police everything I knew."

"It's funny, no one ever mentioned that fact to me."

"Well, I told him."

"Who was *him*?"

"One of the detectives that spoke to me."

"Do you remember his name?"

"Uh, let me think for a second. He was a homicide sergeant from a precinct here in Manhattan. I remember that. His name was . . . Sgt. Markham."

"Sam Markham?"

"Yes, do you know him?"

CHAPTER 26

"I HAVE A PROBLEM," I said to Janet Wood.

"A problem involving what?"

"Men."

"That's a pretty far-reaching topic."

"This problem involves three men."

"No surprise there, given your history."

"It isn't personal this time, Janet. It's professional. I've got three men that I can't figure how they figure into the Wendy Kyle story. Even though I'm pretty sure they do."

We were walking down Madison Avenue on a sunny day amid the lunch hour crowds on the street. We were having lunch too. Janet had a yogurt she was eating with a spoon as we walked. I had a hot dog I'd bought from a street vendor that was covered in sauerkraut, relish, onions, and mustard. Sure, it was junk food. But I figured walking while I ate it—some good solid exercise—would make up for it. I'm always thinking healthy.

"First, there's Ronald Bannister," I said, between bites of the hot dog. "He's got to be involved, but I can't figure out how.

"His name was mentioned in the diary entry Wendy Kyle left behind in her office, and he sure fits as the kind of guy she would be investigating based on the performance I saw him putting on with the woman at the hotel bar. But his wife says she didn't hire Kyle, and I believe her. She didn't seem to have any problem with what her husband was doing in those pictures I showed her, because they had an arrangement.

"So then why was Wendy Kyle investigating Bannister? Or was she? His name was mentioned in the diary entry found at her office. That was first revealed to me by my ex-husband Sam Markham. Which brings me to man problem #2."

"Sam?" Janet asked.

"Uh-huh."

"How does he fit into your problem?"

I told her what I'd found out about Sam—and about his wife hiring Wendy Kyle to investigate him for cheating on her.

"That sounds like a potential motive for murder, huh?"

"He's your ex-husband, Clare. Do you really think he's capable of something like that?"

"No. But I think he's capable of being unfaithful with another woman. He never cheated on me when we were married, as far as I know, but he tried to get me to go to bed with him a few times since he's been with the current wife. He's also got this new woman partner. She's pretty attractive, and she's really fixated on him. I can see him making a play for her. Or, even if he doesn't, his wife being jealous enough to try and find out if he might be. And his wife's name appearing on whatever client list police turned up, that would explain why he's being kept in the dark on the investigation."

"Because he'd have a potential motive for killing Wendy Kyle."

"Right. He doesn't want his wife to find out whatever Kyle discovered."

"But you don't believe that?"

"Of course not."

"Like you said, it's only speculation."

"Absolutely."

I was almost through with my hot dog, but I had almost as much relish, sauerkraut, onions, and mustard on my hands and face as I'd eaten. Janet, of course, looked impeccable as she took tiny spoonfuls of her yogurt. I used a couple of napkins to wipe some of it away and kept eating as we talked.

"Except," I said now.

"Except what?"

"There's something more, Janet. Sam questioned Wendy Kyle's girlfriend after the murder, I found out from her. Apparently, he was not supposed to be part of the investigation. So why was he still talking to people about it? Maybe because he has a personal interest in Kyle's murder."

"Jeez."

"Yeah."

My hot dog was gone now. I licked the remains off my fingers and saw that Janet was still working on her yogurt. How could I finish a big hot dog like that before she polished off a tiny cup of yogurt? What was wrong with this woman?

"And the third man you have a problem with?" Janet asked.

"My friend, the security guard from the hotel."

"Who really isn't a security guard."

"Right. I have no idea what he was doing that night at the hotel bar. But I gotta figure now that it had something to do with Bannister being there. The guy turns up the next day outside my office too. And then at the restaurant in the building where I tailed the woman Bannister was with that first night."

"What do you think he was doing at that restaurant?"

"Not sure. But I checked the place out. It is an Italian restaurant. But it also supposedly is a notorious hangout for mob guys, and a lot of police from 1 Police Plaza stop in there to drink and eat too."

"Wow! Mobsters. Cops. What do you think he is?"

"Maybe neither, maybe someone with his own agenda. But I have no idea what that is."

"Do you think this guy is dangerous?"

"I sure hope not."

It was time for Janet to go back to the office. Time for me too. She threw out the remains of her yogurt, then asked me before she left about Lucy again. I told her about our phone conversation and about the lawyer she had retained. Janet said that all sounded good for Lucy.

"What about you though?" she asked.

"What about me?"

"Bannister, Markham, and your mystery man."

"Ah yes. My three problems."

"What are you going to do next?"

"I do have a plan."

"What's your plan?"

"I'm going to buy another hot dog."

"And after that?"

"I'm going to break a promise I made my old boss, Jack Faron. I told him I'd let this business with my ex-husband play out before I did anything. But I can't do that, Janet. I realize that now. So I'm going to try to find out the truth about Sam Markham and Wendy Kyle."

"You're going to confront Sam?"

"No, not yet. First, I'm going to talk to his wife."

CHAPTER 27

THE HOUSE WHERE Sam Markham and his wife and young son lived was in a nice middle-class neighborhood of Midwood, Brooklyn. People always think about New York City being about Manhattan and skyscrapers and busy streets and stores everywhere. Sometimes even I thought that. But there's also a world of quiet residential neighborhoods in the city, and Sam Markham seemed to have found a good one.

I remembered when Sam and I were married we used to have arguments about this sort of thing. He talked about us buying a house back then, and I would tell him how much I loved Manhattan and had no plans to ever leave it. Sometimes the arguments would get pretty heated, like a lot of the arguments did between Sam and me before we got divorced. Well, Sam had finally found someone to share his house dream with. But had he screwed the whole dream up now with his infidelity?

I didn't expect I'd get a warm welcome from his wife as I knocked on her door. But I was wrong about that.

"Mrs. Markham, my name is—"

"Clare Carlson."

"Uh, that's right."

"Glad to finally meet you."

She stuck her hand out to me. I shook it.

"Mrs. Markham—"

"Call me Deborah."

"Okay, Deborah. We need to talk. About Sam."

"I know. Please come in."

We sat in the living room. At some point, she went out to another room and brought back their son. His name was Keith and he was almost three now. He said hello to me with the precious kind of cuteness little children of that age have. I never got to see that in my own daughter at that age. It took me until she was a young woman before I was able to catch up with my Lucy. I regretted how much I missed of her life because of that.

I explained to Deborah Markham why I was there.

To find out about her hiring Wendy Kyle to spy on her husband.

She didn't seem surprised by the question.

Or angry about it either.

"Yes, I did. I love Sam, but I never trusted him. I saw he had an eye for other women. And I became increasingly concerned he was acting on those urges. I began to suspect every woman he came in contact with. Especially that new partner of his. I always wondered about you too. Sam always seemed to have a thing for you. Even after you split up. I could see him making a play to get you to go to bed with him. Did that happen?"

"No, never. I've never done anything like that with Sam since our divorce."

Which was technically true.

I hadn't done anything with him.

Even though he had propositioned me on more than one occasion.

"And so when he got paired up with this new partner—and I found out she was an attractive woman—I began to worry. Especially because of the way he talked about her all the time and how great she was. It made me jealous. And so I hired this Kyle woman to see if anything was going on."

"Was there?"

"No. Nothing at all. She got back to me and said that it was all perfectly professional between Sam and his woman partner. She said the woman was in another relationship, and that it appeared to be strictly a mentor-type relationship between Sam and her. Nothing sexual about it."

"Wendy Kyle was certain about that?"

"Absolutely. She did ask me if I wanted to do the 'Honey Trap' thing with Sam. Where she would come on to him herself, to see if he made a play for her. But I said no. I'd found out what I needed from her."

Thank goodness for that, I thought to myself. I'd have bet the house on Sam going for the Honey Trap. Especially with a woman who looked as hot as Wendy Kyle.

"But then when this Kyle woman was killed, my name turned up in her client list. They went to Sam and questioned him. They believed he had nothing to do with it. In fact, he didn't even know I'd hired her until after she was dead. But he got very angry at me for doing it. Said I'd ruined his career. And then . . . he left."

"He's gone?"

"He moved out. I'm sure he'll be back though. He loves Keith. It's just that . . . well, I'm going to have to learn to trust him. Even though I'm not sure I ever totally can when it comes to other women. Do you understand?"

"I understand all too well," I said.

At least I was pretty convinced now that Sam had nothing to do with Wendy Kyle's murder.

But my God, what a mess of a marriage!

Were all marriages like this?

Sam's latest one to this woman.

Ronald Bannister's playing around regularly on his wife.

My daughter's unfaithful husband.

Scott Manning and his wife.

I guess that's why someone like Wendy Kyle had such a booming business exposing marital infidelities—until someone murdered her.

CHAPTER 28

LOOKING BACK ON my notes for this story, I tried to think of something I might have missed or could go back on for more information now. The one name that jumped out at me was Alex Sinclair. Wendy Kyle's girlfriend—or partner? I still wasn't sure how serious they were.

Alex Sinclair. She must know more than she told me.

I needed to go back and talk to her again.

I dialed the number she'd given me. It turned out to be the main number at a place called the Cochran Law Firm. I asked to speak to Alex Sinclair. The receptionist put me on hold for a short time. When she came back, she said that Alex was in a conference meeting with the firm's partners now, but I could leave a message on her voicemail.

I started to do that, but then changed my mind. While I'd been waiting on hold, I googled the address of the Cochran Law Firm. It was only a few blocks away from where I was in midtown at the Channel 10 News office, so I decided to walk over instead and talk to Alex Sinclair in person.

Face-to-face conversation was always better than on the phone. Especially for this conversation. I wanted to find out exactly how much Alex Sinclair knew about the diary, and Kyle's activities, and anything else about her life.

I needed to convince her to open up to me about everything.

And, even better, maybe I could convince the Sinclair woman to go on the air with it. That would be a ratings bonanza. WENDY KYLE'S LOVER TELLS ALL TO CHANNEL 10 NEWS' CLARE CARLSON IN EXCLUSIVE INTERVIEW!

Wow! Now that would be must-see TV!

All I had to do was convince Alex Sinclair to go public with the details of her romance with the murdered Wendy Kyle.

The Cochran Law Firm turned out to occupy two entire floors of the office building. Plush carpeting, expensive-looking paintings, modern furniture, and soft classical music playing in the entry area. Yep, it looked like it was a very lucrative law firm.

Of course, you never knew about a place like this. It could all be to put on an impressive front, while the bank was about to foreclose on unpaid loans and the landlord of the building was preparing eviction papers because they owed so much back rent. But, on the face of it, Wendy Kyle's woman worked for a damn impressive law firm.

I approached the receptionist's desk, told her I was the one who had called looking for Alex Sinclair, and asked if she was free to meet with me now.

"What is your name?" the receptionist asked.

"Clare Carlson."

"And what is your business with Ms. Sinclair?"

"I'm with Channel 10 News."

I handed her one of my cards.

"And this is concerning . . . ?"

"She'll know what it's about."

"If you could just give me the subject of your business—the type of legal advice you're seeking—that would help. Personal injury, disability, divorce, estate planning..."

"Wendy Kyle?"

"Excuse me?"

"Tell her it's Clare Carlson from Channel 10 News, and I'm here to talk to her some more about Wendy Kyle. Believe me, she'll know what this is about."

The receptionist gave me a funny look, but then disappeared through a door toward the rest of the offices.

When she came back, she directed me to a chair in the waiting room and said Alex Sinclair would be out shortly to see me.

There were several magazines on the table next to my chair. One was about Bloomberg business, the second was *Architectural Digest*, and the third was a celebrity magazine with Beyoncé and Jay-Z on the cover. I went for that one. It was always important to know the status of their marriage in order to keep up with conversation at the next celebrity party I went to.

Just when I was getting to some juicy gossip stuff, the door opened again and a woman came out. It was not Alex Sinclair. But she walked over to me and stood there with a quizzical look on her face.

"Can I help you?" she asked.

"I'm waiting for Alex Sinclair."

"Why does a Channel 10 newswoman want to talk to Alex Sinclair?"

"How about I discuss that with Ms. Sinclair?"

"Go ahead then..."

"What do you mean?"

"I'm Alex Sinclair."

I stared at her. Not only wasn't she the Alex Sinclair I had met, she didn't even look like her at all. She wasn't glamorous. She wasn't particularly pretty. She had short dark brown hair, a stocky build, and definitely did not come across as the type of woman who would be in a lesbian relationship with Wendy Kyle.

"Do you know Wendy Kyle?" I asked her.

I was so stunned I couldn't think of anything else to say.

"I know who she is. I read the papers. I watch TV news. But no, I don't know her. Why would you think that I did?"

"Then I guess you're not in a personal relationship with her."

"What kind of personal relationship?"

"A sexual one."

She sighed. "Ms. Carlson, I am married to Joseph Keough, one of the senior partners in this firm. I have three children, two in college and one that has graduated. I have never been in a sexual relationship with another woman in my entire life. Now what is this all about?"

"I have no idea," I said.

By the time I'd left, I was convinced she was telling me the truth. She was Alex Sinclair. She did not have any kind of a sexual relationship with Wendy Kyle; she did not even know Wendy Kyle.

Which left me with a very large unanswered question.

Who was the woman I met in Wendy Kyle's apartment?

If she wasn't Wendy Kyle's partner, then what was she doing there?

And why did she make up the phony story claiming she was someone else?

There was only one reason I could think of for her to do all this.

She had come to Wendy Kyle's apartment looking for something.

Just like me.

CHAPTER 29

"CLARE CARLSON, this is Norma Daniels," the woman said to me over the phone.

"Okay."

I wasn't sure who this was or what it was about.

"You asked me to call you."

"I did?"

"You said if I saw anyone at the apartment Jessica Geiger used to live in I should call you. You gave me your card with your number on it."

Ah, the elderly woman who lived above the Italian restaurant where I'd followed the redheaded woman who was with Bannister that first night.

"Is Jessica Geiger there?"

"No, she's long gone. But someone is in the apartment now. I heard the door slam, and I can hear noises coming from inside."

"You hear that from your apartment?"

"Well, I went out in the hall and listened by the door."

I laughed. "You'd make a helluva reporter yourself, Norma. Wait in your apartment. I'll be there as soon as I can."

When I got to Norma Daniels' place, she said no one had left the apartment, to the best of her knowledge. Which meant someone was still in there. I thought about knocking on the door to see who opened it, but instead I decided to wait it out a bit more. I thanked Norma Daniels, then told her I was going to wait outside the building to see what happened next.

It didn't take very long.

The door of the building opened about five minutes later, and someone came out.

It wasn't Norma Daniels.

And it wasn't the redheaded woman either.

It was the big security guard from the hotel. The security guard who wasn't really a security guard there. But then what the hell—and who the hell—was he?

I had hidden myself behind some parked cars on the street so he couldn't see me if he walked past. But he didn't look in my direction. Instead, he turned and went into the Italian restaurant again.

Was he connected to the people running the restaurant? Was he meeting someone there for a big sit-down? Or was he simply going in to eat lunch? It turned out to be the last one, from what I could tell. I made my way to one of the side windows in the restaurant and saw him sitting by himself at a table. A few minutes later, he was dining on a plate of what looked to me like tortellini.

The way I figured it, I had three options of what to do next. I could:

A) Go into the restaurant and confront him.
B) Sit down at his table and eat some of the tortellini with him.
C) Wait outside the restaurant to see where he went after he left.

I decided that A) was too dangerous; B) would be a diet buster for my plan to look fabulous on my fiftieth birthday; and so I went with C) instead.

There was a Starbucks kind of place—same idea, different chain—on the corner. I went there to get myself a coffee and a grilled cheese sandwich to eat. Then I went back to a position outside the restaurant where I could see my man eating inside. Damn, that tortellini dish looked delicious. My grilled cheese, on the other hand, was a tad on the greasy side. I thought as I ate it about all the crappy food I'd eaten as a reporter, standing around waiting for a story to happen.

Fortunately, this time it didn't take too long. Less than fifteen minutes later, he came out of the restaurant. I guess he was a fast eater. He surveyed the street outside, or at least I thought so anyway, and I ducked behind one of the cars.

No indication he saw anything on the street he didn't want to see.

He turned and started walking south on the street, heading farther downtown. Once or twice, he stopped to look in windows at a men's store and at a sporting goods place. He did not appear to be in any kind of a hurry. An ordinary guy going for a midday walk on the streets of Lower Manhattan.

It looked to me like he had no idea he was being followed. Which was a bit surprising. I mean, I'm not an experienced detective who knows how to put a tail on someone without being spotted. I really thought he would have noticed me behind him by now.

But then he wasn't very good at tailing people, either. I'd spotted him right away that morning when he was trying to watch me outside the office building at Channel 10.

He sped up his pace a bit now.

I did too.

I worried about him maybe going down in a subway station or hailing a cab or calling an Uber to pick him up. I wasn't sure what I'd do if that happened. Keep following him the best I could, I guess.

But instead, he kept going on foot, eventually heading toward Park Row. He clearly had a destination in mind.

And it didn't take me long to figure out what it was.

He climbed the steps and opened the front door of a big building on Park Row. Then he went inside.

I knew the building pretty well.

I'd just been inside it myself a few days ago.

It was the Police Headquarters building.

CHAPTER 30

I WAS ON a roll now.

Things were in motion.

Pieces were coming together.

I'd linked the hotel security guard—who wasn't really a hotel security guard—to the NYPD at One Police Plaza. I'd discovered the mystery woman who was so intent on getting herself into Wendy Kyle's apartment, just like I was, had lied about who she was. No, I didn't have all the answers on the story yet. But I had that feeling of adrenaline I get as a reporter whenever I'm on the right track.

I love the rush I get on a story like this. It's what I live for. What a great feeling it is to be on the verge of breaking a big scoop. Scoring another exclusive. It excites me, it turns me on more than anything else can. Drink. Food. Even sex. Well, maybe not more than sex—but it's damn close between the two.

Yep, this was going to be a great moment for me.

I was on the verge of a triumph that could make me forget—at least for a while—about Susan Endicott, the new owners taking over Channel 10, my daughter's broken marriage, and my own upcoming half-century milestone.

I would keep digging and digging now until I finally found out who killed Wendy Kyle—and why.

That was my plan anyway.

And then . . .

Then everything fell apart.

*   *   *

The police unexpectedly put out an announcement that they had tracked down one of Wendy Kyle's ex-husbands, Ted Lansmore—and that they had determined he was the killer.

Lansmore had committed suicide before he could be taken into custody, but he left behind a confession note and other evidence of his guilt in his ex-wife's death.

The cops had found him in a cabin outside of Woodstock in upstate New York, about a hundred miles north of the city. They'd got on to him because he had apparently cashed a recent NYPD pension check in that area.

When no one answered the door at the cabin, NYPD officers—along with local police and state troopers—broke down the door to get inside.

They found Lansmore lying dead on a bed, blood covering his head and hand still grasping a 9 mm Luger—the gun he had used as a police officer. There seemed to be little question as to what had happened. He had eaten his pistol, as they say in police parlance—a former cop suicide.

There was a note on the table next to his body. It turned out to be a confession. In it, he admitted to murdering his ex-wife and said he was traumatized by regret over it. He said he loved her. But that she'd told him she was going to reveal secrets about police corruption he was involved in that would ruin his pension and his retirement and his life.

He said he begged her not to do it. But she just laughed, so he decided to kill her. Later, after he realized what he had done, he said his guilt and grief were so overwhelming he could no longer go on.

"I loved Wendy, I really did," he said in the note. "I'll always love her, no matter what she did. And when I killed her—I killed myself too. So now it's time to finish the job."

There were several pages that appeared to be from Wendy Kyle's diary—like the opening diary page police had found in her office—scattered around the room. They were pages she had written about Lansmore. In them, she revealed mistakes he'd made on the street and during arrests; money and drugs he'd stolen; and— perhaps most painful of all for him—mocked what she called his ineptitude as a sexual partner.

Also in the room was material on how to make a car bomb that he had downloaded from the internet. One of the sections gave a step-by-step instruction guide that said could be done by someone with no previous knowledge of explosives.

Bomb making for the beginner.

Beautiful.

"Based on all this information, it is clear to NYPD investigators that Ted Lansmore murdered his ex-wife to prevent her from revealing incriminating and embarrassing information about him," a police statement said. "There is no indication that anyone else was involved in Wendy Kyle's murder. We believe Wendy Kyle's murder has been solved, and the case is now closed with the suicide and confession of Ted Lansmore."

*   *   *

I broke into our regular programming with a breaking news bulletin—and then I led the 6:00 p.m. newscast with my report on all the shocking developments.

> ME: *Police announced today they have solved the shocking midtown car bombing case that killed controversial law enforcement figure Wendy Kyle.*
>
> *Her ex-husband Ted Lansmore was found dead from a self-inflicted gunshot wound in an isolated upstate New York cabin—and left behind a suicide note in which he confessed he had killed her.*
>
> *There were also materials found in the room that helped him build the bomb that exploded in her car, according to police.*
>
> *It's been speculated that many other men—some of them prominent and powerful figures—were linked to Kyle and her investigations prior to this.*
>
> *But investigators now say they are convinced that none of Kyle's actions—either while she was on the police force, or later when she employed sensational tactics as a private investigator to catch men cheating on their wives and costing them money in divorce cases—had anything to do with her murder.*

*   *   *

The police might be convinced of that. But I wasn't.

I told that to Maggie after the broadcast.

"I checked and there's no evidence of any injuries to him besides the fatal wound from the gun," I said. "We said earlier police believed a second person appeared to have suffered some kind of damage from the attack. There should have been some indication of that—even a damaged piece of clothing—in that cabin. But there wasn't. Why is that?"

"Maybe it just nicked him and took off a piece of the clothing, but didn't cause any significant damage to him. That's possible. Just because there was no evidence of it doesn't mean he wasn't hit—at least superficially—by the blast."

"I still have a lot of questions."

"The police say the investigation is over. They've got their man."

"My investigation isn't over. You know me, Maggie. Remember the time a year or so ago when they said that Army veteran killed a college student. They claimed that case was closed too. Until I opened it for them and caught the real killer."

"I know, Clare. You have done that a few times in the past. But the police aren't always wrong. They're not stupid. And maybe they're not as stupid on this case as you'd like to think. And maybe, just maybe . . . you're not always right."

"I didn't say the police were stupid on this case."

"Then what?"

"A cover-up. An ingenious cover-up. What better way for someone in power to prevent any further investigation than producing a patsy who can be blamed for the crime? A patsy like Ted Lansmore who conveniently commits suicide before anyone can ask him questions about his confession note."

"C'mon, you're really reaching on this one."

"Am I?"

"There's no evidence of anything you're saying."

"Then I'll find evidence."

Maggie sighed.

"So this is not over, is it?"

"Nope."

"You're going to keep working on this story, no matter what I or anyone else tells you."

"What could stop me?"

CHAPTER 31

THE WORD I got when I arrived at Channel 10 News the next morning was that our new owner was here to meet us.

Well, not our new owner yet.

But our impending owner, as soon as the deal for the station went through with Kaiser Media and its head, Brendan Kaiser.

"The new owner is here," Dani said to me when I ran into her while getting coffee downstairs.

"The new owner just showed up," Vic Zizzo, the traffic reporter, said when I got off the elevator.

"Guess who's here?" Maggie said to me when I walked into my office.

"The new owner."

"How did you know?"

"I'm an investigative reporter, remember?"

"He's in Susan Endicott's office with her right now. She said you should go in there as soon as you got here. She's going to introduce you to him."

"Oh, this should be a fun morning."

"Even more *fun* than you think."

"What do you mean?"

"Wait until you meet this guy."

I sighed and started walking toward Endicott's office.

"Got any advice for me?" I asked Maggie before I left.

"Yes, keep your mouth shut, Clare."

"Everybody keeps telling me that these days."

*   *   *

The guy in Endicott's office didn't exactly look like a new media owner to me. His name was Owen Lasker, and he was probably somewhere in his thirties. But he seemed even younger. He had short, light brown hair and fair skin with a kind of a baby face, and he was dressed in a conservative and very serious-looking blue suit, with a blue and red striped tie and a white shirt. I guess he thought it made him look professional and important. But it didn't. At least not to me. He looked . . . boring.

"This is Clare Carlson, our news director," Endicott was saying now. "Clare, this is Owen Lasker. He's the man we'll be reporting to going forward as soon as the sale of the station is finalized."

"I've heard a lot about you," Lasker said to me.

The way he said it, without a smile or any warmth, made me wonder if that was a good thing or not.

"And you're the new owner?"

"I'm not the owner. This isn't going to be like it's been under Brendan Kaiser, with him running things himself a lot of the time. We're a conglomerate of investors at Kellogg and Klein, and we assign the operations supervision of our properties to different supervisors in the corporation. I'm the one they chose to run Channel 10."

"Lucky for us," I said.

Endicott shot me a nasty look, but Lasker didn't seem to pick up on the sarcasm at all.

"I will tell you right now that things will be a lot different than working with Brendan Kaiser. We at Kellogg and Klein operate with a much more multifaceted business approach aimed at maximizing profitability in all aspects of the operations at our properties."

He then went into a long spiel of corporate-speak—using a lot of terms I didn't understand—until I thought my head was going to explode.

I looked over at Endicott and rolled my eyes. She looked away quickly. My God, I couldn't believe that Susan Endicott was at the moment the person I liked most in this room. That's how much I disliked this Owen Lasker guy. I'd only known him for five minutes or so, but that was enough to make my decision on him.

Could this get any worse?

And then . . . it did get worse.

"I'd like to speak to you specially about your role here at Channel 10, Ms. Carlson," Lasker said.

Uh-oh.

"How do you see your role here?"

"I'm a journalist. I break big stories. Carlson's the name, exclusives are my game." I smiled.

He did not smile back.

"But you are supposed to be the news director."

"I am."

"How can you effectively do your job as news director when you're running around the streets chasing stories like a reporter?"

"I multitask very well."

Lasker shook his head. "I—we at Kellogg and Klein—need you to focus entirely on being the news director. Our profit/loss margin will be determined by ad sales, viewer demographics, and audience share—all of which are your responsibilities to perform well at as the news director of this station."

"But I've broken a lot of big stories for Channel 10!"

"It doesn't matter."

"My exclusives don't matter?"

"Not really."

"But good journalism is important and—"

"No, the journalism part isn't important for us. Oh, I know there's the romantic notion that you will break something like Watergate and change the world with your story. But it doesn't work that way anymore. All your exclusives, your big stories—they don't really move the numbers for us. All of these business decisions we're making, and you should be a part of them, that's what pushes the needle."

"Journalism doesn't matter to you," I muttered.

"Carrying out all of your duties as news director is what matters to us. Those business factors I talked about will be much more important in the end than any of your *so-called big scoops*. Are we clear on that?"

"Absolutely."

Endicott jumped in before I could say anything more. "I've been telling Clare this myself. Leave the reporting to others and concentrate on your job as news director. And that's what Clare will be doing from now on. You've got my promise on that."

*   *   *

Once Lasker had left, I glared at Endicott.

"Wow, you were really in there pitching for me, all the way. What about our agreement to put up a united front with the new owner? I didn't exactly see you backing me up there with the boy wonder Lasker."

"I saved you," she said.

"Exactly how did you do that?"

"You can't mouth off to a guy like that. You can't charm him with your wit and smart remarks like you did a lot of the time with Kaiser. Kaiser liked you. He bent the rules for you and allowed you to get away with a lot because you had a personal relationship with him. These kinds of corporate people aren't like that. They are all about the bottom line; they are all about money. And I know more about them than you do. You don't talk back or argue with them about their corporate strategy. If you do, they'll just get someone else to carry it out the way they want. That's why you're only going to be the news director here going forward. No more reporting for you."

"But you're the one who wanted me out there on camera. Talked about my star power."

"That was for Kaiser. Things have changed now. I understand that, even if you don't."

"Look, at least let me finish up the Wendy Kyle story."

"The Wendy Kyle story is over."

"I'm not sure about that."

"You don't believe the police ruling of it as a murder and then a suicide?"

"There's still a lot of unanswered questions. A lot of loose ends. About Bannister. About the security-type guy I ran into. About the woman posing as Kyle's girlfriend. About the missing diary pages. About Wendy Kyle's claims of corruption in the police department. About—"

"Are any of these a story we can put on the air?"

"Not yet. But they could be. We have to do more digging."

"Then assign other reporters to do the digging for us."

"It's my goddamned story!"

"Not anymore, Clare," Endicott said. "This story's over for you."

PART II

B-ROLL

CHAPTER 32

I ONLY HAD a few weeks of my youth left until I turned fifty, so I decided to make the most of it while I still could.

I thought about a lot of options. Things I wanted to do before I got too old. Maybe I could learn how to skydive. Or water-ski. Or play tennis. Or travel to Timbuktu or Antarctica or some other fascinating place.

On the other hand, I liked the idea of focusing my attention on another subject—men. I could go looking for a man to dazzle with my sex appeal and cuteness and overall adorable qualities before they started disappearing as I headed into middle age after I turned the big 5-0.

But which man?

The top men on my wish list at the moment, I decided, were Brad Pitt and Ryan Gosling. But I found out Brad was shooting a movie down in Mexico, and that seemed like a long way for me to travel—even for Brad Pitt. And Ryan Gosling continued his puzzling behavior of refusing to respond to any emails, tweets, or phone calls from me.

I thought about some of the men who had been a part of my life in the past.

At the top of that list was Scott Manning, the ex-cop who was now an FBI agent. Scott was good-looking, smart, funny, and we had shown in the past that we had great chemistry together—especially in the bedroom. The problem, of course—and it was a big problem—was that he was married and still with his wife and family. Strike one on Scott Manning.

Next up was my ex-husband, Sam Markham. I knew Sam was still interested in me, even after we'd gotten divorced. But Sam was mad at me now. He'd gone back to his wife, who told him about our meeting, and he confronted me angrily about that afterward. I guess people get upset when you suggest they might be a murderer. I was glad Sam turned out not to be a murderer. And he'd made it clear on more than one occasion in the past that he wanted to go to bed with me again. I'd always said no to his advances. But now, with the looming drama of my fiftieth birthday coming up, maybe it was time to reconsider that decision. Except Sam wasn't speaking to me at the moment. He was married too, just like Scott Manning. Two strikes against Sam Markham.

Pete Bevelaqua wasn't married. He had that going for him. But not much else. I'd dated him for a while about a year ago until I found out 1) he lied to me and wasn't the real Pete Bevelaqua, 2) he was working for the mob, and 3) he may have played a part in the deaths of several people by his actions for the mob. That's strike three for ol' Pete. Three strikes and out.

There were plenty of other men from my past that I looked at, too, and then rejected as possibilities.

All in all, I'd been pretty active—sexually speaking.

But now—on the cusp of turning AARP age at fifty—I was all alone.

I was running out of men in this town.

*   *   *

It felt strange for me not to be chasing stories or appearing on the air anymore.

In TV news, there's a term we use called B-Roll. B-Roll refers to video you use with the live coverage of a story. Stock footage of old scenes, or past events, or from previous stories. It doesn't really tell the news story you have on air—it's only there to help flesh it out for the viewer.

That's kind of how I felt now about my life at Channel 10. I was B-Roll. I was there for support and background help and all the behind-the-scenes stuff. I was still busy running the newsroom and putting on the 6:00 p.m. and 11:00 p.m. shows each night. But I wasn't actually breaking news stories anymore. I wasn't covering the news. I missed the actual reporting I'd been doing until recently.

Oh, I'd gone through streaks before when I wasn't on air—just being a news director running things behind the scenes. And I'd been able to deal with that then. But this was somehow different for me. I guess I felt I still had unfinished work to do. An unfinished story in Wendy Kyle.

I had a lot of angles and leads I wanted to check out. But I couldn't do it now that I was off the story for good. And, even though I still cared, the story had ended with the suicide and confession of Wendy Kyle's ex-husband, and everyone had forgotten about it now. Everyone except me.

The sale of the station from Brendan Kaiser and Kaiser Media to Kellogg and Klein hadn't officially gone through yet, but everyone was acting as if it had. Owen Lasker was on the phone or in the newsroom a lot giving us his ideas on how to run the newscast. His big idea—and he acted as if he was the first person who ever thought of it—was for us to be the "Happy News" station. Everyone would laugh and joke around on air as if we were all great friends. I think this concept was first proposed back in the '60s and it had been used at countless TV stations since then. But Lasker thought he had a swell idea in turning us into the Channel 10 Happy News Team.

The news itself kept happening, of course. Whether I was reporting it myself or not. The news never stops. Jaime Ortiz—New York's new political star—had won the primary election, and he was overwhelmingly favored to get to the governor's mansion in November. Some people thought we should be giving him more on-air coverage, but politics didn't really move our ratings very much on TV news. Unless it was the right kind of politics for us. Like a story out of Brooklyn about a councilman who used his campaign funds to pay for hookers, strippers, and porn videos. Now that's a political story! There was also all the usual crime, mass transit, human interest, sports, and celebrity stories.

But it was almost summertime now, and much of the news on TV this time of year is about the weather. It didn't used to be that way when I worked at a newspaper. I remember I had an editor there once who hated doing weather stories, especially in the summer. "We're gonna ask people to pay money to buy a paper so we can tell them its hot outside?" he used to say. "They already know its goddamned hot outside!"

But on TV you can never have too much weather news. I'd done it all. One standby is a feature on the hottest job in New York during the summer—it was a tie between a pizza parlor worker and a guy who poured asphalt on the highway. Another time we even tried to prove the old adage that "it's hot enough to fry an egg out there." We cracked an egg and waited in front of the camera for it to fry. It didn't. But it was still a memorable TV moment.

Sometimes the ideas get even crazier and sillier—it makes people downright giddy.

Like at a recent Channel 10 news meeting.

"How about we come up with some fresh, different ideas on how to cover the weather?" I said to everyone. "Any ideas?"

"First man to get eaten by a shark at the beach gets a free TV set."

"Tenth man with sunstroke wins a Channel 10 T-shirt."

"Worst case of sunburn gets a tub of butter to put on it."

The most surprising thing that happened in the news meeting that day came when Brett and Dani suggested their own weather stunt. They said they would get married at the beach wearing bathing suits and standing in the water off of either Rockaway Beach or Coney Island.

"What do you think?" they both asked pretty much in unison.

"Uh, aren't you already married?" someone pointed out.

"Or are you getting divorced?" I asked. "I keep losing track of the exact status of your marriage."

"We love each other—we know that now," Dani said. "And we want to declare our love to the world, especially the TV viewers who watch us every night. So we've decided to reaffirm our vows at another public wedding ceremony. And this one will be broadcast by Channel 10 News."

Wow! I didn't see that one coming. But I had to admit it sure would be must-watch TV. I gave the go-ahead before the meeting was over, although I hoped they did it quickly before they changed their minds about being married to each other again. Like I've told them in the past, we could do a reality show on the two of them. They think I'm kidding, but I'm sort of serious.

*   *   *

I took a few days off at one point and went to visit my daughter in Virginia. I'm certainly not—nor have I ever been—a traditional mother to Lucy. I mean I wasn't there to see her take her first step or speak her first words or help her navigate her way through puberty in her teen years or watch her graduate like a normal mother–daughter relationship.

I always felt like I was playing catch-up as a mother since it had been only a few years ago that we were reunited. But she needed a mother now. I wanted to be there for her as best I could.

"I really need your advice, Mom," she said to me once I was there.

"About what?"

"Marriage."

I laughed.

"You're asking me for marriage advice?"

"Well, you certainly have a lot of experience in it."

"Bad experiences. Three of them. But go ahead, ask me your question."

"Why do things go wrong in a marriage?"

"Lots of reasons. Infidelity. Money. Boredom. Sometimes it's simply the realization that you're not with the person you want to spend the rest of your life with, even though you once thought you did. That's what happened to me. What happened in my marriages wasn't really the fault of any of my husbands, it was mine. I woke up one morning—in all three marriages—and realized I didn't want to be married to this person anymore."

"Do you think that's what happened with Greg?"

"I don't know, kiddo."

"What about the other woman? The woman he's seeing now? How can she do something like this? Break up a family. Take him away from me and from his daughter. How does a woman do that?"

I did have an answer to this question. Because I'd been the *other woman* before. More than once. But most recently with Scott Manning and his wife. I was sleeping with him—hoping he'd leave her for me—while she was with their children waiting for him to come home. Did I feel guilty about this? Not at the time. But now I did.

"How's Emily dealing with it?" I asked.

I'd spent time with my granddaughter after I arrived, but I didn't feel comfortable bringing the topic up with her.

"She's fine. At least for now. Greg and I agreed to take her to counseling to see if our breakup was having any traumatic effect on her. The counselor said it's always better for a child her age to deal with a separation than to live in a home where the parents are stressed out and fighting with each other. I think that's right. At least I hope so."

Lucy talked about how she wasn't sure what she was going to do with her life now. She had been a stay-at-home mom, raising Emily while Greg went to work every day. Now she said she wanted to have some kind of a career and a life of her own, but she wasn't sure how to do it.

"There's a lot of options," I said. "Go back to school for starts. Pick something you're interested in and throw yourself into that. It's what I do with being a journalist. What excites you? What would you like to do? Teaching? Law? Painting? Working in the financial world? Opening up a store of your own?"

She thought about it for a second.

"I like to write," she said.

"Then write."

"What would I write?"

"Write what you care about."

"Maybe I could be a journalist like you, huh?"

"You've sure got the bloodlines for it." I smiled.

"I wish I was as confident about that as you. I'm thirty years old. I don't have any experience in anything other than being a wife and a mother. I don't see how I could get hired by any TV station or newspaper or website. I'm not like you, Mom. Everything comes easy for you."

"Not really."

I told her about everything I was going through now: my new owners about to take over the station, the boss I hated in Endicott, being forced to stop reporting on air, my trauma over my impending fiftieth birthday, and my overall anxiety about what was ahead for me in the future.

"I didn't know all that," she said when I was finished.

"Nothing comes easy. Not for any of us. But you'll be fine," I told her.

Then I gave her a big hug.

"You, too, Mom," she said, hugging me back.

*   *   *

Back in my office at Channel 10 again, no matter how busy I was, I kept thinking about the Wendy Kyle story. All the unanswered questions I still had. The missing pieces to the puzzle. My doubts about the official ruling that she'd been murdered by her ex-husband, who then conveniently left a confession note and committed suicide.

I really wanted to know more.

But there wasn't much of anything I could do.

I was off the story, and that was that.

The Wendy Kyle story was over.

I told myself that one more time, then I began pulling up all the files and interviews and broadcasts I'd done on Wendy Kyle at Channel 10.

Damn, there were so many loose ends to this story still out there. Sitting and going through all this material again now, I suddenly thought about one of them. One loose end, one trail I hadn't really followed. Something I'd never really checked out about the redheaded woman who'd been in the bar with Ronald Bannister. Yes, I'd tracked her back to the apartment over the Italian restaurant. But I'd tracked her somewhere else before that: the office building where she went after leaving Bannister.

Why did she go there at night?

*   *   *

It was called the Lavelle Building, and the place was much busier than it had been the night I was there before. I was able to blend in with the people going in and out of the lobby. There was a different security guard on duty now, and this one wasn't paying any attention to me.

I walked over to the directory and began looking through the names of offices located here. Not like I did that night, just wanting to find a name I could use to try to bluff my way upstairs to follow the redhead. But now I went through list of names and companies more carefully, hoping something would jump out at me as being significant to the story.

There were a lot of insurance offices, real estate brokerages, finance companies, medical people, some retail outlets. None of the names on the directory meant anything to me at first. But then I found one that did. It was on the 9th floor. It said:

COMMITTEE TO ELECT

JAIME ORTIZ FOR GOVERNOR

It was a campaign office for Jaime Ortiz.

The security guard still wasn't paying any attention to me, so I made my way past him to the elevator bank. I got on one, pushed the button for 9. When I got there, the door was shut. But there was a buzzer. I pressed it. A few seconds later, the door opened and a woman stood there asking: "Can I help you?"

I was tongue-tied for one of the few times in my life.

The woman clearly didn't recognize me.

But I sure knew who she was.

It was the redhead from the bar now here in Jaime Ortiz's campaign office.

"Is this Knowlton Realty?" I blurted out, remembering the name of one of the offices I'd seen on the list.

"No," she said. "I believe they're on the 6th floor."

"Oh, I'm sorry. Thanks so much."

I could have confronted her right then and there, I suppose.

But I wasn't ready to do that.

Not until I knew more.

No, I didn't want to tip my hand to this woman, whoever she was.

But my reporter's instinct—and my reporter's adrenaline too—had kicked in big-time now.

Maybe I'd been chasing the wrong thing all along in this story.

I'd assumed—like most everyone else—Wendy Kyle's murder most likely had something to do with her sensational PI business.

The Honey Trap. The cheating husbands. And all of the other sensational and controversial things she did at her Heartbreaker Investigations detective agency.

But what if it was really about the police and Wendy Kyle's previous links to the NYPD?

Her ex-husband had been fingered as her killer by the police.

Her former commanding officer had risen through the ranks of police brass to the top of the department after she got fired for their altercation.

And now Jaime Ortiz—the former police chief she'd worked under during her tumultuous time on the force—was running for governor.

Yes, Wendy Kyle had made a lot of enemies digging up dirt on cheating husbands for salacious divorce cases.

But she had also made enemies on the police force by talking about corruption and threatening to reveal NYPD secrets.

I needed to find out if that's what got her killed.

PART III

LAW IS WHERE
YOU BUY IT

CHAPTER 33

"You want me to do what?" Brendan Kaiser asked me.

"Hold off for a while on the sale of Channel 10."

"That's crazy."

"Give me one good reason you can't do it."

"Money. Millions of dollars are at stake here."

I had to admit, that was a pretty good reason.

"Look, I'm not asking you to blow up the sale. Or flush millions of dollars down the drain. I'm wondering if maybe you couldn't slow things down a little bit. At least for a few weeks. That's all I need."

"Need to do what?"

"Break a big exclusive story about the Wendy Kyle murder."

"What does that have to do with me selling Channel 10 to Kellogg and Klein?"

"A lot."

I told him how I'd been ordered not to do reporting anymore or go on air with a story of my own. That my job now was simply to act behind the scenes as news director. I figured he already knew that, but I wanted to make sure he understood my situation.

"I can't do this story without your help," I said.

"Clare . . ."

"I have an idea I want you to hear."

"I'm not going to like this idea, am I?"

"Just hear me out . . ."

I'd gone to see Kaiser because I couldn't think of anything else to do. I knew Owen Lasker and his people at Kellogg and Klein would tell me they didn't want me on the air reporting again if I made a plea to them. I knew Susan Endicott would back them up because she was trying to save her own career, which took precedence over any agreement she and I might have.

I knew, too, if I tried to go ahead and report the story again anyway, I might get fired by Lasker. And, most of all, I knew—or at least I truly believed—that I was the only one that could do this story. I couldn't simply hand it over to Janelle Wright or Cassie O'Neal or any other reporter, which Lasker and Endicott would want me to do.

Either I did this story myself—or it didn't get done.

That's when I thought about going to Brendan Kaiser for help.

Sure, it was a long shot that I could convince him to do what I wanted.

Yes, this was a real Hail Mary.

But, when you're all out of other options, sometimes you have to take a chance on that long shot / Hail Mary to pull off a miracle.

Kaiser and I had a history of working together. More than you would normally expect with the owner of a TV station and an on-air reporter.

A few years ago, his name had come up in a big murder story I was doing. The killer had left behind a list of names he said motivated him to kill, and one of them was Brendan Kaiser. It turned out to have been from a chance encounter Kaiser had with the killer years ago when they were both young. Kaiser was grateful to me for getting him the answers that explained it for him.

We'd had a number of one-on-one encounters since then. He took me out to lunch to personally tell me he was bringing in Susan Endicott to replace Jack Faron as executive producer of the Channel 10 News. And he'd gone to bat for me a few times in my battles with Endicott since then. I knew he liked me. No, not liked me in *that* way. Actually, who knows? Maybe he really did like me. What's not to like about me?

"Do you know Owen Lasker?" I asked him.

"Sure, he's the guy who's going to be running the station for Kellogg and Klein."

"What's your opinion of him?"

"He's a very valued and respected member of the Kellogg and Klein team."

"He's an unsufferable jerk."

"Well, there is that too."

"I need you to get him off my back."

"How do I do that?"

"How long before the sale goes through?"

"Probably another few weeks. They're still working out some of the language in the contract. Why?"

"Owen Lasker is already making his opinions—bad opinions in my view—apparent to Endicott and everyone else at Channel 10. And they're listening to him. Especially Endicott. Everyone wants to make the new guy happy. Except me. I need to get back on the air to break this story."

"The Wendy Kyle story? The one everyone else thinks is over?"

"I think the story may be about Jaime Ortiz."

"The gubernatorial candidate?"

"Un-huh. And Ronald Bannister too."

He looked confused.

"How do Ortiz and Bannister fit together in this? What's the connection?"

"That's what I have to find out."

"How much do you know already?"

I told him everything I'd found out. Ending with the redhead I'd seen at the bar with Bannister showing up at the campaign headquarters of Jaime Ortiz.

"This could be about politics, about money, about police corruption—or maybe all three," I said. "I'm not sure which yet. But what I am pretty damn sure about is that poor confused Ted Lansmore did not blow up his wife and then kill himself in remorse with a confession note left behind."

"Do you have any hard evidence for this?"

"I have my reporter's instinct."

"That's all?"

"My reporter's instinct has worked pretty well for us in the past."

One of the things a good reporter needs to do is read people. That's what I was doing now with Brendan Kaiser. Most wealthy station owners like him would reject an idea like this out of hand. But Kaiser was different. I remembered from our first meeting on the murder story when he told me he never wanted to be a business tycoon, he wanted to have fun in life. He wanted excitement. I always felt he got some kind of vicarious thrill out of the exclusives I broke for him and Channel 10. That he wished he could do something like this story.

That's how I read Brendan Kaiser.

I hoped I was right.

"Lasker isn't really in charge of Channel 10 until after the sale," I told him now. "Until then, it's technically still your station. At least for the next few weeks. Until the sale to Kellogg and Klein goes though. Maybe you can push that sale date back a little more. Make Lasker back off until then. Then you're still calling the shots for the newsroom."

"And one of those shots I'd call would be to put you back on the air as a reporter for the Wendy Kyle story."

"That works for me."

He smiled.

"Works for me too. I owe you, Carlson. You've done a lot for me and for this station. So this will be my parting gift for you."

"In lieu of severance if I get fired afterward?"

"That's a real possibility."

"Because of Lasker?"

"He's probably going to find out that it was you who came to me and set all this in motion."

"I imagine he will."

"Owen Lasker is not going to be happy with you, Clare."

"People like Lasker rarely are."

CHAPTER 34

I ALREADY KNEW some stuff about Jaime Ortiz. He'd been around for a while on the New York scene—as police commissioner for several years and now as a political candidate running for governor. But I wanted to know more. A lot more. I pulled everything that I could find in our files. Including a lot of the video we'd shot of Ortiz in the past. It was all very impressive.

In many of the videos and interviews, he kept hammering away at the crime issue in New York.

A few years ago, the NYPD had taken down a gang of "subway thrill killers"—a gang of brutal teens who had been pushing people on platforms in front of moving trains just to watch them die. These were horrifying crimes—even for a place like New York City—and people were terrified.

Ortiz held a press conference where he hailed the capture of the killers as a monumental victory against crime for the city.

"No longer will New Yorkers have to live in fear when they go into a subway station," he said. "No longer will they have to allow people like this to run wild in our city. We are taking back New York for us, people. And this is just the first step."

In a more recent appearance while running for governor, Ortiz continued to hammer away at this anti-crime theme. He talked about setting up citizen "crime stopper" organizations to help local police keep towns and streets safe throughout the entire state if he was elected to office.

"We all can become crime stoppers," he said. "Looking for anything that seems suspicious. Alerting the police and stopping the criminals even before they can carry out any violent or illegal acts. This will be a new grassroots movement of citizen crime stoppers stretching from New York City to Albany to Buffalo and across the entire state. Let's all become CrimeStoppers for New York."

Ortiz was a good-looking guy too. Probably in his fifties, but he looked younger. Dark hair combed straight back, a friendly smile on his face in most of the pictures and videos I'd seen, a snappy dresser.

He was Hispanic. Both of his parents had come here from Puerto Rico when he was a baby, I had found out. He spoke with no hint of an accent. Except maybe a slight New York accent. Clearly, he had spent most of his life here in New York City, growing up and then later during all his years with the NYPD.

All in all, Jaime Ortiz looked to be an ideal political candidate.

A very convincing guy for the voters.

Hell, all this even made me want to vote for him to be governor.

*   *   *

"What do we know about Jaime Ortiz?" I asked.

I was with Maggie and also with Vic Malone, a longtime Channel 10 reporter who knew a lot about politics and police and stuff like that.

"Was on the force for twenty-seven years," Maggie said. "Worked his way up from street patrolman to detective to precinct commander and then deputy commissioner before he became police commissioner in 2012. Spent eleven years in that job before stepping down—and retiring from the NYPD—a year ago. All sorts of awards and acclaim."

"No black marks or complaints?"

"A few, but nothing major that ever stuck."

"So he didn't retire to avoid some big scandal?"

"If there was a scandal he was hiding, he probably wouldn't run for governor," Malone pointed out. "It would be sure to be exposed then."

"Right," I said.

"He also made big inroads for diversity in the department during his time in office," Malone continued. "He was the first Hispanic officer to rise as high as he did. And he set in motion a lot of initiatives to encourage people of color to join the NYPD. Hispanic and Black both. The number of Black and Hispanic recruits rose dramatically under him. And so did the number of promotions for Hispanic and Black police officers to higher and better-paying jobs on the force."

"So white people in New York like him because he stops crime in their neighborhood," I said. "Hispanic people like him because he's one of their own. And Black people like him because of all the progress he's made for them and all people of color. Is that about right? This guy Ortiz is perfect?"

"Well, no one's perfect," Malone said.

"But he sounds like about as much of a Mr. Clean as you're going to find running for public office these days."

"I guess that sums it up."

I looked over at Maggie.

"And everyone is pretty sure he's going to get elected governor?"

"He's definitely the big front-runner at the moment."

"Any political weaknesses at all?"

"Just that he's never had any political experience," Malone said.

"That could be a plus in today's political climate."

I had one more big question to ask.

"Where does Ortiz's campaign money come from?"

"Looks like the usual stuff," Maggie said. "Unions. Political action groups. Lots of grassroots fundraising asking individual citizens for small amounts of campaign donations. He talks about this being a good idea for political campaigns to avoid a candidate being beholden to rich and powerful donors and lobbying groups. This is actually a big topic of his—getting financial support from little people instead of the wealthy ones. Although I imagine he'd take a big contribution from a wealthy donor if it was offered."

"What about Ronald Bannister? Does he have any connection at all to Ortiz's campaign? Has he given him any money?"

"Nope, nothing I found about Bannister," Maggie said.

"Damn."

"C'mon, Clare." Maggie laughed. "That would be too easy."

"And no connection of any kind we can find between Wendy Kyle and Ortiz?"

"They were on the NYPD at the same time. She joined the force when he was commissioner."

"But no direct connection or interaction that we know about?"

"Nope. And, for whatever it's worth, Ortiz has been married to the same woman since he was twenty-one. They have four children, no hint ever of any discord in the marriage—according to everyone who knows him. It seems unlikely that he or his wife would have been involved with Wendy Kyle and Heartbreaker Investigations for any reason."

"So how does this connect Ortiz in any way to the Wendy Kyle story?" Malone asked.

"I was kind of wondering the same thing myself," Maggie said. "What does Ortiz have to do with Wendy Kyle?"

"That, my fellow crime stoppers, is the question we have to answer," I said.

CHAPTER 35

THE FALLOUT FROM my visit to Branden Kaiser's office came swiftly and pretty much predictably.

The worst, of course, was from Owen Lasker. When I told him I was going back on the air to keep covering the Wendy Kyle story, he accused me of insubordination for not following his specific instructions. I pointed out to him that it was not insubordination to take my orders from the man who owned the station. Which was not him or Kellogg and Klein. For good measure, I added that Kaiser—and me—did not want him around the newsroom at all until the sale was final.

Susan Endicott was mad at me too. At first, anyway. I mean, I had defied her directions to stay off the air and stop chasing the story, just like I did with Lasker. She also pointed out that under the "agreement" we'd made, I should have told her first what I was doing. She was right about that. But I think a part of her admired me for doing it. Her position was pretty precarious, like mine, once the new ownership was in place. Hanging me out there as the main target for Lasker's wrath helped cement her position with him as the one of us that would remain standing. Or at least that's the way I figured she saw it.

To the Channel 10 staff, I was kind of a hero once I told them what had happened and what I was doing. Albeit a crazy hero. And maybe one courting career suicide. I couldn't disagree with any of that.

"Damn, you got a pair on you, girl," Vic Zizzo said when he heard the news.

"You're not going to win any popularity contests with Lasker or Kellogg and Klein," Cassie O'Neal said with a laugh.

"This could be the biggest story of your career, I get that," Dani Blaine said. "But, if you fail, this frigging move could also end your career. Have you thought about that?"

"What the hell," Brett said. "If Clare goes down for this, we all go down. So if we have to go down, let's go out in a blaze of glory. I love it!"

That night I took everyone out to Headliners. It's a bar not far from Channel 10 that has been a media hangout for years in New York City. I used to go there a lot when I worked for a newspaper in the area. I still like it as a TV journalist.

There were pictures on the walls of many of the greats who have worked in New York City media. Walter Cronkite. Jimmy Breslin. Barbara Walters. Even Matt Lauer still had his picture up there, even though he had left the media in disgrace after the *Today Show* sex scandal. Once you get your picture up at Headliners, it's hard to lose that place of honor. Maybe someday I'll get my picture on that wall. That is, if I still have a job in the media once this story is over. But then I've always been a glass half full kind of gal.

After a few drinks, as is usually the case, everyone started telling media stories.

This time it was about the crazy ways people in our business can lose their jobs.

One of the editors had been around for a long time, and he talked about how there had been twelve newspapers at one point—and that number suddenly dropped to three by the end of the '60s.

No one at a newspaper knew if they'd have a job from one day to another, he said.

He talked about one legendary story where a reporter from a New York paper went into the bank to cash his paycheck. The bank rejected the check. "Why won't you cash my payroll check?" the confused reporter asked. "I cash it here every week." Not anymore, he was told by the bank teller: "Your newspaper just went out of business." And that's how the reporter found out.

Another reporter, at the old *New York Journal American*, was working a story on the phone at his desk when the line suddenly went dead. He looked down and saw a phone man on the floor disconnecting the wires. "What are you doing?" the reporter yelled. "Taking out the phones. Your paper just folded."

I didn't have any firsthand old newspaper stories like that, but I talked about my favorite newspaper movie on the topic. *Deadline—USA* from the 1950s. "Humphrey Bogart is the editor of a newspaper that's going to shut down the following day. But for the last edition, Bogart wants to break this big exclusive mob story that could be really dangerous to cover. He assigns a reporter to do it, but the reporter refuses: 'Why should I risk my life for a newspaper that's not even going to be here in another twenty-four hours?' he says. Bogart tells him: 'You're absolutely right. And you're fired.' They then broke the big story on the last edition the paper ever printed. God, I love that sort of thing."

There were also stories about media people who had crashed and burned on their own by screwing up.

"I heard once that Linda Ellerbee, before she became a TV star, got fired from the Associated Press because she wrote a personal note to someone and then accidentally sent it out on the AP wire to the world," Maggie said.

"How about the weatherman at the New York station who got canned for the rape remark," Monica McClain, our own weather person, said. "For some reason, during his nightly report on the weather, he said: 'To quote Confucius, if rape is inevitable, just lie back and enjoy it.' This was back in the '70s, but even in those pre–politically correct times, that was pretty much a career ender."

"Megyn Kelly jettisoned her NBC career by talking about dressing up in blackface for Halloween. She never said she did it herself, just that it was okay when she was a kid," someone said. "That was it for her, even though she'd recently signed a massive contract. But the truth is, I think they wanted to get rid of her before that. This gave them the excuse to do it."

"How about Jessica Savitch?" I said. "That was probably the worst meltdown I remember on live TV. She was NBC's Golden Girl for a while. But then one night she did the network newscast slurring her words and looking completely out of it. No one ever knew for sure if it was alcohol or drugs or maybe some combination of both. Then, not long afterward, she drowned in a car accident."

"Hope you wind up better than Jessica Savitch," Brett said.

"She will," Dani said. "Oh, she may lose her job, but I don't figure she'll die."

Everyone was laughing and drinking and having a good time. I was happy about that. Happy for them. And happy for me too. We needed some feel-good moments like this at Channel 10.

It was Maggie, as usual, who brought us back to our real-world problems when she said, "I'm worried about this Lasker guy."

"He can't do anything as long as I have Kaiser on my side."

"But what about afterward? He's going to be out to get you. You showed him up, Clare. Guys like Lasker don't like being shown up. And they don't forget about it either. They try to get even."

"I'm well aware of that."

"And?"

"And what?"

"Do you have a plan to deal with Lasker?"

"I do."

"What's your plan?"

"To break the Wendy Kyle story wide open. If I can do that, if I can bring down some of these people like Bannister and maybe even Ortiz with it, I'll be the biggest journalism story around. And Lasker won't be able to get rid of me. No matter how much he wanted to. It would be a bad business decision for him and Kellogg and Klein, and he doesn't like to make bad business decisions."

"You've got a lot riding on this story, Clare."

"I've always got a lot riding on any story I do."

"But this time . . . well, I just hope that even if you pull it off, it's enough to protect you from the new owners. You can't be sure of that. No matter how big a story it is."

"Don't worry," I told everyone. "A big story always makes everything better."

CHAPTER 36

"I NEED YOUR help," I said to Scott Manning.

"Again?"

"Again."

"Okay, what do you want?"

"A police report."

I was still looking for answers on some of the loose ends I'd uncovered earlier about Wendy Kyle. One of those was her sudden descent from NYPD star recruit to controversial complainer and troublemaker whose conduct eventually got her fired. According to what I'd learned, that rebellious behavior seemed to begin when she responded to the murder of a woman named Troy Spencer that had been ruled a suicide, even though Kyle said she thought it was murder. Maybe there was something in the details of the Troy Spencer case that could be a lead for me. I couldn't know for sure until I read the complete police file on the case.

"You realize that I don't work for the Police Department anymore?" Manning said.

"But you still know people there. You were able to get me that information on Wendy Kyle's client list and diary before."

"I understand, but still . . ."

"This is important, and I can't think of anyone else to ask but you."

"Don't you have any sources in the NYPD?"

"I did. My ex-husband, Sam Markham. The homicide sergeant. He was always my go-to guy when I needed something from the police department. But he's not speaking to me at the moment."

"Uh, because you said you suspected him of murder?"

"I was wrong about that, and I apologized. But he's still really mad at me."

"Go figure."

We were sitting in my office again. I'd asked Manning to stop by. I felt more comfortable—or at least less likely to do something stupid with this guy—if I met him in an official setting like the Channel 10 office.

"A few years ago, Wendy Kyle was the first police officer on the scene at the death of a young woman in Murray Hill. Her name was Troy Spencer. The NYPD classified the death as a suicide. But Kyle apparently disagreed and became very upset. And, from what I can tell, that's when her battles with the NYPD began. Ergo, I think there might be something more significant to the death of Troy Spencer than a simple suicide. That's why I want to see the case file."

I told Manning then about my suspicions involving Jaime Ortiz, the former police commissioner now running for governor; Ronald Bannister; the mysterious guy at the hotel I thought was a security guard; the missing red-haired woman; the woman posing as Kyle's partner; and all the rest.

"And how do you figure this all fits together?" he asked when I was done.

"I have no idea."

"What about Ortiz and Bannister? Do they know each other?"

"Not that I'm aware of."

"Had Bannister made political campaign contributions to Ortiz?"

"Nothing on record."

"So you don't know if any of this has anything at all to do with Kyle's murder?"

"No, I don't."

"Here's something else: the murder case you're looking for the report on happened several years ago. If that case had anything at all to do with Kyle's death, wouldn't they have killed her then— not now after all this time? Why wait years to put a bomb in her car, if that case really is connected as some kind of motive?"

"I don't know that either."

He shook his head.

"Your brain works in strange ways, Clare Carlson."

"People tell me that."

"It's not necessarily a compliment."

"Look, I still think there must have been something significant about this case for Wendy Kyle. That's why I want to see the report. That's the way I work. I want to check out everything, even if it doesn't make sense right now. I've broken a lot of big stories with that approach. Will you help me to get the Troy Spencer police report?"

Manning said he'd see what he could do.

"So are you seeing anyone these days?" he said as he stood up to leave.

I was surprised by that.

"Uh, not at the moment, no."

"But you have been in a relationship since we . . . we . . ."

"Ended our relationship."

"Yes."

"I didn't join a convent or anything, Scott. I've been out with other guys. And you?"

"I'm still with my wife."

"Good for you."

"Yep, good for me."

"How's that going?"

"Well, we haven't had sex in eight months," he said.

Definitely wasn't expecting that one either.

"I miss you, Clare."

Then he closed the door of my office, walked over to where I was sitting at my desk, leaned down, and kissed me. I think I kissed him back. I'm not sure. It all happened so fast that I guess I was in a state of shock.

"I'll let you know what I find out about the report," Scott Manning said.

And then he was gone.

*   *   *

The next morning there was a package waiting for me on my desk when I got to the office.

It was from Scott Manning.

There was a note inside that said:

"Always good to see you, Clare. Hope what I came up with here helps you with your story. Hope that other thing I did in your office gives you something to think about too. We still make a pretty good team."

There was a file folder filled with papers inside the package.

It was the police report on the death of the woman known as Troy Spencer.

The one I'd been wanting so desperately to see.

Now I had it right in front of me.

So why was I still thinking about the other stuff with Scott Manning when I opened the file?

CHAPTER 37

ON THE FACE of it, the Troy Spencer file seemed like a pretty straightforward case of suicide.

A tragic story of a woman coming to New York with her dreams and then self-destructing when those dreams didn't come true.

Fairy tales didn't always come true, and Troy Spencer seemed to be a classic example of that.

Her actual name was Ruth Landau, and she grew up in Boise, Idaho, fantasizing about coming to New York City and becoming a star on Broadway. She performed in high school plays and local theater productions, and she took acting classes as best she could in the Boise area. Then one day, she boarded a bus, rode across the country, and arrived in New York.

There was a picture of her in the file. Several pictures of her actually. A headshot and also a full body shot, which she must have used for actress auditions. It had been collected as evidence and then presumably forgotten about in the file. I looked at the pictures now. She was a pretty woman. No, she was more than that—she was a knockout. But there were a lot of really attractive women in New York, and she somehow got lost in the mix.

At first though, she did surprisingly well. There were some backstage jobs at theaters. Then a few parts off-Broadway, and even a small role in a Broadway show for a period until it closed.

At some point, the jobs dried up and—struggling to survive in the big city—she turned to alcohol and pills to ease the pain, according to people who knew her that had been interviewed by police.

On April 8, 2016, after a woman friend had tried repeatedly to reach her at her apartment in a high-rise building on East 33rd Street off of Second Avenue, the friend went to the building and knocked on the door. Inside, the friend could hear a TV playing, but there was no answer. After repeated tries, she went to the building superintendent and convinced him to open up the door to make sure she was all right.

They found Troy Spencer lying naked on the bed. There was a half-filled glass of vodka and empty pill bottles next to her. The landlord ran back to his office and immediately called the police.

Among the first to arrive on the scene was Police Officer Wendy Kyle.

This was followed by more police, medical personnel, and a detective.

The detective—after examining the body, looking at the crime scene, and conferring with medical personnel—said there was no evidence of foul play and that her death was being classified as a suicide.

Nothing there that jumped out at me as unusual or suspicious.

People commit suicide all the time.

And it seemed like Troy Spencer was a prime candidate to off herself.

Still, I kept reading through the file. I wanted to know the name of the detective at the scene with Kyle. And also the name of the woman friend who went to the building looking for Troy Spencer.

The detective, Jack Bladlow, turned out to be retired. Even worse, he was dead. Retired in 2017 and died in Livingston, Nevada, two years later.

I had better luck with the woman. Her name was Gretchen Grimsditch. Because her name was so unusual, I was able to track her down. Not in New York, she didn't live here anymore. But to Los Angeles where she moved a few years ago. She was an actress too, and she had gotten a number of parts in movies and TV. She said she wished Troy was still alive so she could have joined her out there.

"Funny you calling me about Troy," she said on the phone.

"I guess it is kind of out of the blue. Something way back in your past."

"No, I mean it's funny to be asked questions about it all so soon again."

"Someone else was asking you about it?"

"Right. A week or two ago. Not a reporter like you. She worked as a private investigator now, she said. But she told me she was there at the apartment that first day as a police officer. I remember her too. She was very kind, very comforting to me. Some of the men were . . . well, I was very upset as you can imagine, and it was nice having a woman there. She made sure I was okay."

"We're talking about Wendy Kyle?"

"Yes. In fact, I thought that was her when you called. I saw the New York area code. She told me she was going to call me back and tell me about anything else she'd been able to find out."

I told her about Wendy Kyle being dead. She was shocked. Especially when she found out how it happened. I let her pull herself together for a little while, and then I asked her more about her conversation with Kyle.

"What did she ask you about?"

"She asked me if I remembered seeing bruised areas on her neck and face when we found her. I did see them at the time, but the others there—that detective, I remember—told me she must have gotten them when she'd fallen down from the booze and pills before making it to the bed and dying."

"Kyle thought she might have been beaten?"

"I think so."

"What else?"

"She talked about everything in the room that day. The half-filled vodka bottle, the empty pills, the TV playing so loud to get attention from outside the door, even the naked body on the bed—this Wendy Kyle woman said it all seemed *staged* to her. Like someone set it up like that to make it look like it was a suicide. Even if it wasn't."

I remembered reading in the police report that an autopsy had revealed potentially lethal amounts of alcohol and sleeping pills mixed together in Troy Spencer's blood. But what if she didn't ingest them voluntarily? What if someone beat her and forced her to take them? Or even forced them down her throat in death. It was just speculation on my part, but I thought justified speculation.

"She also asked me about the last time I'd talked with her. I said it had been at least twenty-four hours before I found her. But that I had tried repeatedly to call and text her with no success. She said she didn't think much about that at the time when I'd been questioned about my last dealings with Troy. But now she thought it might be important."

"Why?"

"She said it would have given a killer plenty of time to set up the apartment to make it look like suicide before anyone found her."

"Did she have any idea who this killer could be?"

"She didn't tell me." Her voice trailed off.

"But..."

"But what?"

"I think she had someone in mind."

There was something else about Troy Spencer that was bothering me. The location of her apartment. It was a high-rise on Second Avenue and 33rd Street. That was a pretty high rent district. How did a struggling actress like Troy Spencer afford that kind of expensive place?

Gretchen Grimsditch hesitated for a minute when I asked her that question.

"Troy did some outside work," she said finally.

"Must have been lucrative work."

"It was. Very lucrative."

There was one obvious thing that came to mind.

"Was she selling sex?" I asked. "Was she turning tricks?"

"Yes."

"In the apartment?"

"Right. Men came to see her there, and they paid her for her time. She had a very high-class clientele. She made a lot of money. I kept telling her to quit, but she said it paid all her bills in a way that her acting never could."

Well, that sure raised some intriguing possibilities about her death.

"Did you tell this to the police that day when you found her body?"

"Yes. But they didn't seem to care. They still thought she just got depressed and killed herself with booze and pills. Everyone said that except for one of them. The woman cop."

"Wendy Kyle?"

"That's right."

After I hung up, I read through the details of Troy Spencer's death all over again in the report.

It made perfect sense—the pills, the alcohol, the suicide—when you saw it on paper like this.

But not so much if you believed Wendy Kyle's suspicions about maybe being beaten to death or forced to consume the pills and alcohol, then everything else was set up to make it look like suicide—not murder.

I looked at the names in the report again. Jack Bladlow, the detective. Gretchen Grimsditch, the friend. The landlord was someone named Jack Hertz. I could go back and talk to him too, but I doubted it would be of very much use. All he did was let the Grimsditch woman in and then called the police.

And, most importantly, Wendy Kyle was there.

Wendy Kyle—who didn't believe Troy Spencer's death was a suicide.

But the police did.

That was their official ruling.

I noticed one other name in the report now. At the very end. The person that approved it. Confirming the ruling of suicide as the official NYPD ruling on the death of Troy Spencer. The name was scrawled at the bottom.

Jaime Ortiz.

The police commissioner at the time.

CHAPTER 38

"Scott Manning kissed me," I told Janet.

"He did more than that as I remember."

"No, I mean recently."

"How recently?"

"Just the other day."

"Where?"

"In my office at Channel 10."

I told her the details of our meeting.

"Do you figure this means he's still interested in you?"

"I do."

"Anything else?"

"He said he misses me."

"That's it?"

"Oh, and he mentioned that he and his wife hadn't had sex in eight months."

"Jeez."

"Yeah, I know, it was all kind of weird."

"What are you going to do about all this?"

"Nothing, right now."

"What if he tries to kiss you again?"

"I'll probably kiss him back."

"And then?"

"I guess I'll follow my instincts."

"That's not always a good approach for you when it comes to relationships."

We were sitting in Janet's office on Park Avenue South. I generally went to her office when I wanted to discuss work she might be able to help me with, as opposed to a purely personal conversation. And, despite my confession to her about the Scott Manning kissing moment, I wanted to talk to her about the story. Janet had a logical, legal mind and could frequently sort out extraneous matter to get to the heart of the issue. I could use a dose of logical thinking like that now.

"Let me tell you how I see the Wendy Kyle story right now," I said.

"I can hardly wait."

"Remember, this is all hypothetical."

"Is it based on any facts at all?"

"Of course. There are always facts. I'm only adding some speculation to put the facts I have together. Here's the scenario I came up with,"

I ran through all the details with her.

"I think the Troy Spencer case was the start of it all a few years ago. She's dead, and everything looks like a suicide, according to police. Except her friend who found her said she saw bruises on her face and neck. The cops say she must have fallen, presumably because of the booze and pills. But what if she was beaten and strangled, then forced to swallow the alcohol and booze to make it look to the medical people afterward like that was what had killed her?

"Who would do this? A male client? Troy Spencer was supposed to be paying her bills at the end by having sex with men for money in her apartment. So maybe one of her clients killed her in a violent rage and did whatever it took to make sure the police covered it up.

"Now here is where it gets interesting. Who would have the clout—or money—to get the police to do something like that? One man immediately comes to mind. Ronald Bannister. Let's say Bannister kills the girl during sex, then buys off the cops. Not just any cops. All the way right up to the top. To the police commissioner himself.

"That would take a lot of money to buy a man like Ortiz. But Bannister's got a lot of money. An obscene amount of money. Ortiz is already thinking about his political future, and he wants to get a money man like Bannister on his side.

"But then Wendy Kyle—for some reason we may never know—decides to open the Troy Spencer case up again. She starts reaching out to Ortiz and Bannister looking for answers. They panic over this. There's a diary out there somewhere too. Wendy Kyle's diary. We know there's a first page, but there's got to be more. Why did she keep a diary? Presumably to go public with everything she knew about Bannister and Ortiz too. Maybe she was going to write a book or something. Bannister tries to buy her off to keep her quiet, but she refused. And so they decide they have to get rid of her. Bannister and/or Ortiz—well, not them, but someone hired by them—puts the bomb in her car and BOOM! Problem solved."

Janet didn't say anything at first. I wasn't sure if that was good or bad. It was a lot for her to digest in one dose like I'd hit her with. Finally, she shook her head.

"You don't have anything there, Clare. No evidence, no real facts, nothing that could ever work in a legal sense in any court in the world."

"I said it was all hypothetical."

"It's not even hypothetical. It's all guesswork on your part."

"Then what do I do?"

"It seems to me you need to confront Ortiz or Bannister. Ask them questions about this directly. That's the only way you're going to find out if you're on the right trail."

"I've tried with Bannister. He's tough to pin down. I did talk to his wife. But she can't really tell me anything about her husband. It sounds like the two of them live really separate lives."

"What about Ortiz? He's a public figure. He's out in public all the time running for governor, right?"

Damn. She was right about that.

Ortiz was always holding press conferences here in the city and around the state.

Maybe I should go to one of them.

And bring up Wendy Kyle.

That might be interesting.

"What exactly are you going to do now?" Janet said to me before I left.

"Solve the Wendy Kyle case, win my corporate war with Kellogg and Klein and with Susan Endicott, and then maybe sleep with Scott Manning again too."

"That's a lot on your plate."

"Oh, and I want to complete this all before I turn fifty."

"Then you better get off your ass and start moving on it really quickly."

I laughed, stood up, and headed for the door.

"Where are you headed next?"

"To find Todd Schacter."

"The crazy computer guy?"

"I'm hoping he can track down some more information for me online about Wendy Kyle."

Janet shook her head.

"Like I've told you before, that's a slippery slope, Clare. You're really pushing the envelope with Schacter. Not everything he does is strictly legal."

"Me neither," I said.

CHAPTER 39

I MET TODD SCHACTER on a sunny afternoon in Madison Square Park.

The meeting spot was his choice, but I was fine with it. That's because it had a Shake Shack there. Not just any Shake Shack either, the original New York City one that came before the franchise spots around everywhere now. This was still one of my favorite places to eat.

I surveyed the menu. The specialty was their hamburger. A big juicy burger covered in cheese and all sorts of toppings. Hmm, good. But also loaded with calories. I wanted to make sure I could still fit into my clothes on my fiftieth birthday, so I passed on that. Instead, I went for something more healthy. Another hot dog. Okay, maybe a hot dog isn't particularly healthy food either, but it had less calories than the burger. I was tempted by the creamy chocolate milkshake too, but I settled for a Diet Coke. You can see how serious I am about this health thing.

I was on my last few bites of the hot dog when Todd Schacter slipped onto the park bench next to me.

"What do you need?" he asked.

"How are you doing, Todd?"

No answer.

"Me, I'm fine."

Still nothing.

"Well, I do have this fiftieth birthday thing coming up, which has me a little concerned about getting old. There's some difficult stuff I'm dealing with about my daughter too. And I really don't like the people I work for anymore. But hey, thanks for asking. Good to know you care."

I finished off my hot dog and took a sip of Diet Coke.

"You know, you're getting a little sloppy, Todd."

"What do you mean?"

"Meeting here in Madison Square Park."

"What's wrong with it?"

"We met here once before."

"So?"

"I always thought you liked to switch up meeting places to make sure no one was watching you, spying on you."

"I do. I have several places where I meet people. Different places. This one just came up again on my list of meeting spots today."

He was probably right about that. I'd met Todd before in Bryant Park, Madison Square Park, and a Starbucks. He had a rotating list, I guess, and this spot came to the top again today.

"We could move somewhere different if that would make you more comfortable."

"No, this is great, Todd. I was just having some fun with you."

"I don't have fun."

"Right."

"Let's get down to business . . ."

Todd Schacter sure is a bizarre character. He is a tall, skinny guy with wild-looking long hair. I had no idea how old he was. He looked like he could be in his forties, but I had a hunch he was younger. Mostly, though, he was really wired. Nervous all the time, moving and twitching and blinking his eyes. Looking around constantly at everyone around him like he was afraid of being watched.

All I really knew about him was that he was a computer hacking expert. I'd met him a few years ago through Janet. She'd represented him—and gotten him acquitted—on charges of breaking into corporate computer files and looking for personal information about top executives he wanted to expose for malfeasance. I'd secretly used him first to help me find my daughter, Lucy, then worked with him on a few other cases too.

"I need you to find out any information you can online from— or about—a woman named Wendy Kyle."

"The one who got blown up in Times Square."

"You follow the news, huh?"

"I never miss watching you on the Channel 10 News, Clare."

He smiled. Not a big smile, but a smile. He was being sarcastic, I knew that. But I'd take any emotion from this guy—even a bit of sarcasm.

"Do you have access to her computer?" he asked.

"No."

"Phone?"

"No."

"Tablet?"

"Uh, no."

"Email address or Twitter account or Instagram login?"

"Again, no."

"Not much to work on."

"That's why I came to you."

"I don't know . . ."

"You don't think you can do it?"

"Without any place to start, it's almost impossible."

"I guess I must have overestimated you, Todd. Maybe I can find someone else instead who knows more and could—"

"Okay, okay, I'll look into it."

I figured that would work. Making it a challenge for him. Todd always liked to see if he could beat impossible odds and pull off a computer miracle. I'd found that out from him myself in the past, especially when he tracked down my daughter.

I told him all the information I had on Wendy Kyle. Her home address. Office location. Marriage history. He took out a laptop from a bag he was carrying and punched in the information.

There was one more thing I wanted to ask him about.

"I'd like you to check on a license plate number for me," I said. "It's for a dark blue Lincoln."

I gave him the plate number I'd written down from the car driven by the phony security guard I'd met that night at the Stratton Hotel. The one I'd seen waiting for me outside my office the next day.

"I can pay you for all this," I said.

Todd Schacter had never taken money for any of the work he'd done for me at Channel 10, but I figured I should ask.

"How much?"

"$1,000? For starters anyway . . ."

"You're going to give me $1,000?"

"We'd put you on the freelance payroll at Channel 10. It's all very simple."

"This information would go to the IRS?"

"I'm not sure. I suppose so."

"And you would need a social security number?"

"That's normal procedure.'

"Date of birth, too?"

I nodded.

"Thanks, but no thanks then."

"But you will try to find the information for me?"

"I'll see what I can do."

He stood up to leave. I turned away briefly to throw my hot dog wrapper and Diet Coke container into a trash can.

"I hope everything works out well with your daughter," he said, which really surprised me. He remembered my daughter. "Give her my best."

But, by the time I turned around, Todd Schacter was gone.

"Thank you," I said to nobody.

CHAPTER 40

WENDY KYLE'S DETERMINATION to find out the truth about the death of Troy Spencer—her seeming obsession not to accept the verdict of suicide like everyone else—made me remember another troubled woman she had felt strongly about and tried to help.

That was Reby, the homeless woman in her Upper East Side neighborhood that people said Wendy Kyle had befriended and looked out for.

I decided I wanted to find Reby.

I wasn't exactly sure why I wanted to do this.

But a few years ago, I'd gone looking for information about a homeless woman named Dora Gayle after she had died on the streets of New York. No one really cared about Dora Gayle, and she didn't seem very interesting at first, but I kept digging into her life and uncovered a fascinating story.

It was a good lesson in journalism.

And a good lesson in life.

Everyone has a story if you go looking for it.

I needed to find out Reby's story.

Why? Well, maybe she knew something about Wendy Kyle that no one else did. Not likely, but it was always good to track down as many people as I could on a story like this. And, even if she couldn't help me in that way, she might make a good human interest story. Give the viewers a different side of Wendy Kyle besides a lot of the bad stuff that had come out from her time on the NYPD and as a controversial PI. More of the Wendy Kyle paradox.

Of course, looking for a homeless person in New York City can be a frustrating experience. Reby had no address to go to or phone number to call, at least as far as I knew. But I remembered some of Wendy Kyle's neighbors had said Kyle volunteered at a nearby shelter for homeless women. That seemed like a good place to start.

I went through this when I got there with the woman who ran the place. She was able to give me some more information about Reby, including her name.

"*Reby* is short for Rebecca. Her full name is Rebecca Kirkland. But her street name and her name around here is Reby. That's what everybody calls her."

The woman I was talking to was named Stacy Gilman. She was an older Black woman with graying hair—and I had the feeling she'd been at this place for a long time. She certainly talked that way.

"And yes, Wendy Kyle spent a lot of time with her. Wendy tried to help as many of the women here as she could. She sometimes brought them food or even nice clothes to wear so they'd feel pretty. She wanted them to feel good about themselves again, she said. It's a simple concept. But not a lot of people understand how important that is to the women here. But Wendy . . . well, Wendy did.

"Reby was special for Wendy. She spent more time with Reby, trying to help her, than with anyone else. She took her shopping, she took her out to eat in restaurants, she invited her up to her own apartment sometimes so she could shower and clean up. It was almost like they were friends. Even though they lived in different worlds. But Wendy was determined to help because of what happened to Reby . . ."

"Uh . . . what happened to Reby?"

I always like to ask the tough, probing questions.

"She was in an abusive marriage. Physically abusive. Her husband used to beat her all the time. She went to the emergency room numerous times, but the system failed her. No one stopped it from happening.

"Then one night he came home drunk and angry and looking to beat on her some more. Only this time he didn't stop like he usually did after a series of punches. He kept going with the beating. She was convinced that he was going to kill her this time, and I think he would have.

"She managed to get into the kitchen, grabbed a butcher knife, and then stabbed him with it in the throat when he came at her again. I don't know if she intended to actually fatally stab him, but she did. He collapsed on the floor and bled to death very quickly.

"Wendy was with the NYPD then, and she was the first officer on the scene. Reby was traumatized and hysterical and crying that she didn't want to go to jail. Wendy comforted her, then was by her side as best she could when the detectives arrived and she went through everything that followed. It was a bond that continued up until now."

"But how did Reby end up here?" I asked. "And living on the street?"

"There were never any charges filed against her for killing her husband. Her story of self-defense stood up, and Wendy did everything she could do to make sure of that too. But she had no money and no home without the husband. She'd never been on her own before, and she didn't know how to handle it. That's what happens to a lot of women in this situation. They stay with their husbands because they feel their only other alternative is to be out on the street.

"At some point, that's what happened to Reby. We've tried to get her into some kind of permanent housing, but it never lasts. Sooner or later, she's back on the street. Her husband did a lot of damage to her. Not only physically, but emotionally too. She's never recovered from that. Maybe she never will."

"Is she here now?" I asked. "I'd like to talk with her."

"No. Reby doesn't really stay here. She comes and goes. Gets some food, maybe some clothes or whatever. Then she's back on the street again. A lot of the women are like that. But Reby, well—I'm going to have to tell her about Wendy being gone. That's going to be very difficult for her to handle. I only hope it doesn't push her over the edge. She really depended on Wendy."

"Any idea where I could find her?"

"Just keep looking on the streets."

"That's all you can tell me?"

"Sorry, these people don't provide us with a schedule once they leave here."

"Whenever she does come back, will you let me know?"

"I don't see why not."

I handed her a card with my phone number on it.

"I'd also like to put you on the air talking about this relationship. As part of our Wendy Kyle coverage. I think it would put her in a different light—a good light—for all the positive things you said she did for the women here."

"As long as you talk about the center here too and let people know what we're doing. Allow me to ask them for any help they can give us."

"I'm okay with that."

She smiled. "Then you can put me on the air."

"One more thing, Stacy. Do you have a picture of Reby? Something I could use to illustrate her for our newscast?"

She sifted through some drawers and pulled out a file. Rebecca Kirkland's file. There was a picture of her on top. She looked it over and handed it to me.

I looked at the picture of Reby, aka Rebecca Kirkland. She probably was pretty once, and there was still some beauty in her face. But she looked tired and broken down. She had short brunette hair and brown eyes with a vacant look in them. I wondered if the defeated look came once she was out on the street, or if she'd had it for a long time before.

The look on her face made me sad.

But it also touched me deeply.

Just like it had touched Wendy Kyle—so much so that she and Reby had shared a unique kind of friendship.

Maybe Reby knew something about Wendy's murder.

Maybe Reby knew about secrets that Wendy had been hiding.

Maybe Reby knew a lot of things about Wendy that could help me.

All I had to do was find her.

CHAPTER 41

LOOKING FOR A missing person under any circumstances can be a tough thing to do.

Especially in New York City.

And even more so when the missing person is homeless—without any apparent roots or trail to follow—like Rebecca "Reby" Kirkland.

But missing people can be, and usually are, found in the end. I once heard an investigator who specialized in that sort of thing say: "No one—absolutely no one—can stay hidden forever if the right person is looking for them."

I've found a few missing persons in my life. The most notable being my own daughter, Lucy, who disappeared when she was eleven. It took me fifteen years to locate her, but I eventually did thanks to some emails and the computer genius of Todd Schacter.

Social media and all the modern devices in the world now made it almost impossible for a person to totally disappear forever. Eventually, they will be found.

The problem was I didn't have much time to try to find Rebecca Kirkland. I had to talk to her immediately. I wasn't exactly sure why she was so important to me. But I had a feeling—that damn reporter's instinct again—that she might well possess information about Wendy Kyle's last days that could be crucial to me.

After hearing about the death of Troy Spencer—and how emotional Kyle had been after that—it made me think about her strange relationship with Reby too. Another woman had endured a horribly abusive early life, and she was struggling now in the same way Troy Spencer had been—although in a different way—to survive.

First, there had been Spencer—and how much that had affected Kyle. Then came her relationship with the homeless Reby.

Kyle had suffered a similar kind of tough early life, and she clearly identified with these women. It was another example to me of the good side of Wendy Kyle. Yes, there were a lot of bad things I'd found out about her—but she seemed to be a caring, kind person. Really made me wonder exactly what Magnuson had done that made her kick him in the balls that day, which got her fired.

*   *   *

I went back to the area around 96th Street and Third Avenue—where Wendy Kyle had lived and where the women's homeless shelter was—and began to walk the streets. I had the picture of Reby I'd gotten from the shelter. It isn't like I expected to run into her walking down the street or panhandling on a corner or sleeping in an alley. But I was also looking for information. Information that might help me find Reby.

I discovered that one of the places where she hung out sometimes was a bar called Dalton's on Lexington. She didn't actually buy drinks at the bar or anything—she hardly ever had money enough for that. But the owner, a guy named Nick Dalton, told me he would give her free drinks and food on many occasions. He also said he let her sleep there sometimes in bad weather, in one of the back rooms.

"People told me I was crazy to do that, that she might steal stuff from the bar or do something violent. But that's never happened. She's a nice woman. Down on her luck. But that could happen to any of us. I always have done whatever I could to help her."

I asked him about Wendy Kyle and Reby.

"The Kyle woman came a number of times with Reby. Paid me for a lot of the stuff I'd done for Reby. I told her she didn't have to do that, but she insisted. She was a nice lady too. Sorry to hear about what happened to her. Who would do something like that?"

I said I sure didn't know.

"When is the last time you saw Reby?" I asked.

"Oh, it's been a while. A week or two, I guess."

"Since before Wendy Kyle's killing?"

"Yes, I guess so. Why?"

"Does she often disappear for long periods like this?"

"No, she doesn't, now that you mention it. She's always been a pretty regular visitor here. Do you think she's all right?"

"I hope so. That's why I'm looking for her." I gave him my card. "Will you call me if she does turn up?"

Nick Dalton said he would.

I was fascinated by the fact that both Kyle and Dalton wanted to help Reby so much. Not so much out of pity, but more out of compassion. Reby must have good qualities to elicit that kind of a response.

I heard pretty much the same story about Reby wherever I went. I found a bank vestibule nearby where she sometimes slept. The bank security guard said he was supposed to not allow her to do it, but he rarely threw her out. "She never bothered anyone," he told me. "She was just trying to get a peaceful night's sleep. I felt like we owed her at least that."

There was a grocery store where she turned in bottles and cans for money when she could. A Goodwill store that gave her used clothes when they were able to. And even a church where the pastor said she sometimes showed up to pray.

"She didn't look very good, and sometimes she smelled of alcohol," he explained to me. "A few parishioners complained about her being there. But the church is open to everybody. God is here for all of his creations. Maybe even more so for someone like this woman who was in such need of salvation. So yes, Reby was always welcome in our church."

Except none of them—the bar owner, the pastor, the grocery store clerks, the people at Goodwill—had seen Reby recently.

Which worried me a lot.

She had been a visible presence in this neighborhood for a while, and now suddenly she was not.

She also had a close relationship with Wendy Kyle, who was now dead.

I wanted to find Reby because I thought she might know some of Wendy Kyle's secrets.

But what if someone else had the same idea?

Did they kill Reby to keep her quiet, like I thought they did with Kyle?

Or was Reby aware she was now in danger too and disappeared after hearing about what happened to Wendy Kyle?

Either way, I had to find Reby.

Find her alive or find her body.

But I had to know.

There were a lot of missing pieces to this story.

A lot of things that didn't fit together in any logical way.

And one of them was Rebecca—Reby—Kirkwood.

CHAPTER 42

I STOPPED AT a place called the Madison Coffee Shop down the street from the Channel 10 building to grab some coffee for Maggie and me before I went upstairs. Black for me, and an espresso for Maggie. I was in a hurry to get to work to plunge back into the Wendy Kyle story, and I sure didn't want to waste time talking with anyone at the coffee place. Until someone did start talking to me.

"You can get me a coffee too," I heard a voice say. "Dark roast, skimmed milk, and two Splendas."

I whirled around and saw Todd Schacter standing behind me.

"We should talk," he said.

"How did you know I was here?"

"I know a lot of things, Clare. That's why you use me."

"Did you do some kind of search thing on my phone again?"

That's what he'd done the first time we met. Surprised me at another coffee shop by tracking my phone there.

"Not this time."

"Well, you know I work around here. But how did you find out I was going to this specific place for coffee? And that I'd be here at exactly this time?"

"I read your email."

"What?"

"At 7:34 this morning, you emailed your assistant Maggie something to the effect of: 'Meet you in the office at 8:30. I'll grab you an espresso and me a coffee on the way up there.'"

"That's really scary," I said.

"It's what I do."

Schacter had done something like that the first time we met too. He gave me the number—and balance—of my bank account and my IRA balance. I think he does stuff like this just to prove a point, although I'm not really sure.

We sat down at a table in the corner with our coffees in a spot where he could survey the entire room.

"Don't you have to take that espresso up to Maggie?" he asked. "It's going to get cold."

"That's what microwaves are for."

He was still nervous and twitchy like the last time, looking around to see if anyone was listening to us. Damn, this guy was weird and paranoid.

"What have you got for me?" I asked.

"Google searches."

"Huh?"

"I was able to access her Google searches in the days before she died."

"What about email?"

"No."

"No emails at all?"

"Nothing that I could find."

"You found my emails pretty easily."

"From what I can tell, Wendy Kyle didn't use email. I guess with the kind of work she did she didn't want to leave an email trail behind. It was all supposed to be confidential, right? That's why she probably avoided using email because she was afraid of some kind of a security breach."

"Who in this day and age doesn't use email because they're afraid of a security beach?"

"I do," Schacter said.

"Right."

Of course, he would. I should have expected that.

"Damn, I was really hoping to read her emails," I said.

"Do you want to hear about her Google searches?"

"Of course."

"Okay, she spent a lot of time online. Most of it seemed to have to do with her private investigation business. Going on dating sites, checking hotels and restaurants—the kinds of places where a cheating husband might take his mistress. But all of that part seemed scattered. Very hit and miss, nothing she was looking too deeply into on the web."

He stopped talking and waited.

I waited.

"Aren't you going to ask me what she did spend a lot of time on?"

I sighed.

"You're really enjoying this, aren't you?"

"Immensely."

"Okay then, what did she spend a lot of time on?"

"There were two main topics—two names—that she was googling numerous times—almost obsessively in the period before she was killed. The first name was . . . Ronald Bannister, the billionaire."

Bingo!

"And the second name was . . ."

"Jaime Ortiz, the former police commissioner now running for governor."

"How did you know that?"

"Lucky guess."

Bannister and Ortiz.

It made sense.

And yet it didn't.

How did the two of them fit into all this?

"There's more," Schacter said. "I also hacked into some of the police files about her when she was with the NYPD."

"You hacked into police files?"

"Uh-huh."

"Isn't that illegal?"

"Probably, yes. I wanted to find out what the personnel files said about Kyle. All the confrontations and fights and suspensions she had. Most of the stuff in her official file sticks pretty closely to what you already know, leading up to the altercation she had with her commanding officer."

"I already read that file."

"But did you know about the other file?"

"What do you mean?"

"There was another file about her. One I couldn't access. It was marked CLASSIFIED, and I couldn't get through the firewall. But I was able to determine the subject of the file. The name of the file was WENDY KYLE / DEATH OF TROY SPENCER, dated 4/8/16.

Wow!

Why did the death of Troy Spencer—and Kyle's actions at the crime scene—wind up in a classified file?

This was all very interesting, even if it left me more confused than ever.

"Thank you," I said. "This helps."

"There's more too."

"All right."

"The license plate you asked about. I got into the DMV records and found a name for the plate. It belongs to a man named Steve Healy. Turns out he's another PI here in town, just like she was. And he's ex-NYPD too. Left the force a few years ago—like she did—to set up his own PI business."

He took out a laptop now and called up a website for Healy's PI company.

There was a picture of Steve Healy on the site.

"Mean anything to you?"

It sure did. He was the same guy, all right. The one I saw first at the hotel bar, and thought he was a hotel security guy; then outside Channel 10 when he tried to follow me the next day; and finally, at the downtown apartment over the Italian restaurant where I watched him eat and then walk over to Police Headquarters at 1 Police Plaza.

Steve Healy.

At least I had a name for him now.

But the man I was most interested in now was Jaime Ortiz.

Why was Wendy Kyle spending so much time looking up information on him?

Jaime Ortiz was the new player in all this.

Maybe the biggest player, along with Bannister.

Who could I talk to about Ortiz?

CHAPTER 43

I REALLY DIDN'T want to have to go back to Warren Magnuson again. But I needed to talk to someone high up in the NYPD about Jaime Ortiz. And Magnuson seemed like my best chance to do that.

"The current police commissioner, Norm Garrity—the one who replaced Ortiz—has been on sick leave for two months," Maggie said when I asked her to come up with information on the power structure these days at 1 Police Plaza. "Some kind of a heart condition, seems pretty serious. The word is he's probably going to have to step down soon from the commissioner's job."

"Who's running the department at the moment?"

"It's a combination of a few top NYPD officers."

"And one of them is Warren Magnuson?"

"That's right."

"If Garrity does resign, who will be the next police commissioner?"

"I hear Magnuson is the favorite choice."

"Terrific. The Peter Principle at work."

"Huh?"

"That's the old business adage about companies promoting people higher and higher until they reach their level of total incompetence."

"You don't think Magnuson is competent?"

"I have no idea, but I don't like him."

"Because Wendy Kyle didn't like him?"

"I guess that's part of it. But I also met the guy myself."

"Was he rude or obnoxious or engage in some kind of inappropriate behavior with you?"

"Not exactly."

"Then why did the meeting make you not like him."

"You had to be there."

*　　*　　*

The one good thing is I wouldn't have to talk about Wendy Kyle with Magnuson this time. My questions were about Jaime Ortiz. Sure, I hoped the answers might help me uncover answers about Wendy Kyle's murder too. But I didn't have to mention her name to him. She clearly was a sensitive topic with the guy.

"I'm looking for information about Jaime Ortiz," I said to Magnuson. "Background stuff about him and his time at the NYPD."

"Is this for a profile or something on his gubernatorial run?"

"Yes, right. You worked with him here, didn't you?"

"I did. But not very closely. I got promoted to this job as chief of department after he left. Norm Garrity had the job, and he moved up to commissioner."

"So Ortiz's departure was a good thing for you?"

"It was a good thing for everyone."

"You didn't like him?"

Magnuson hesitated before answering.

"Can we be off the record here?" he asked finally.

"Absolutely."

"Jaime Ortiz was—and still is—a PR creation of himself and of people in the media. People like you who bought into everything he said. Those of us here knew Jaime Ortiz much better. We knew the real Jaime Ortiz. Not the heroic crime fighter that he liked to make himself out to be."

Interesting response.

"Did you ever see him—or suspect him of—doing anything corrupt while he was in the office of police commissioner?"

"Corrupt how?"

"Taking payoffs. Bribes. Covering up crimes to protect rich and powerful people who could help him."

"Are you talking about anything specific?"

I brought up Troy Spencer's death that had been ruled a suicide. I did not mention Wendy Kyle's involvement. But I said there was some suspicion that she might have been murdered, and the evidence of that covered up. Possibly by people high up in the NYPD.

"I wasn't involved in that case," Magnuson said. "Hard for me to answer any questions you have about it."

"Jaime Ortiz was involved in it."

"How?"

"As police commissioner. He signed off on the suicide ruling. I saw his name in the report."

"Then you'd have to ask him about it."

I nodded.

"Let me ask you one thing: even though you don't know anything much about the Spencer case, is that something you could see Ortiz doing? Covering up a crime for a wealthy and influential person who could help him in a lot of ways? Like even running for governor? With money and with political clout? Is that totally crazy to think about for someone like Ortiz? Or is it a potentially viable scenario?"

"What kind of story are you working on?"

"We're still off the record here. I only want to know your honest reaction."

Magnuson was quiet for a long time.

"Off the record . . . well, then yes. I could see Ortiz doing something like that. Again, I don't know anything about this specific case. For all I know, the woman really was a suicide. But I could believe that Ortiz would sell out himself—and the department—for his own benefit and advancement. And, between you and me, it pisses me off that Ortiz is going to very likely wind up getting elected governor. If you could figure out a way to stop that, it would be a great thing for all of us."

As I was leaving, I asked Magnuson about the speculation that he would be replacing Garrity soon as the next police commissioner.

"There's nothing official yet," he said.

"The word I hear is you're the most likely candidate."

"I'm going to keep doing my job here. I'm a police officer. I've dedicated my life to the NYPD. I will do my duty for the department, whatever that is."

"Well, good luck on getting the top job," I said to him.

I meant it too. Well, sort of. I still didn't like the guy. And I was pretty sure he had been a creep to Wendy Kyle before she attacked him. He'd probably made a lot of other mistakes along the way too. But whatever things Magnuson had or hadn't done, they were nothing of the magnitude I now suspected Jaime Ortiz to be guilty of.

Magnuson wasn't the bad guy here.

Jaime Ortiz was.

CHAPTER 44

JAIME ORTIZ WAS scheduled to have a press conference the next day. It was supposed to be for announcing new members of his campaign team, receiving endorsements from several political leaders, and announcing new initiatives for his CrimeStopper campaign. But I had other things I wanted to talk about.

I did not tell Susan Endicott I was going to the press conference. I certainly didn't tell Owen Lasker. And I didn't even tell Maggie. I knew that all of them—Maggie included—would try to convince me why this was a bad idea once I told them what I was going to do at the press conference. They probably would have been right. But I didn't want to hear that right now.

Instead, I arranged on my own to have a Channel 10 film crew there to get it all on video, and I showed up at the Ortiz press conference unannounced.

I was a bit late, and he was already into his anti-crime stump speech when I got there.

"We've made great inroads, amazing progress in getting crime off the streets here in New York City," he was saying. "But crime is not only a New York City problem. It plagues all of the towns and the cities in this great state. Protecting all New Yorkers is my priority. And, as governor, I will dedicate the same amount of time and effort and new strategies—including our ingenious CrimeStopper program—to do the same thing for this entire state. From Buffalo, to Syracuse, to Albany, and to all the smaller towns in between and back here to New York City—we can do this! We can beat back crime! We can make our homes and our neighborhoods safe places again!"

There were questions from the press, but none of them were very interesting or noteworthy. Then I stood up.

"Mr. Ortiz, you say that crime fighting is a priority of yours. But what about the horrendous crime here in Times Square? A woman blown up in her car in broad daylight. Could you tell us your reaction to that?"

Ortiz looked confused.

"Well, that just happened, Ms. . . . ."

"Clare Carlson. Channel 10 News."

"I'm not the police commissioner anymore, so I can't really comment on something like that at all."

"Her name was Wendy Kyle."

"I'm aware of that."

"She was an ex-NYPD officer. Don't you remember her from the force?"

"I had 35,000 officers under me on the force. I don't remember them all."

"Are you saying you didn't know Wendy Kyle?"

"I knew of her. Because of her record—much of it embroiled in controversy while she was on the force."

"Did you ever meet her or talk to her?"

"No, I did not. I don't understand why you're asking me questions about Wendy Kyle. Yes, it was a tragic death. But the police solved the crime, found out who did it, and why. I'd really like to move on with other questions."

I was hoping to rattle him, but so far it hadn't worked.

"You may not have remembered her, but she sure seemed to remember you," I said. "I've seen her Google history. She was searching numerous times for information about you. Almost obsessively. Why do you think she was doing this?"

"Maybe she liked my campaign and wanted to be a part of it. I have no idea. But I don't want to waste any more time on this. There are other reporters with questions to ask about relevant topics. I am very sorry about former NYPD officer Kyle's death, but I don't see what any of this has to do with me."

Damn.

No nervousness at all.

He still looked cool and confident.

But I wasn't done yet. I had one more thing to try.

"What if I were to tell you that I obtained access to Wendy Kyle's cell phone records, and she made numerous calls to your number in the days before she died?"

Ortiz didn't look so cool and confident anymore.

"What if I were to tell you that these calls were to a personal cell phone number that only you answered?"

More squirming.

"Why would she be calling you?"

"I . . . I don't know . . ."

"You don't know why she called you?"

"No."

"But she did call you, didn't she?"

"I mean . . . I never spoke to her."

"You never answered any of the calls."

"No, no."

"The big question is why was she calling you?"

"I have no idea."

"Did she leave messages?"

"Only asking to call her back. She never said why on the messages. And I never called."

"Mr. Ortiz, don't you think this is very relevant to the investigation into her murder?"

"What investigation? The investigation is over. The police know who killed Wendy Kyle. The case is closed."

"Yeah, well, I want to try to get it reopened again."

*　　*　　*

"Wow!" Susan Endicott said to me once I got back to the office. "That was really something."

"Are you happy or mad at me for doing this without telling you?"

"I was mad at first. But then I got happy. I'm not sure exactly what all that means going on between the two of you but it was really dramatic and riveting. This is going to be must-watch TV when we put it on the air tonight."

"That's what I was going for."

"You were struggling there at the beginning. But damn . . . it really was lucky you were able to get those cell phone records showing Kyle trying to call him so many times. That's what really got him shaken up on camera. Those cell phone records of the calls to him that you somehow found. Nice work."

"I didn't have any records of calls to him."

"Huh?"

"I don't even know what his number is."

"But you told him you did have the records of the calls Kyle made to the number."

"No, what I said was 'what if I told you I had cell phone records showing Wendy Kyle making calls to your number?' Ortiz filled in the rest of it on his own."

"You bluffed him!"

"Yes, and I got lucky. It worked."

"You goddamn bluffed Ortiz into telling you what you were looking for."

Endicott shook her head and chuckled.

"Remind me never to play poker with you, Carlson."

CHAPTER 45

RONALD BANNISTER HAD been floating around this story from the very beginning, even though I had never been able to figure out how he fit in with Wendy Kyle.

Now, with the revelation from Schacter that Kyle had been researching him extensively online before her death—along with Jaime Ortiz as well—I needed to find out more about how in the hell Bannister fit into the Wendy Kyle story. Maybe that could give me answers about a possible Ortiz connection too.

"What can you tell me about Ronald Bannister?" I asked Nick Pollock, who worked for the U.S. Treasury Department.

"He's worth a lot of money."

"Always pays to go to an expert."

"Why are you asking me about Bannister?"

"He's involved in a story I'm covering."

"A financial story?"

"A murder story."

Nick Pollock's specialty was going after tax fraud cases, but he was pretty plugged into a lot of big money stuff that the federal government monitored. He was a good-looking guy. Damn good looking. In fact, the first time I saw him I described him to Janet later as a Brad Pitt look-alike.

We'd met on a big story I was doing a few years ago, and we'd become friends. Only friends. Unfortunately, Brad was one of the men I knew who was happily married. To another man. But I think the fact that he was off my sexual radar made it easier for us to be closer to each other. Lack of sexual passion always makes things easier when you're dealing with someone.

He'd become my sort of male version of Janet, a close friend that I talked with and went to when I needed help. I needed help now. I told him about Wendy Kyle and Ronald Bannister.

"Are you people in Treasury looking at Bannister for anything right now?" I asked.

"We're always looking at people like Bannister. That's our job."

"And?"

"There's a lot of money moving around to all of Bannister's business dealings. There always is. The same as there is with Bezos and Musk and Gates and Murdoch and all the other mega-billionaires out there. Is all of it being handled strictly within the boundaries of the law? Probably not. But we're only looking for big targets in terms of prosecution. We only go into action when we spot some major red flags in their financial transactions."

"Any red flags you've seen with Bannister?"

"Nothing I'm aware of. Why? Do you know something about Bannister?"

"He cheats on his wife."

"Excuse me?"

"He's got a lot of girlfriends he sees on the side."

"That's not illegal, last time I checked."

"No, but it exhibits a certain lack of class by the guy."

"You don't like Bannister?"

"Never met him."

"But you still don't like him."

"Can't stand him."

I asked him about Jaime Ortiz.

"The guy running for governor? The former police commissioner?"

"That's him."

"Why would I know anything about Ortiz?"

"No recent history of any money dealings between Ortiz and Bannister? Maybe some kind of a large campaign contribution?"

"I have no idea about that. But campaign contributions from a big business to a political candidate aren't illegal either, Clare."

"I know."

"What exactly are you looking for here?"

"The idea that Bannister paid Ortiz a lot of money to help his campaign back up a theory I have that Ortiz might be covering up something—some big secret—from Bannister's past. I keep thinking there's got to be some kind of money trail between Bannister and Ortiz. But I haven't been able to find it."

"Well, there are ways to hide that kind of a campaign contribution, if it did exist."

"Okay."

"Say someone like Bannister doesn't want it known he's backing a particular political candidate. Maybe he doesn't want to piss off the other candidates, in case they win. Or maybe he's hedging his bets and giving money to several of the candidates in the same race. So he funnels a large amount of money to some company or fund or enterprise besides the candidate. But, after maybe a series of financial transfers, the money winds up in the candidate's campaign chest. It's not easily traceable to Bannister."

"And this happens a lot in campaign financing?"

"More than you would think."

"Could you maybe take a look and see if anything like that might be happening in Bannister's financial transactions records?"

"Clare, I'm backed up here with a full slate of work."

"I know you're busy."

"And even if I had the time . . ."

"Oh, and I really need this in a hurry too, Nick."

He sighed.

"Okay, I'll see what I can do."

Before I left, I asked him about the rest of his life outside the office, including his marriage.

"It's good," he said. "We got a little dog a few months ago. A beagle. Cutest dog you ever saw. And, nothing definite yet, but we've talked about adopting a child. Maybe more than one. We'd like to raise a family."

"That's good, Nick," I said.

And I really meant it.

I was happy for Nick Pollock.

I'm always happy when good things happen for people I like.

"How about you?" he asked.

"Still looking for that right guy."

"You'll find him."

"I'm running out of time."

I told him about my fiftieth birthday coming up fast on the horizon.

"You don't look fifty, Clare."

"Good to hear."

"Hell, you look great."

"Just for the record, if you ever do decide to switch teams and join us on the hetero side of the sexual equation, well . . . keep me in mind."

"If I was ever looking for a woman, Clare."—He laughed—"you would be at the top of my list."

"Then there is hope after all."

CHAPTER 46

"WHAT HAVE WE got for tonight's newscast?" I asked everyone at the morning news meeting.

"At the moment, about sixty minutes of dead air," Maggie said.

"C'mon, people, let's be optimistic."

"Wait until you hear the story list."

I was still running the news meetings. Even though I was doing the Wendy Kyle story too. Handling both jobs like I did before. I wasn't sure how much longer that might last—but, for now anyway, it was business as usual for me at Channel 10.

"The best story we have right now," Maggie said, "is about a possible shark attack off Jones Beach."

"*Possible?*"

"Well, no one is quite sure. Someone thought they saw a fin in the water and reported it to the lifeguard. They cleared the beach for a while. Then they let everyone back in the water but warned them to be on the lookout for sharks."

"Not exactly *Jaws*, is it?" someone said.

"Now if the shark had only eaten someone . . . or at least taken a bite out of them."

"We can still make it dramatic. Terror at the beach, right, Clare?"

"No, let's be responsible. We don't want to scare the hell out of people for no reason. We simply say what happened, but maybe also get some shark experts to talk about the likelihood of any kind of shark attack happening on our beaches now."

"We're still going to scare people," Monica McClain, the weatherwoman, said.

"Yeah, but at least we'll do it responsibly."

The rest of the news was pretty routine. Schoolteachers were threatening to go on strike in the fall, but no one really cared yet because the deadline was so far away. There was talk about raising toll charges on the East River bridges and tunnels. Shootings were up in the city for the sixth consecutive week. A new plan was being unveiled for the redevelopment of Penn Station.

"So, basically, we've got a shark attack that didn't happen and a lot of stories not even that good," Maggie said when she was finished.

"Be patient, ye of little faith," I said.

"What does that mean?" someone asked.

"The news gods will save us."

There were groans around the room. Because they'd heard me going on about the news gods before. The same way I did to Susan Endicott the other day. That didn't stop me from doing it again.

"Pray to the news gods; they will never let us down," I said before winding up the news meeting.

And, sure enough, by the time of the afternoon news meeting several hours later, we did have a lead story.

"It's a murder," Maggie said. "A good murder."

Calling something a *good murder* might sound cold and heartless, but that was the way it was in the news business. There were a lot of murders in New York City. We didn't cover all of them.

Just the good ones. The sexy ones. The sensational ones. The ones we knew our viewers would care about.

"A young woman, twenty-five years old, named Becky Ayers. Shoved in front of a moving subway train in Grand Central Station as she waited for a train to come in. She was an aspiring actress from Indiana, looking for her big break in New York. No one knows yet who did it. But they say it looked intentional."

This was a good murder story on several levels.

First, there'd been a spate of subway pushing in recent weeks around the city—and many people were becoming afraid of going down into the stations to wait for a train on the platform. This was just one more horrifying example of this danger that lurked below the streets.

Second, the cautionary tale of a young woman who came to the big city to be a star and found tragedy instead—as old as it was in the news business—never failed to get people's attention and attract ratings.

But the best part, at least the best part for us, Maggie said, was that Becky Ayers was an attractive woman.

And attractive woman murder victims were also always good for TV news.

Maggie put a picture of Becky Ayers up on a screen in the conference room for us.

Yes, she was attractive, all right.

A real knockout.

A charming smile, big blue eyes, and the kind of cheekbones you'd see on a high fashion model.

That's not what I was looking at though.

I was looking at her hair.

She had red hair.

Just like the woman at the bar with Ronald Bannister.

And that's who she was.

The same woman.

The woman Ronald Bannister had been canoodling with and then disappeared into a hotel room—presumably for an hour of sex.

It was Becky Ayers.

And now she was dead.

CHAPTER 47

I WANTED TO talk to Ronald Bannister.

I needed to talk to Ronald Bannister.

I really had to talk to Ronald Bannister.

I always had, right from the very beginning after his name turned up in Wendy Kyle's diary page. Now, with the death of the woman I'd seen him with at the hotel bar that first night—along with the strange Jaime Ortiz connection—I needed to find out exactly how he was connected to the Wendy Kyle story.

How did I do that?

Well, there were three obvious ways I could confront him:

1. Follow him from his office to whatever woman he was seeing that night, like I did before. Except this time, I wouldn't let him go up to the hotel room with the woman. I'd confront him right then and there in hotel bar or lobby.

But there was a problem with that.

A major problem.

I was pretty sure Bannister would be mad at me if I turned up unexpectedly like that to ruin his tryst with questions about whether or not he was involved in Wendy Kyle's murder. Then he'd probably have me thrown out of the bar, out of the hotel entirely, and I wouldn't get to interview him.

2. Like I thought about earlier, I could pull a Wendy Kyle and do the Honey Trap on him. Dress up in a sexy outfit, come on to him, and then—when he's about to take me to bed—I hit him with the news that I'm a TV reporter doing a story about him.

But, as I said, would Bannister even go for me? The woman I'd seen him with looked to be in her twenties, so I assumed he liked that age for his sexual encounters. Not an old broad like me pushing fifty.

Plus, there was the question of journalism ethics. I'm not sure— I mean, I'm not sure about a lot of things in these crazy times—but I believe there is still a journalistic code for a woman reporter not to use sex to get a story. I mean I never heard of Katie Couric or even Barbara Walters back in the day doing that. I didn't want to be the first.

3. I could simply go directly to Bannister's office, put in a request for an interview, and wait for him to get back to me. The problem was I knew what his answer would be. Either no response or else a flat turndown for an interview. Then I'd be back at square one where I started.

No, this required a more ingenious approach. A brilliant idea. I sat there at my desk in the Channel 10 newsroom and tried to think of something ingenious or brilliant. I could not. So I contacted Bannister's wife again. At least she talked to me.

"I need to speak with your husband," I said.

"So do it."

"I don't think he'll agree to talk to me."

"That's between you and him."

"Ms. Bannister, this is a murder story. A murder story your husband might be involved in. Don't you care about that?"

"You should talk to him about that, not me."

The conversation went on like that for a few minutes.

She made it clear to me again that she and her husband went their separate ways.

Whatever he did—whether another woman or murder or anything else—had nothing to do with her, I guess.

I did have another idea forming in my head now, though. A way to smoke Bannister out. By putting a lot of public pressure on him. So much public pressure that he couldn't stay silent.

"Ms. Bannister, I'm planning on running those pictures of your husband at the hotel with the redheaded woman he later accompanied to the hotel room. That woman is now dead. I'm going to make that connection on the air. He's not going to be able to hide once I do that. Tell him I'm going to put it all out there."

"Do whatever you want," Ms. Bannister said.

Then she hung up.

*　　*　　*

And so that night, on the 6:00 p.m. broadcast, I went public with the sexual relationship I'd seen in the hotel with the now dead redheaded woman.

ME: *We have breaking developments in the Wendy Kyle murder story. From the very beginning, billionaire investment tycoon Ronald Bannister has been mysteriously linked to Kyle because of a document found in her office mentioning his name for some reason. And now he's connected with another dead woman.*

These pictures show him with Becky Ayers, 25, in a midtown hotel where they disappeared into a room. Now Ayers is dead too—the victim of a fatal subway pushing incident.

Ronald Bannister, we need you to come forward and answer questions about what your relationships were with these two women—what you might know about their deaths.

None of this exactly made a lot of sense, of course.

But it didn't matter.

It was out there now.

What would Ronald Bannister do about that?

CHAPTER 48

No, I HADN'T forgotten about Steve Healy.

I wanted to talk to him too, especially now that I knew his name.

About being at the hotel with Ronald Bannister, about being interested in me enough to follow me the next morning, about showing up at the same apartment building as the redhead from the bar who was now dead, and about what he was doing that day visiting NYPD headquarters.

The problem was I couldn't find Healy anywhere I looked.

If Wendy Kyle had made a lot of noise and controversy as well as enemies on the NYPD—and then more recently as a private investigator—Steve Healy appeared to be the exact opposite. There was almost no record of him as a cop. Or as a PI. He seemed to be the ultimate Nowhere Man who blended into the background without leaving any type of trail or indication he'd been there.

Still, Healy had been around the story since that first night at the bar, and I needed to find out why.

From what I could find out about Healy—and it wasn't a lot—he'd been on the force several years, leaving a year after Kyle was dismissed for her attack against her commanding officer, Magnuson.

There was no indication of any crossover between him and Kyle during that period, or at least none that I could find. But, like I said, all of the information on Healy was pretty damn sparse.

One reason for that was that I did find out Healy had been assigned during those final years with the NYPD to the Internal Affairs Unit. Which was the shadowy department that investigated police officers for potential corruption.

Could Wendy Kyle have come in contact with him during the time she was talking about police corruption a lot and making other allegations against the NYPD about cover-ups and wrongdoing and malfeasance by top people there?

Possibly.

But there was no hard evidence of that.

What made it tricky was that the Internal Affairs Unit did much of their work in secret, so there's wasn't a lot of transparency about what they might be doing behind closed doors. Which seemed to fit Steve Healy's persona perfectly.

I figured I'd be able to reach him through his private investigator office, but I was wrong about that too.

There was an address listed on his website. It was in Chelsea, on West 22nd Street between Seventh and Eighth Avenues. But, when I went there, it turned out to just be a mail drop. And no one there could—or would—tell me how to reach Healy directly without going through the mail there.

The phone number on the website was the same thing. It simply went to some kind of group answering message. Didn't mention his name at all. I thought about leaving a message, but didn't. I still hoped to catch him somewhere by surprise, even though that was looking less and less likely.

I mean this guy was hard to find.

Not sure exactly what kind of PI business he ran.

But it sure wasn't a high-profile operation.

I had another idea.

I'd seen Healy twice now at the apartment house where the redhead had gone after her meeting with Bannister—after the stop at the building I now knew housed the campaign office of Jaime Ortiz.

At lunchtime, I went back downtown to the restaurant where he'd been both times.

I went inside the restaurant this time. It was filled with a lunchtime crowd. A waiter offered to take me to a table. But I asked to see the manager instead.

A few minutes later, a big man—with dark hair and an even darker mustache—came out of an office in the back to greet me. He said he was Raymond Grieco and asked what I wanted.

I gave him my card with my name and number for Channel 10 News—and told him I was a reporter.

Then I showed him a picture of Steve Healy I'd downloaded with Todd Schacter from the internet.

I asked Grieco if he knew this man or how I could find him.

He looked at the picture, then back at me.

"Do you know our special today is pasta primavera?" he said. "Everyone loves it, we get rave reviews. I recommend it highly."

"Uh, that sounds wonderful. But what about the man in the picture?"

"It is indeed a quite exquisite pasta."

"You're not going to tell me about Steve Healy, are you?"

"Are you sure you won't try the primavera? No charge for you. On the house."

"Maybe some other time."

I looked down at my business card still in his hand.

"If you do talk to this man, Steve Healy, tell him to contact me at that number. It's very important. Tell him I know all about him and Wendy Kyle. I have a lot to talk to him about. Make sure he hears that."

If the name meant anything to Grieco, he didn't show any emotion. He looked down at the card one more time and then put it in his pocket. I walked out through the restaurant. As I did so, I saw a waiter deliver the pasta primavera special to one of the tables. It looked good. Damn good.

Maybe I should have taken Grieco up on that free lunch offer.

CHAPTER 49

BRENDAN KAISER WANTED to see me. I got a message telling me that. Not a good sign. My last meeting with him had been successful in getting me back on the Wendy Kyle story. But why did he want to talk to me again now? Had he changed his mind? Was the sale of Channel 10 about to take place, which would put Owen Lasker and Kellogg and Klein in charge? Whatever it was, this didn't sound good to me.

He wanted to meet for lunch, the message said. At a downtown restaurant called Tri-Bar in SoHo. It was his favorite spot. The only time I'd ever had met with him outside the office before was when he took me there a year or so ago to break the news that he was bringing in Susan Endicott to replace Jack Faron as Executive Producer.

Maybe Tri-Bar was his spot for giving people bad news.

So what bad news did he have for me now?

*　　*　　*

Kaiser was sitting at his regular table—yes, he had a regular table!—when I got there. He greeted me warmly, which was nice—but didn't really mean anything. He was drinking white wine and asked me what I wanted to drink. It was barely noon. I don't normally start drinking at this time of day. But I guess you can drink at noon or anytime you want when you're the big boss. Me, I'm just a working girl, and I had to go back to the office to put out a newscast. I asked for iced coffee.

The menu had a lot of exciting items, but what caught my eye was the hamburger. The reason it caught my eye was it cost $36. I wondered what a $36 hamburger tasted like. Would it really be that much better than . . . say, a Whopper from Burger King? I decided to order it and find out. Kaiser gave me a funny look when I did. He went for some kind of a duck confit dish.

I filled in Kaiser on some of the things I'd found out about the Wendy Kyle story and the questions I still had.

I wanted to blurt out "what's this lunch all about?"—but I waited to find the right moment to do that.

And then I didn't have to.

As I was about to bring it up, Kaiser said to me: "I have some news about the sale of Channel 10."

"Oh?" I said, as if this were the last thing on my mind.

"I wanted to tell you directly."

"Is the sale final now?" I asked anxiously.

"Not exactly."

"Then what's happening?"

"There's been another potential bid for the station."

"Besides Kellogg and Klein?"

He nodded.

"We got a notification of a new offer."

"A bigger offer than Kellogg and Klein?"

"Much bigger."

"How much bigger?"

"The new offer blows the Kellogg and Klein one out of the water."

"So you're gonna take that one?"

"It's not that easy."

He played with his fork in the duck confit for a bit, without actually eating any of it. I had a feeling the big news he'd brought me here to tell me was still to come. I took a bite of my $36 hamburger and waited. It wasn't a bad hamburger, but definitely not worth $36. I wasn't even sure it was better than a Whopper.

"The new potential buyer is Ronald Bannister," Kaiser said.

I suddenly stopped eating, put down the hamburger, and stared at him across the table.

"*My* Ronald Bannister?"

"Same one."

"Has he ever expressed any interest in buying the station from you in the past?"

"None."

"Then . . ."

"I think he's worried about what you might find out if we let you keep covering this story."

"Wow! So a man like Ronald Bannister would spend millions and millions of dollars to buy a TV station just to make sure some bad or embarrassing story about him doesn't get on air. That's crazy. Who would do something like that?"

"A man like Ronald Bannister."

"C'mon, you're rich too. Would you spend money on something like this?"

"I'm not Ronald Bannister."

"I'm sure glad about that."

"He doesn't really want the station, Clare. He wants you. He wants to get control over you."

I guess I should have felt flattered. But I wasn't. I was mad. Mad that someone like Bannister thought that he could buy me like one of his shopping malls or oil wells or yachts. And mad, too, because I was afraid he might get away with it.

"Are you going to sell the station to him?"

"I'd be crazy not to at the price he's offering."

"That wasn't my question."

He smiled.

"No, I'm not going to sell the station to Ronald Bannister no matter how much money he offers me for it."

"And that's what you brought me here to tell me."

"I thought you should know."

I finished off the rest of my hamburger. I was starting to like it better now. Maybe I could stop off for a snack here sometime with the gang from the newsroom and put it on my expense account.

"I don't have to tell you what this means, do I, Clare?"

"It means I'm on the right trail with this story."

"You've hit on something that has Bannister really worried."

"Which means I need to keep doing what I've been doing."

"That's right."

"Keep digging until I find out what it is that Ronald Bannister doesn't want me to find out about him."

"Yep."

"And you're going to let me do that?"

"I wouldn't have it any other way." Kaiser smiled.

CHAPTER 50

FOR SUCH A seemingly smart guy—and you had to be smart to be worth $50 billion, right?—Ronald Bannister had made a pretty big mistake.

I didn't realize it at first while I was talking to Kaiser about Bannister's mega-offer to buy the station.

And presumably me—and my silence—along with it.

But, after I left Kaiser, the realization of what this meant hit me.

Bannister had basically sent up a red flag alerting us he was somehow involved—in a way he didn't want anyone to know about—in the Wendy Kyle story. I mean, a day or so after I call him out on air, he tries to buy my damn station. It might not be enough to convict him of anything in a court of law, but it was easy for anyone to connect the dots. And those dots now led directly to him.

All I had to do was go public with all this.

I'd do a follow-up story on Bannister, confronting him about the offer to buy the station—then put it on the air with whatever he said—or didn't say.

Whatever his response was—even a no comment or more legal threats or trying to ignore me and my questions—would make him look guilty in the perception of the viewing public.

The only problem would have been if Kaiser didn't want me to go public with the Bannister offer for the station. But when I went back and asked him, Kaiser was fine—even enthusiastic—about doing it. I think he was offended that Bannister thought he could buy him off with a ton of money. Two rich guys' egos going at it, I guess. But it worked out great for me.

I made plans to confront Bannister at his office the next morning. I'd bring a video crew with me. If he refused to see me, I'd get that all on camera too. One way or another it was going to be a media event. A win-win either way for me and Channel 10.

I made arrangements to meet up with the video crew outside Bannister's office building at seven a.m.

Early enough that we'd get him on the street outside his building coming to work later that morning.

Yep, it all seemed pretty straightforward.

Yep, this was going to be easy.

Or so I figured.

*　　*　　*

On my way there in the morning, my only real decision was if I should stop to buy coffee—or go directly there without coffee?

Decisions, decisions.

I decided to hold off on the coffee until later in case Bannister got to the office early. I didn't want to take any chance on missing him.

There'd be plenty of time for coffee later.

I thought about how satisfying it was going to be to finally be face-to-face with Ronald Bannister. I thought I knew him pretty well at this point because of everything that had happened, even though we'd never actually met. The closest was that first night at the Stratton Hotel bar. He looked cool, calm, and collected then. A man who had everything he could want—money, women, power.

What would his reaction be now if he thought I was a threat to take all that away from him?

Maybe try to buy off me or Kaiser or the station with even more money than he offered before?

I was still thinking about that when I approached Bannister's building.

That's when I saw them outside.

The police.

Police cars lined up in front of the place.

Other vehicles with detectives.

An EMS vehicle too.

And I realized at that point it was going to be a long wait before I could get that morning coffee.

I looked around for my video crew, but I didn't see them anywhere yet. I tried to approach the front of the building, but I was stopped by one of the uniformed cops.

"No one is allowed in," he said.

"But I have business inside."

"What kind of business?"

I showed him my press credentials.

"I came here today to try to interview Ronald Bannister."

"Well, that's going to be kind of hard to do."

"What do you mean?" I asked, even though I was pretty sure I knew what his answer was going to be.

"Ronald Bannister was found murdered upstairs in his office."

PART IV

BROADCAST BLUES

CHAPTER 51

THE DETAILS WE knew about Ronald Bannister's murder went like this:

At a little after six the previous evening, he'd left his office building on Madison Avenue and walked over to the Stratton Hotel bar again. He was planning to meet a woman named Marsha Hunt. Authorities knew that because he had sent text messages earlier, talking to her about meeting up there.

The two of them had checked into the same room there a little after 8:30—then he was seen walking out through the lobby and leaving by hotel security video around 10:00. Clearly, he wasn't a man who spent a lot of time during sex, even though he did it a lot.

He then walked back to his building and went to his office there. A series of texts and emails were found indicating he worked for at least an hour. There were communications with financial leaders and business associates and employees who worked for him. People who knew Bannister said he frequently worked late into the night like that.

There was nothing in any of the messages sent by Bannister to suggest he was upset about anything or worried or under any kind of duress. There were a series of other messages to people too, including even one to his wife to tell her he "was working late." Not that his wife probably cared where he was at night, based on my conversation with her. But I guess he liked to keep up appearances for everybody.

A night security guard noticed the door of Bannister's office was open at some point during the early morning hours. The guard went inside to check, found Bannister dead at his desk, and called the police.

Bannister was shot three times at point blank range. Authorities believed Bannister knew his killer. It didn't look like a robbery. Nothing was missing. No sign of a break-in either. No indication Bannister made any effort to run or get away from his assailant. He was just sitting at his desk when he was shot.

There was nothing from the security tape in the building's lobby of anyone suspicious coming or going out during the night after Bannister returned there. Only a handful of people, none of whom would have had any reason to go to Bannister's office.

Marsha Hunt, the woman he'd been with at the hotel, was quickly cleared as a potential suspect. She'd ordered room service sent up to her in the room after Bannister left to return to his office. It had been delivered to her in person by a member of the hotel staff—who saw her in the room—while Bannister would have still been sending messages at his office.

Also, the hotel had a security service that could tell if a door was opened or not at any specific time. The room where Marsha Hunt was—the one she'd shared earlier with Bannister—had not been opened following the delivery of the room service food. She'd been there all night.

She had a perfect alibi.

Police said that at the moment they had no suspects and no motive and had not been able to pinpoint anyone with a specific reason to want Bannister dead.

I couldn't help but feel I had some responsibility for Bannister's death. I mean, I'd gone on TV and practically threatened to expose him. To come after him about the things he'd done. To reveal his secret deals and relationships. And, maybe most importantly of all, to link him with the Wendy Kyle murder.

I still believed he had been involved.

But now it was clear he wasn't alone.

There was someone else in the picture.

Someone as powerful as Ronald Bannister.

Someone who wanted to make sure Bannister's secrets were never revealed.

And murder was the most effective way to do that.

But who?

Who was worried enough about Ronald Bannister possibly revealing what he knew to resort to murder to keep him silent?

The one name that jumped out to me was Jaime Ortiz. He had the motive, if he was involved with Bannister like I believed. He had the means too—he was a former police commissioner running for governor, so he presumably knew a lot about how to kill someone and not get caught.

And I had another scary thought too.

What about me?

If someone like Ortiz was that worried about Ronald Bannister talking to me, why wouldn't he come after me next?

Nevertheless, I had my job to do. To report the news. And this was goddamned big news. So that night at 6:00 p.m.— after breaking news bulletins and special reports through the day—I led our newscast with the story of the murder of Ronald Bannister.

ME: *One of the richest men in the country was murdered in his New York City office last night—and the big questions now are who killed Ronald Bannister and why.*

Was it connected to one of his controversial financial transactions?

Was it because his public romancing of women had gotten one of their husbands or boyfriends mad enough to kill him?

Or was it—as we believe here at Channel 10—that Bannister's death is somehow linked with the murder of former NYPD officer and private investigator Wendy Kyle?

* * *

There was a lot of reaction to what we ran on Bannister's shocking death. Rival business leaders who hailed his achievements. People he worked with in the financial world. Coworkers, friends, and others he came in contact with. Everyone said nice things. Even his wife went on camera and spoke tearfully and emotionally about the pain of losing her "love and lifelong companion" so suddenly and tragically. It was all the traditional stuff people said at the time of a shocking death like this whether any of it was true or not.

To balance out our coverage of the man and his life, I re-ran the pictures of him at the Stratton bar carrying on with Becky Ayers, the redheaded woman—who eventually wound up at the hotel room upstairs. Normally that might have seemed inappropriate when someone had died in a shocking murder. But since Becky Ayers, the woman in the pictures, had been murdered, it now seemed very relevant. It was hard to believe the two murders were not somehow connected. Which is what I pointed out to the viewers.

There were also lots of pictures from the files of Bannister living the beautiful life of the super-rich. Dining at fine restaurants, attending theater openings and lavish parties, even one of him lounging on the deck of a yacht, cruising the Mediterranean off the coast of France. His wife was in the yacht picture. The caption said it was a wedding anniversary cruise for them. I guess he had to do some things in public with her like this. Both he and his wife were smiling at the camera in the picture. But they still didn't look happy.

All the wealth, all the power, all the fame. The man sure lived a glamorous life with his money.

And now it was all gone.

Just like him.

In death, Ronald Bannister was just like everyone else. No longer Ronald Bannister, the billionaire. Like they always say, death is the great equalizer. We all wind up in the same place, even someone like Bannister.

CHAPTER 52

"So what do we do next?" Maggie asked me the next morning when we got to work.

"Keep working the story about the killing until we find out who did it."

"Bannister?"

"And Wendy Kyle too."

"You figure they were both killed by the same person?"

"It's the only theory that makes sense to me."

"And the redheaded woman?"

"Her too."

"Damn."

"It's all gotta be connected."

Maggie and I were in my office drinking coffee and munching on bagels before the morning news meeting. I always liked to do this with Maggie before the actual meeting. So that we had some kind of a game plan going in.

I knew the bulk of the news meeting today would be about our follow-ups to the Bannister murder. But the question was where to go and who to do it. That was complicated by the fact that I was still the lead reporter on this story, as well as having to be the news director running the entire Channel 10 operation.

I couldn't complain though. I'd lobbied for this, and I wanted it. I was all-in on this story. At least I was until the station was sold. All I had to do was break this story wide open before then.

What could go wrong?

"Here's my theory," I said. "I think Bannister was involved somehow in the Wendy Kyle murder. That Kyle was working on something—maybe close to exposing it—involving a scandal for Bannister. Now what kind of scandal would scare a man like Ronald Bannister? Not a sexual one, he was pretty damn open and public about what he was doing with other women besides his wife. A money scandal? I don't think that makes sense either. He'd been implicated in a bunch of financial investigations in the past—all of that kind of messy stuff was probably part of doing business for him. No, this had to be something bigger. A lot bigger. Something like murder."

"The woman who died in Murray Hill that was ruled a suicide?"

"That's my best guess. Troy Spencer was a hot-looking woman, from what everybody says. And she was using her physical attributes to get money out of rich men for sexual pleasures, we now know. Sounds like Bannister's type of woman. So she meets up with Bannister, they go to her place and start having sex. But something goes wrong. Maybe it was supposed to be rough sex, maybe it was an accident—but Bannister killed her. That's where the bruises on her neck and face came from, not because she fell or slipped.

"What does Bannister do now? He could run, but maybe he's worried people had seen him or knew about the girl, especially if he put on a public display with her like he did with the redhead at the Stratton Bar. Or maybe he just panics and doesn't know what to do. But he's rich, and he's powerful. Which means he knows a lot of other powerful men. Maybe some of them are on the NYPD.

"He calls one of them who can make the murder look like a suicide. Then the entire scene in the apartment is *staged* to make it look like a suicide, not a murder. Bannister is off the hook. But he has to pay whoever helped him a huge amount of money—and maybe he was still making those payments.

"The only problem is one of the police officers who showed up at the scene—a young recruit named Wendy Kyle—didn't buy the suicide angle. She began trying to press for a murder investigation. Whoever helped Bannister tried to discredit her so she wouldn't be believed. That's when all the disciplinary actions and suspensions against her occurred. Nobody believed anything she said, she was a troublemaker—a loose cannon.

"But then recently—we're not sure why—she opened up the case again, reaching out to some of the key people. She wasn't with the NYPD anymore so they couldn't stop her the way they did in the past. Instead, the solution was a fatal bombing so that her secrets went to the grave with her.

"Except then I come along and start reporting on all of this. Things about Bannister and about his possible links to the Wendy Kyle murder. They didn't count on this kind of publicity, and that freaks them all out. Bannister and the people he bought and paid for on the NYPD. Maybe they decide Bannister is too dangerous because of what he knows—he's a liability now. So Bannister has to die."

"Someone on the NYPD kills their golden goose—the one who's been paying them off for years," Maggie asked. "Does that make sense?"

"If they thought he might give them up. He's presumably paid them a lot of money over the past few years for the cover-up. They decide to take the money they have and eliminate the risk of exposure by Bannister."

Maggie didn't say anything.

"What do you think?" I asked her finally.

"Very thin on facts."

"I realize that."

"How do we get more facts?"

"Go after the person we believe was involved with Bannister on this."

"Are you talking about Jaime Ortiz?"

"I am."

"Jesus."

"He's the only one I can think of powerful enough to pull something like this off—have Kyle killed, the redhead Becky Ayers, and then get rid of someone as important and influential as Bannister himself when he began to be too much trouble. Jaime Ortiz wants to be the next governor. How far is he willing to go to win the job? I think whatever it takes. People like Ortiz will do anything to get that kind of power."

"And you're convinced now that Ortiz is the person behind all this?"

"Well, there is someone else involved that I need to find out about too."

"Who is that?"

"An ex-cop named Steve Healy. He's been around this story since the beginning for me. I have to find out why."

I told her about trying to find Healy and finally leaving a message for him at the restaurant where I'd seen him twice on the Lower East Side.

"I don't expect him to call me back," I said. "It was something I decided to do for the hell of it. Hey, at least maybe it will shake

Steve Healy up a little bit—make him nervous and do something stupid—if he does get my message."

But then, to my surprise, I got a text a short time later at the number I'd left with Grieco at the restaurant.

Amazingly enough, it was from Steve Healy. *Meet me tonight at 6 at the Stratton Hotel bar. The same place I saw you before. It will be well worth your time, I can assure you of that. I have a lot to talk to you about too.*

CHAPTER 53

STEVE HEALY WAS waiting for me at the bar when I got there. He was sitting in the same spot where'd I'd met him last time. Funny how things had come full circle since that first chance meeting—or so I thought. Now he might hold the answers to both the Wendy Kyle and Ronald Bannister murders.

"Why meet here?" I asked him as I slipped onto the stool next to him.

"I thought it was a nice touch."

"Never thought I'd see you here again after that first time."

He smiled. "Never thought I'd see you here again either."

It was a nice smile. A damn charming smile. Healy was a good-looking guy. Curly blond hair, rugged features, big shoulders and body—not fat at all though, he looked like he was in perfect shape. I didn't think much about his looks the first time I saw him. But now I was very aware of the fact that I was sitting here with an attractive man.

Healy already had a drink in front of him.

"What do you want?" he asked.

"Diet Coke is fine."

"I think you're going to want something stronger."

"What do you mean?"

"What I'm going to tell you is going to shock the hell out of you."

I nodded.

"Jack Daniels, on the rocks," I told the bartender.

Once my drink came, Healy picked up both his and mine off the bar and led me to a single, secluded table in the corner. He said he wanted to make sure we could talk privately. I followed him. What the hell else was I going to do? I had a million questions for this guy, but I decided to let him talk first.

"How much do you know about Wendy Kyle?" he asked. "Or think you know?"

"A lot."

"Did you know Wendy and I were partners on the street when we were both with the NYPD?"

That did surprise me.

"I thought you worked out of Internal Affairs," I said.

"That was later. Before that, Wendy and I shared a police car together."

I thought about what it must have been like when he was paired with Wendy Kyle as NYPD partners. She was a knockout of a woman, and he was . . . well, they had to be the sexiest crime fighting duo out there back then.

"I'd lost touch with Wendy over the years," Healy said now. "But then she reached out to me out of the blue. About a crime scene and a case that she'd once been involved with. She said she had new information, blockbuster information—and she wanted my help to get the truth out there once and for all."

"The Troy Spencer death," I said.

"Yes. That's it. Wendy was really worked up about that one, right from the very beginning when she got to the crime scene and they ruled it a suicide. I didn't have any opinion one way or the other; we weren't partners then. But—from what I found out later—Wendy began arguing with the detective and the ME's people and claiming it should be investigated as a murder. I was never sure why it affected her so deeply. I asked her, but she would never talk about it."

"She went through a lot of bad stuff herself as a young woman," I said. I told him about her background and even about the way she had even befriended the homeless woman Reby in her own neighborhood recently. "I think she empathized with women who had been through things like her. She likely empathized with Troy Spencer."

I had a question for Healy before we went any further.

"Who do you work for?" I asked him.

"I work for a lot of people."

"Was one of them Ronald Bannister?"

He nodded.

"My agency is a special security company," he said. "I work for a lot of VIPs here and around the world. Not only Bannister. I'm not the kind you'll find listed under PIs somewhere. My work is very . . . let's say discreet. I work with some good and some bad elements, which is a necessary part of this kind of thing."

"Is everything you do legal?"

"A lot of what I do is in what you might call a *gray area*."

"And Wendy Kyle knew you worked for Bannister?"

"Yes, she found out Bannister had hired me after I left the force. That's why she came to me, why we reconnected. Because she was out to get Bannister. To make him pay for getting away with murder. I never put Bannister together with the Troy Spencer case for any reason until then. But Wendy told me how she believed Bannister murdered Troy Spencer and covered it up. She said she'd always been convinced someone had murdered the

Spencer woman, and now she knew it was Bannister. She said she'd found out he paid off people in the NYPD—top people there—to make sure that Troy Spencer was never considered anything else besides a suicide. She wanted to expose Bannister and all the police corruption involved in the cover-up now. And she wanted me to help her."

"Why would you do something like that—why would you help her—when you work for Bannister?"

"She was my partner."

"I know, but . . ."

"If you've never been a cop, you probably can't understand it. But there's a pact between a cop and his or her partner. A loyalty that exists. Even if you're not on the force anymore. Plus, I wanted to find out the truth. I didn't know Bannister was a criminal, at least not that kind of criminal. A murderer. But, if he was, I wanted to expose him too. Along with all the corrupt people in the NYPD that had protected him. Once a cop, always a cop, I guess. I wanted to see justice done too. The same as Wendy did. That's why we agreed to work together on it."

He took out a piece of paper and showed it to me. It was the opening page from Wendy Kyle's diary that police had found in her office. I wondered where he had gotten it from. I'd seen the same page when Manning showed it to me from the police files. Maybe Healy had gotten it from there too. I remembered seeing him go into 1 Police Plaza that day I tailed him from the Italian restaurant on the Lower East Side. But who had he gotten it from there? Or maybe Wendy Kyle gave him a copy before she died. In any case, he had circled a key part of Kyle's diary entry. It said:

Wendy Kyle is the kind of woman who deals in facts for a living, the kind of woman who doesn't let emotion cloud her judgment and—maybe most importantly of all—the kind of woman who never blindly puts her trust in anyone.

Especially a man.

Hey, I'm not some man-hating bitch or anything like that, no matter what you may have heard or think about me. I like men. I love men, or at least I've loved a few men in my life. It's just that I don't trust them anymore.

So wouldn't it be ironic—or maybe a little bit fitting, to look at it completely objectively—if trusting a man this one time was what wound up costing me my own life in the end.

"That man was me," Healy said. "She depended on me. I couldn't save her life. But I'm determined to expose the corruption the way she wanted to do."

I asked him a lot more questions. Like about the redheaded woman from the bar who I followed back to the same building where I later saw him. He said she'd been working for him, trying to get information out of Bannister. And people he thought were involved in the Bannister cover-up.

"Who killed her?" I asked.

"I'm not exactly sure."

"Do you think she really got pushed in front of that subway in a random crime?"

"No, I think someone found out who she was and wanted to make sure she didn't tell anyone whatever she knew."

"And Bannister."

"They had to make sure he didn't talk too."

"Who is *they*?"

"The people at 1 Police Plaza who are trying to hide all of this. Not just people there now. People who've been involved in this from the very beginning, when they took big money to do a big favor for Ronald Bannister. Cover up the fact that he murdered a woman."

"Are we talking about Jaime Ortiz here?"

"I believe so. That's why I need your help now. To expose him."

"What do you want from me?"

"To do a story that puts enough of this stuff out there that it shakes Ortiz up. Gets him to make a mistake. Then we can jump on that and hopefully nail him. That's what Wendy and I wanted to do. But you—with your TV news platform—you can put things out there for all the world to see. Especially Jaime Ortiz."

"How do I know I can trust you?" I asked when he was finished talking.

"Wendy trusted me."

"And now she's dead."

"That's why we need to do something about this. To avenge her death. To make her sacrifice worthwhile and meaningful. We have to make Jaime Ortiz pay for his crimes. We can do that. You and me, Ms. Carlson. What do you say?"

I had to make a decision about this guy.

To trust him or not.

Wendy Kyle had trusted him.

But should I?

CHAPTER 54

I DIDN'T HAVE a whole lot of people I knew I could trust right now. I sure couldn't trust Jaime Ortiz, because of what I'd found out from Healy. According to him, I couldn't really trust anyone in the NYPD hierarchy at this point. And, for that matter, I wasn't sure I could trust Healy either. I didn't trust Owen Lasker or anyone at Kellogg and Klein. I'd already been to Brendan Kaiser for help. I didn't want to go back to him again. I trusted the people I worked with at Channel 10, especially Maggie. But I needed to find someone higher up at the station to talk to about what I planned to do next.

And so in the end, to my astonishment, I decided to trust Susan Endicott.

Well, not really trust her.

Not totally.

But at least enough to go to her with my idea and work it out together.

Susan Endicott seemed as surprised as I did when I told her what I wanted to talk to her about.

"We made a pact to stick together because of the sale of the station, right?" I pointed out to Endicott.

"We did."

"So why are you surprised?"

"Well, you sort of broke the pact when you went to talk to Brendan Kaiser about the sale without telling me what you were going to do."

"Still, it got the job done. It held up the sale. At least for a while. And the basic guidelines of our pact agreement are still there."

"In other words, you have something else you want to do. But you're worried about it. You want me to back you up."

"More than that. I want to talk about it with you first. Work out a game plan between us. Then, once we do that, we put up a united front. Even if it all goes up in flames. Which it very well could."

"You don't seem to have a lot of confidence in this plan."

"It's got some potential pitfalls."

"Journalistically speaking?"

"Maybe personally too."

"But you think that maybe—just maybe—you can break open the Wendy Kyle story with it?"

"I do. And the Ronald Bannister murder too. Plus, a big corruption scandal at the top of the NYPD, possibly involving gubernatorial favorite Jaime Ortiz."

I told her everything I'd found out. About Ortiz. Bannister. All the stuff from Healy about the murder of Troy Spencer that he believed top people in the NYPD tried to cover up. About how Jaime Ortiz's name was the signature on the official police report confirming it was a suicide. About the links to the redheaded woman, Becky Ayers, who'd died in the subway attack. About how Bannister had tried to buy Channel 10 by making an over-the-top offer to Kaiser before his murder. And, most of all, how Healy was investigating Ortiz and other top people at the NYPD in all this.

"We put a lot of this out there on our broadcast tonight," I said. "As much as we think we can get away with saying. But we definitely point the finger of suspicion at Ortiz and other top people from the NYPD. Talk about him and Bannister and the rest. We won't actually accuse Ortiz of anything criminal, of course. But we don't have to. We go with everything I know, and then see what happens. Ortiz can't ignore it. He'll have to respond. Maybe he'll make a mistake."

"And we'll be the one breaking the story," she said.

"Well, I'll be."

"And if you're wrong and this all goes bad and blows up in your face?"

"Then I'll take the blame. You can do what you've always wanted to do. Fire me."

Endicott didn't say anything at first. But I was pretty sure she was going to go for it. The upside was just too good for her. She was thinking about all the attention and big ratings that could come for her and the station if she let me do this. She could take a lot of the credit. Hey, if it worked, she might even try to act as if it was all her idea. I didn't care about that. I only wanted her backing now.

"What the hell," she said finally. "Sometimes you got to take a chance."

"Great! I'll put together a segment for the 6:00 p.m. broadcast."

"We'll start doing teasers for it during our afternoon programming. Blockbuster exclusive report coming from Channel 10 on the Ronald Bannister murder."

"Sounds good."

I started to get up to leave. I had a lot of work to do before the newscast. I needed to get everything right. Exactly right. I might not get another chance if I screwed up any of this right now.

"Did you tell Brendan Kaiser what you planned to do?" Endicott asked me before I left her office.

"No, I didn't."

"I thought he was your friend."

"He's not my friend. He's the owner, at least for now. He's also involved in a big money deal to sell Channel 10. He helped once. Twice, I guess, if you include him telling me about the Bannister offer. But I don't want to push it."

"You're afraid he might change his mind about helping you?"

"I don't want to find out."

"What if I'd said 'no' to you about doing this?"

"You didn't."

"But if I did . . ."

"I was pretty sure you'd say 'yes.'"

"Why? After everything you and I have gone through?"

"Because you're a journalist at heart. Like me. Well, not like me. But you still know the value of a good story. This is more than a good story. It's a great story. This could be a career-maker for a journalist. For me. And for you too. Everyone will be talking about us here at Channel 10 News, one way or another—once we do this."

Endicott smiled. She really smiled.

Hard to believe, but the smile was there.

"Just don't screw it up, Carlson," she said.

But she was still smiling when she said it.

CHAPTER 55

I WENT TO see Scott Manning in his office at FBI headquarters in downtown Manhattan the next day.

"We have to stop meeting like this," Manning said.

"I haven't been to your office in a few years."

"But last time we met in your office."

"Only trying to keep it professional between us."

"I did kiss you that last time we were in your office," Manning pointed out. "Do you remember that?"

"Now that you mention it, it does ring a bell."

He laughed.

"That was some helluva broadcast you put on last night," Manning said now. "You sure threw a lot of stuff out there. About Bannister. Speculation about Ortiz. The NYPD brass. You must be getting a lot of flak for all that."

"Yeah, I figure the shit's really gonna hit the fan when I get back to the office. In a lot of ways. Which is why I'm here, Scott. I need your help again."

"I don't think I can be of much more help to you in investigating the story."

"I'm not talking about the story. I'm talking about me. I need someone to watch my back. You're the best person I can think of to do that."

He looked confused.

"What do you mean?"

"Someone murdered Wendy Kyle, Becky Ayers, and now Ronald Bannister. Presumably because they knew too much. That leaves one person who knows a lot about this story. Me. I'm afraid they might come after me next. And I'm not talking about court orders or angry public statements. I mean trying to take me out too. Is there some way you could watch me to make sure nothing happens? Or set up some way that you'd know if I was in any kind of danger or trouble?"

"I can't watch you 24/7."

"Well, I don't mean you personally . . ."

"And I can't ask anyone from the Bureau to do it."

"Why not?"

"Do you have any idea the kind of trouble I'd get into if someone found out I was using FBI resources on my girlfriend, the TV reporter?"

"I'm not exactly your girlfriend."

"That's the way they would see it."

He was right, of course. I knew that.

"What about the police?" he asked. "Have you gone to them?"

"I can't. From what I know so far, the police might be the people I should be afraid of. Especially the police at the top at 1 Police Plaza. That's probably who's behind all of this. I think it goes up to the top of the NYPD. Likely all the way up to Jaime Ortiz, from when he was the police commissioner."

"What about your ex-husband? The homicide cop?"

"Not an option either."

"Right. Because he found out you suspected for a while that he might have been the one who killed Wendy Kyle."

I sighed.

"That's a tough one to come back from. You can't simply say 'my bad, sorry' after something like that."

We talked some more about it.

"Is there some way you could put a wire on me or something?" I asked. "That way you'd overhear any conversations I had that seemed suspicious or threatening or from someone who sounds like they're about to do something bad to me. Couldn't you do that, Scott?"

"Only if we were close by. We'd have to be stationed with listening equipment outside your office and apartment. I don't know if that's possible. Besides, if someone was going to do something like that to you, they'd probably do it somewhere else—like on the street or subway—the way they did with Kyle and Ayers."

"What about my phone?"

"What about it?"

"Can't you trace me from that?"

"Sure. There's lots of ways to trace you. Phone. Apple Watch. GPS Dot. I mean the GPS Dot is really small and can track anyone anywhere. So small we could hide one in your shoe, your clothes, even your hair. But then what? We'd know where you were, but that's all. We couldn't listen to you on a wiretap once you got out of range. Unless . . ."

Manning thought about it for a minute.

"How about this? We do our best to listen to you on a wiretap set up at both your apartment and your office. I can't promise we can do it full-time, but we'd do our best to monitor you that way.

Then, if you're going anywhere else, you call us or text us to let us know. That way if we see from the locator that you're headed somewhere we don't know about, we'll know something is wrong. And we'll go looking for you there."

"And you can get the FBI to do all that?"

"Well, I'll be doing a lot of it myself."

"You'd do that for me?"

"I don't want anything bad to happen to you, Clare."

"Thank you."

"You should have some kind of codeword," he said. "A signal that will let us know if we're listening to you on the wiretap—at your home or your office—that something unexpected is happening. It should be a word that seems innocent enough to whoever you're with at the time, but will alert us to a potential problem."

"Okay."

"What's that word?"

I thought about it.

"How about 'Kim Kardashian'?" I asked finally.

"Kim Kardashian."

"Right."

"How are you going to work 'Kim Kardashian' into the conversation with someone?"

"I'll think of something," I said.

I smiled at him. He smiled back. That was nice.

"There is a quid pro quo for all this," Manning said.

"Uh, what are we talking about here."

"If I do help you survive this, you have to have a drink with me one night. It's been too long since we had a drink together."

"A drink?"

"Right."
"One drink?"
"Yep."
"Nothing else you're looking for?"
"We'll see how it goes."

CHAPTER 56

To say that the rest of my day back in the newsroom was crazy and busy and pretty much all consuming would be an understatement.

The whole city seemed to be reacting to my broadcast blockbuster from the night before, and all the scenarios and theories and evidence I'd talked about on the newscast.

The biggest reaction came from the things I said about Ronald Bannister and his presumed involvement in so much of this. His blatant womanizing that somehow—despite all the denials—could have been a target for Wendy Kyle's investigation; his name appearing on Kyle's diary page; even his desperate efforts to buy Channel 10 when I started reporting about him; and, of course, culminating in his own death. I couldn't come right out and say I suspected him of paying off cops—all the way up to the top of the NYPD—to cover up the murder of Troy Spencer. That was still speculation. But I threw a lot of suggestions and innuendo in there suggesting something like that by Bannister.

The fact that he was dead made my reporting on him easier. There's an old journalism adage that "you can't libel a dead man." Certainly, his lawyers would have come after me hard and quickly if he were alive. And, as a matter of fact, they still made threats about lawsuits from Bannister's estate and business interests. But it was mostly talk, and our lawyers at Channel 10 thought we were on pretty good ground when it came to speculating what Ronald Bannister might have done or not done.

The NYPD was very upset with me. The head of media relations at 1 Police Plaza called to scream at me. He accused me of maligning the "brave and heroic and honorable police officers of our city" with my insinuations of corruption and malfeasance within the NYPD. I told him I thought most of the city's police officers were brave and heroic and honorable. But I wasn't so sure about some of their bosses at police headquarters. Our conversation really went south after that. But hopefully I'd shaken up a lot of people there.

I also heard from a lot of people who had known or interacted over the years with Wendy Kyle—either as a police officer or a private investigator. Of course, the reaction ran the gamut from good to bad. Same with the overall viewer reaction. Some people loved Kyle, others were critical—even saying she brought her violent death on herself by her controversial actions and behavior.

I had to spend a lot of time dealing with the rest of the media too. Newspapers and other TV stations trying to get me to talk to them about everything I'd found out. That was a tough line to walk sometimes. I wanted the publicity, but also needed to make sure I didn't give away anything that we hadn't already talked about on Channel 10. The bottom line, though, was I was a media star. Again. Like I had been when I broke some other big stories in the past.

The one person I did not hear from—and I wanted some reaction from the most—was Jaime Ortiz.

We'd gone to him for comment, of course. Before putting the piece—with the potential links to Ortiz—on the air. But no one ever got back to us. Not Ortiz or any of his people. I made repeated calls, imploring them to respond and saying how bad it would look for Ortiz if he left what I said about him on the air unanswered. But there was still nothing from his camp.

Steve Healy called me at one point. He seemed happy with it. I'd done what he wanted, putting it all out there for people to hear about. I still wasn't exactly sure how Healy fit into all this. I mean he did work for Ronald Bannister. Still, he seemed to be on my side—and wanted to do the right thing for Wendy Kyle, his old partner—so that was good.

I also had to deal with another broadcast—a follow-up to my story—for tonight. I'd pretty much shot my wad of new information with all I had aired last night. What did I do now?

Maggie and I decided on basically doing a reaction piece. I'd repeat again many of the things I'd already said—then get everything from Bannister and the cops and everyone's comments on air too. Including the fact—which I thought would seem significant—that there had been no reaction at all from Jaime Ortiz.

That was the plan anyway.

But sometimes plans change when you least expect it.

That's what happened that afternoon.

*   *   *

"Ms. Carlson, there's someone down in the lobby that wants to talk to you," the security guard at the front door of the Channel 10 building said to me on the phone.

"Who is it?"

"He won't say."

"Ask him again."

There was a pause, then the security guard came back on the line.

"He says it's about Wendy Kyle."

"Lots of people want to talk about Wendy Kyle. What's his angle?"

Another pause while the guard talked to the visitor.

"He says it's about Wendy Kyle and Jaime Ortiz."

Okay, I had no idea exactly what this was about, but the mention of Ortiz's name made me interested enough to go downstairs to check it out.

When I got to the lobby, I saw a man outside the door standing next to a limo. The guard said he was the one looking for me. I went outside to talk to him.

"You're Clare Carlson, right?" he said.

"Well, I'm not Kim Kardashian."

I figured that ought to get Manning's attention if he was listening in out there.

"Jaime Ortiz wants to meet with you."

I looked into the limo. There was another man in there, sitting in the driver's seat. He was not Jaime Ortiz.

"Where is Ortiz?"

"We'll take you to him."

"How can I be sure you even work with Ortiz?"

He took out his wallet, then showed me credentials—official identification—saying that he was a top aide to Ortiz in his gubernatorial campaign.

I still wasn't completely convinced.

I told him that.

He took out a phone, punched in a number, and then handed it to me.

"This is Jaime Ortiz's," a voice said on the other end that I recognized as Ortiz's voice. It was definitely him. "Please get in the car and come meet with me. I promise you it will be worth your time. I have a lot of things to tell you. I think it's time you—and everyone—knew the truth."

I had to make a decision.

Which wasn't really a decision.

This could be my key to breaking the story wide open, even if I didn't know what Ortiz was going to tell me. That was hard for any reporter to pass up. Especially a reporter like me.

"Let me go upstairs and get my stuff," I said.

I figured I'd call or text Manning from my office and make sure he knew what was going on down here—like we had talked about.

"No, we can't let you do that," the Ortiz aide said, taking the phone back from me. "No one else can know about this. Get in the car, Ms. Carlson. All of your concerns—all of your questions—will be answered by Mr. Ortiz."

I nodded and got in the back seat. I still wasn't sure if Manning or anyone else from the FBI was listening on the wire I was wearing. If they were, I wasn't sure how long that would last. I decided to take advantage of it while I could before the car pulled away and took me out of wiretap listening range.

"Nice car," I said. "Being in a limo like this makes me feel rich and famous. Like I'm Kim Kardashian or somebody."

"Why do you keep talking about Kim Kardashian?" he asked.

"Doesn't everyone talk about Kim Kardashian?"

Then the driver shifted the limo into gear, and we pulled out into the midtown traffic.

CHAPTER 57

I RECOGNIZED THE guy now who'd met me at the door. I'd seen him at press conferences with Jaime Ortiz—including the one where I'd confronted Ortiz the other day—standing alongside him. So I knew him to be the real deal, an Ortiz aide of some kind. He looked like he could have been a bodyguard too. A big guy, short-cropped hair, wearing a suit but you could see plenty of muscles underneath it.

The driver was more nondescript. He was thin, with longish hair and dressed more casually in a sports jacket and slacks. Neither of them gave me their names. Neither of them asked if I was having a nice day. Neither of them said a word to me as we made our way through New York City traffic.

I tried to break the silence with some clever conversation.

"A real spate of hot weather we've been having, huh?" I said.

No response.

"Of course, it's not really the heat—it's the humidity."

Still nothing.

"Me, I can handle the high temperatures, but the humidity is what kills me."

I decided to suspend the weather report at this point—and be more direct.

"Where are we going?" I asked.

"To see Mr. Ortiz."

"And where are we going to do that?"

"You'll see when we get there."

"Which is?"

He didn't answer me.

I figured we'd probably be going to Ortiz's campaign headquarters. I knew about the office where I'd seen Becky Ayers. Also, I'd checked and found out he had a big headquarters in Herald Square. When we went to 34th Street and began heading west, I thought that's where we were headed. But I was wrong. Instead, the driver went all the way to the West Side Highway and started driving north on it.

I was starting to get a bit concerned.

I thought again about the locator device I was carrying. Was Manning or anyone else following via the GPS Dot they hid in my hair? I sure hoped Manning was out there. I mean, I found it hard to believe that Ortiz's people would abduct me off the street in broad daylight. But the farther north we went on the West Side Highway, going through Manhattan and then Riverdale in the Bronx and finally out of the city into Westchester County—well, the more uneasy I was about this whole thing.

"Exactly where is Jaime Ortiz?" I asked.

"Like I said, you'll find out soon enough."

"What if I change my mind and decide I don't want to go with you?"

"Have you changed your mind?"

"I'm not sure."

"Do you want to get out of the car?"

"Right here on the highway?"

"Of course not. We don't want to take you anyway against your will. We'll pull over onto a side road, call you an Uber, and you can be on your way back. If that's what you really want. But you won't get the story. This is a big story, Ms. Carlson. And Mr. Ortiz is prepared to give it you—and you alone—as soon as we get there. Don't you want that story?"

I did want that story.

God, did I want the story!

It was the perfect argument to use with me.

I told them to keep driving.

We kept going through Westchester County, north of the city. We finally pulled off the highway in a small town called Elmsford, right next to the Tappan Zee Bridge crossing the Hudson River between New York and New Jersey some thirty miles north of Manhattan.

I reached up and felt the locator device in my hair where Manning and the FBI technicians had hid it.

It felt reassuring, but only if someone was following it—and following me—on this drive.

Was Manning out there somewhere?

Did I need him?

It was about fifty minutes after we started driving when we finally pulled into the driveway of an ordinary-looking house sitting alone at the bottom of a street, with no other traffic around. We got out of the car and walked to the front door.

Was Jaime Ortiz waiting for me inside? I sure hoped so.

Because if he wasn't, I didn't like any of the alternative scenarios that might be about to play out.

I saw Ortiz as soon as I went in the door.

Yep, it was Jaime Ortiz, all right.

No question about it.

And he was waiting there to talk to me.

Just as advertised.

CHAPTER 58

ORTIZ WAS SITTING on a couch in the living room. He stood up, greeted me with a hello and shook my hand. I sat down in a leather recliner across from him. I'd never seen him up close in person before. We'd only met that one day when I was in the crowd at his press conference.

He was definitely an impressive guy. Early fifties, I knew. Rugged good looks. His hair was still mostly dark brown but with speckles of gray sprinkled throughout that made him look distinguished. He had a nice smile too, which he was flashing at me right now. I could see why he had been such a popular police commissioner, and why he was now so popular with voters as the leading candidate for governor.

"I thought it would be good for you and I to meet in a quiet situation where we don't hurl insults and accusations at each other in a room filled with other media."

"Hopefully, we can still hurl insults and accusations at each other here though."

He smiled. That was a good sign.

"All I'm looking for is the truth," I told him. "I want the real story. I want the whole story."

"I know that. And I think its time you know the truth. That's why I thought this was the best way to show you that you don't have the real story about any of it. Particularly about Wendy Kyle's murder."

"Do you really believe that her ex-husband is the one who blew her up in her car, then killed himself in remorse over what he had done?"

"No, I don't."

"Then why don't you speak up about it?"

"I plan to. But it's a bigger story than that. A much bigger story. You know some of it, but not all. I'm going to give you the whole goddamned story. Then I'll hold a press conference for everyone. But you'll have the exclusive on this, Carlson."

"Why me? Why do you like me so much?"

"I don't like you. I don't even know you. But you already have figured out part of it. That makes it easier to work with someone like you. Anyway, that's how I want to break the news that I have. You may think you already know what happened. But believe me, you're going to be surprised. There is more. A lot more."

He took out a picture of Troy Spencer now and laid it down on a coffee table in front of us.

"You know who this is, don't you?"

"Troy Spencer. Died in her Murray Hill apartment several years ago. Ruled a suicide, but Wendy Kyle insisted it was a murder and that someone in the NYPD—someone high up in the NYPD—was covering up the crime."

"You are a good reporter." Ortiz smiled.

"Well, to be honest, I figured the person high up in the NYPD who was paid to orchestrate the cover-up was you. And that the person doing this—the one who killed the Spencer woman—might have been Ronald Bannister."

"Right idea, but wrong person. Not with Bannister. He killed the girl. Apparently, they were having some kind of rough sex that got out of control. Then he pulled in a lot of favors and paid a lot of money to set it up to look like a suicide."

"But you're saying the money didn't go to you?"

"No, I never knew about any of this until recently."

"Then who took the payoffs?"

"Warren Magnuson."

"The Chief of Department."

"That's right."

"And the same man that got Kyle fired for attacking him."

Ortiz nodded.

"He's had quite the career boost since all this," I said.

"Bannister's money and influence in political circles helped him skyrocket to near the top of the NYPD brass. Now, as you probably already know, he's expected to be the next police commissioner when Norm Garrity retires soon. That's what we've been trying to prevent. We wanted to make sure that doesn't happen."

"Who's 'we'?"

"Me and Wendy Kyle."

Now I really was confused.

"I read the official police report on the Troy Spencer death," I said. "All the way to the very end. All the way to your signature. You were the one who signed the official ruling that Troy Spencer died of a suicide."

"I signed all those documents as commissioner," Ortiz said. "Most of them I had no personal knowledge about. I took the information from the investigating officers or the people who were working under me. That's what happened with Troy Spencer. They told me it was a suicide, and I accepted that finding."

"Who told you it was a suicide?"

"Warren Magnuson."

It was a helluva story, if it was true. Former police commissioner and gubernatorial candidate working with someone like Wendy Kyle before she was murdered to topple a top and powerful police official like Magnuson—and more people around him—as well as taking on Ronald Bannister, who had been one of the richest men in the world.

But Ortiz wasn't finished with telling the story yet.

"I'm the person Wendy was referring to in that diary entry police found in her office," Ortiz said. "The man she said she was going to trust. Even though she was already scared about dying in all this. That was me."

Hmm. Steve Healy had told me he was the man she was referring to in that diary entry. He made more sense than Ortiz. How the hell did Wendy Kyle even know someone like Jaime Ortiz?

I told him about Steve Healy's claim that Healy was the man Kyle was talking about in the diary entry.

"No, it was me."

"Why should I believe you?"

"Because it's the truth?"

"Do you have any hard proof? Proof to convince me that you were for some unknown reason working with Wendy Kyle. And proof to convince me that you weren't really the person who killed her?"

"I have the ultimate proof I didn't kill her," he said.

He stood up from the couch, walked through a door to another room in the house. When he came back, he had someone with him.

A very attractive woman.

Long brunette hair, good-looking figure.

I'd never met her before.
But I'd seen plenty of photos of her.
I recognized her right away.
And she was very much alive.
It was Wendy Kyle.

CHAPTER 59

"I DON'T UNDERSTAND," I said.

It was pretty much the only thing I could think of to say.

"As you can see, I'm not dead," Wendy Kyle said now. "There are a lot of people who wish I was—I know that. But I am still very much alive."

I tried to make some sort of sense out of all this. Wendy Kyle—whose death in a car explosion I'd been covering for days—was sitting here in front of me at the moment. And Jaime Ortiz—the man I thought likely to be the most responsible for killing her—was right here with her.

"If it wasn't you, who died in the car explosion?" I asked Kyle.

I had a million other questions I wanted to ask, but that somehow had to be the first one—the priority—to get out of the way.

"A woman named Rebecca Kirkland."

"Reby?"

"You knew Reby?"

"She's a homeless woman that you befriended at a shelter in your Upper East Side neighborhood. They told me about her there when I went looking for more information about you for my stories. I spent a lot of time in the area looking for her. But she had disappeared after the explosion. Now I know why. What happened?"

"It was tragic," Kyle said. "Even though it saved my life. But I still feel guilty about it. I used to give Reby a place to sleep sometimes—maybe a hotel room, sometimes in my apartment where I had an extra room, and once in a while she even slept in my car. So she knew my car. All I can imagine is that she tried to get inside that morning to get off the street for some sleep like she had in the past. Then, when she opened the door—instead of me—it set off the blast which killed her. I heard the explosion, ran to my car, and saw what had happened. That's when I decided it would be best if people thought I was dead. They wouldn't be looking for me. That gave me a better chance to do what I needed to do."

"Which is?"

"Bring down that bastard Warren Magnuson."

Ortiz jumped in now.

"After the car bomb, Wendy reached out to me for help in pulling off the story that she died in that explosion. We knew someone had tried to kill Wendy. And, as far as we knew, they thought they had succeeded. We decided that she should stay dead for a while."

"How did you make everyone believe it was Wendy Kyle that died in that car blast?" I asked.

"It wasn't hard. Everyone quickly assumed it was her. Then, as a longtime police officer and a former commissioner, I was able to figure out ways to make sure no one questioned that the body in that car was Wendy Kyle. She was officially dead, as far as the NYPD and everyone else was concerned."

It still didn't make sense to me.

"Why call you? Did you and her know each other well? During your time on the force? What's the relationship? I'm having a lot of trouble trying to sort all this out."

"Let's just say we both found out at some point that we shared the same goal."

"Which was to stop Warren Magnuson," Kyle said. "And that's what we plan to do. I've been accumulating information in the past few weeks about him—the corruption, the payoffs, the cover-ups—and turning it over to Ortiz. We're ready to act now. Ready to make big news with this."

"And you want to use me—and Channel 10—to do this?"

"It's a win-win situation for everyone." Ortiz smiled.

I believed him. It was hard not to with Wendy Kyle sitting there right next to him, backing him up and supporting him. But I still had a lot of questions about how all this had transpired.

I looked down at the picture of Troy Spencer that was still on the table in front of us.

"Is that why you attacked Magnuson that day?" I asked Kyle. "Because you found out what he had done to cover up the Spencer woman's murder?"

"I didn't know for sure it was him then. But I suspected it, even though I couldn't prove anything. And when I asked him that day about Troy Spencer—whether he had been involved—he laughed and called her a 'slutty whore' no one cared about. I guess I lost it at that point and went after him."

"But that was years ago, Wendy. Why is all this happening now?"

"Because I slept with Ronald Bannister," she said.

"When?"

"Not long before he died."

"As part of your Heartbreaker Investigations?"

"Yes."

"But his wife claims she never hired you."

"She didn't."

"Then who . . . ?"

"He had another woman he was seeing regularly. He told her he was going to leave his wife for her. She believed him, at least for a while. But then she began to suspect he was seeing other women—and probably telling them the same thing—too. That woman was the one who hired me. It was an opportunity to find out more about Bannister and what he had done to Troy Spencer. So I took the job.

"I did the Honey Trap on him. In this case, though, I actually slept with Bannister. Several times. I established a sexual relationship with him. I'm not proud of that. I'd never gone to bed before with any other man I was investigating. But I was willing to do whatever it took to get the evidence I needed against him. Even if I had to use sex to do it. Men—even men like Ronald Bannister—will reveal their secrets, their deepest innermost secrets, if you push the right buttons in the bedroom. That's what I did with Bannister.

"And, at some point, I got him to start talking about Troy Spencer. He had no idea who I was, of course. Only some woman he had picked up in a bar one night and was having a few flings in bed with. But I got him drunk that last time, and I kept telling him how turned on I was by all his wealth and power. Between the booze and the sex, I was able to convince him to talk about some of the things he'd gotten away with simply because he was Ronald Bannister. He liked that. It turned him on even more. Finally, I asked him about Troy Spencer.

"Bannister told me then what really happened. He said he and Troy Spencer were having rough sex, and it got out of control. She wanted him to stop, but he didn't. And then she was dead and he was desperate not to be involved. He told me about how he used his money and his influence to get it all covered up by the NYPD.

He even bragged about doing it. Getting away with murder was easy when you had money, he said. I think he thought I would be impressed by it all. Best of all, he specifically named Warren Magnuson as the police official he paid off—and was still paying off—to cover up all this.

"I wasn't sure what to do with this information or who to tell. I sure couldn't go to the NYPD. But then I learned more about Ortiz and decided he was a good man. I reached out to him and told him all this. We decided to go after Bannister. And, even more so, to bring down Magnuson. Which is what we were doing when the bomb went off, trying to kill me."

"Is there a diary?" I asked. "More than just that single page found in your office by police?"

"Oh, yes. I kept a diary for years. When I was on the force and then later as a private investigator handling all those salacious divorce cases. I wrote down a lot of stuff in that diary."

"Why?"

"In the beginning, it was to protect myself. I wanted a record of my actions in case of any trouble I got into. But then I realized it could be much more than that. I was going to write a book from the material in it. I still plan to do that."

"A tell-all book?"

"That's right."

"Naming names? Police corruption? Your clients and their philandering husbands and boyfriends?"

"All of it."

"That would upset a lot of people."

"It sure upset Warren Magnuson when he heard what I was doing."

"How did he find out about it?"

She shrugged and said she had done a stupid thing. She had confronted Magnuson at one point, and she told him she was going to bring him down. To stop him from becoming police commissioner by revealing all the corruption he'd been involved in over the years. And that Ortiz, the former police commissioner and likely future governor, was going to help do just that. She even talked about how she had a diary that she was going to make public to expose him.

"I sometimes can't keep my mouth shut." She sighed.

"Yeah, I have the same problem," I said.

"It made us targets for him. Me to be knocked off to keep me quiet and Ortiz to be smeared as the bad guy in all this. But now we want people to know the real story. That's why we've come to you. If you go on the air and tell everyone all this, Magnuson is finished. He can't keep telling his lies. It's a great story, Ms. Carlson. And we're giving this great story to you."

Well, that was the good part. It was a great story. And it was my story. All I had to do was put everyone on the air and tell it. It seemed too good—too easy—to be falling into place like this. And, of course, it was. As I was about to find out.

*   *   *

I was still basking in the glow from all this when I heard a gunshot. Followed quickly by a second shot.

A man burst into the living room. Holding a gun. At first, I thought it was one of the men from the car that had brought me. But then I saw his body lying by the front door. Along with a second body. The driver.

No, this was someone else.

Someone that I knew.

It was Steve Healy.

"Who are you?" Wendy Kyle blurted out.

"That's Steve Healy," I said.

"Who's that?"

"Your ex-partner, Wendy."

Kyle stared at Healy, holding the gun pointed at her and at Ortiz and at me.

"I've never seen him before in my life."

"I was afraid you were going to say that," I said

CHAPTER 60

"WELL, WELL, WELL," Healy said when he saw Wendy Kyle in the living room. He seemed as surprised to see her as I had been. "I figured it would pay off if I followed Carlson and saw where she went after that on-air report. But I wasn't expecting this. I'm glad it worked out this way though. This could have been a nasty surprise if you turned up alive later. But that ain't gonna happen now."

"Who are you?" Ortiz said.

"He worked for Ronald Bannister," I said.

"Actually, I lied to you about that. Just like I lied to you about being her ex-partner."

"You weren't working for Bannister?"

"No, I was working—and am still working—for the man Bannister paid the money to. Bannister's dead. But this man is still paying me. It works out better for me that way. Wouldn't you agree?"

"Who are we talking about?"

"Haven't you figured it out yet?"

"I think so, but tell me."

"Warren Magnuson. The next police commissioner. And that will mean even bigger payoffs for us."

A second person came in from outside. This was a woman. I recognized her. The woman from Wendy Kyle's apartment who called herself Alex Sinclair. She was holding a gun too. I wondered who had shot the two men by the door I'd come here with. Probably both of them.

"Remember me?" she said to me.

"Well, you're not Alex Sinclair."

"No, and I wasn't Wendy's girlfriend either. In fact, I never met her until now. I've got a couple of phony identities I use in situations when I need them. I got Alex Sinclair's name from a court case I was involved in. I wrote it down for future use. Like I used it on you when I stumbled on you in the apartment."

"Okay, but why tell me you and Wendy Kyle were in love?"

"I wanted to shock you. Throw you off your game. So you didn't ask me too many specific questions about who I really was and what I was really doing there that day. It worked too. That and the business about Sam Markham questioning me for the police."

"You never talked to him?"

"No. But I'd checked up on you before. I knew he was your ex-husband. And I knew he was not supposed to be working the case. I figured that would keep you thinking about something else than me."

"How did you know all this?"

"Let's just say we, both of us," she said, looking over at Healy, "have connections with important people in the NYPD."

"Magnuson?"

"It helps to know people at the top."

"Did you work in Internal Affairs with him and Healy too?"

"Actually, she worked for the bomb squad when she was on the force," Healy said now.

"She was the one who . . ."

"Right. Blew up Kyle's car. Of course, it wasn't her fault that Kyle apparently wasn't in it. Of course, we'll make sure she's gone for good now."

I thought Wendy Kyle was going to lose it at that point. I could see the anger and the anguish in her face. Magnuson ruined her life and her career. And now he was doing it again. He was getting away with it. I wondered if she was going to try something against Healy. Maybe if she did, it would be enough of a diversion for Ortiz or me to get the gun away from him.

But she just kept glaring at him, without moving—and I realized nothing like that was going to happen.

"I remember you now," she said to Healy. "You were on the Internal Affairs unit that investigated me. They sent you to interview me—about my allegation of corruption and then about the fight with Magnuson. You never listened to a word I said. You were too busy staring at my ass. I knew you were a jerk then."

"Now, now, no reason to get nasty."

"Why not? You're going to kill us, right?" Ortiz said.

"It's only business. Nothing personal."

"Like Warren Magnuson's business?"

"Hey, Magnuson has a big future ahead of him."

"Being police commissioner."

"That's right. And getting rich from people like Ronald Bannister who'll do anything to cover up a crime they committed. Everyone makes mistakes. But the people like Bannister have enough money to buy their way out of it. And men like Magnuson and me are happy to help them do it. But then Kyle here threatened to mess everything up. She was trying to expose Magnuson and everything he was doing with the payoffs from Bannister and all the rest. And—when I found out Ortiz was helping her—now we have to take both of them out of the picture. We can't let Ortiz here be elected governor, since he knows about Magnuson. He has to die the same as Kyle. There's too much money at stake here."

"How in the hell did you ever hook up with Magnuson?" I asked.

I wasn't sure why I cared, but I figured I should keep Healy talking for as long as I could, in case Manning—or someone else—might be on the way.

"Magnuson spent a lot of time getting to know the people in Internal Affairs, and getting them on his side. It's a good place to go after the people you don't like and mess up their careers. You can wield a lot of power in Internal Affairs. Magnuson understood that, and he has used it to get the things he wants done. Like getting someone demoted or even dismissed from the force. The way he did with this bitch Kyle."

If he was trying to get a reaction from her by calling her a "bitch," it didn't work.

She simply stared at him coldly.

Calm, in control, even in a terrible situation like this.

I realized she probably had been a damn good police officer until Magnuson got her booted from the force.

"What happens now?" she asked.

"I'm afraid you're all going to have to disappear."

"You're going to shoot us all like you did those men when you came in?" Ortiz asked.

"No, that would be too hard to pull off. A mass shooting that involved the leading candidate for governor? They'd have everyone out looking for the shooter who did something like that."

"Then what are you going to do?" Kyle asked. "Blow us up with a bomb like you tried to do to me in my car?"

"Close, but not quite right. Two bombings? Too suspicious—it could lead back to Magnuson. No, this is going to be a fire. A fire that will destroy this house and everyone in it. Namely you, Ortiz and Carlson. Then an official investigation—headed up of course by Warren Magnuson—will determine it was an accidental fire. Started by a faulty gas valve in the house. Terrible tragedy. But everyone in the house will be gone. This place will be burned to the ground. Not sure they'll be able to identify you when its over, Kyle, or if you'll just go down as an unidentified female victim. I mean they already think you're dead anyway."

He turned to the woman I'd known as Alex Sinclair now, and she began walking toward the basement to the house. I could see she was carrying a satchel with her. Presumably materials to start the fire down there that would destroy the house. And us in it. She disappeared down the steps.

"That's what she's doing down there," Healy said. "Setting it all up to start the fire. And then I'll set it off from outside."

I remembered Maggie telling me how whoever set the bomb in Kyle's car hadn't seemed particularly adept or expert at it.

All I could hope for at this point was that this woman might screw up something down there.

"What about the two bodies with bullets in them over there?" I asked. "It's going to be clear they didn't die in an accidental fire."

"I'll make those bodies disappear. No one will ever find them."

He took a device out of his pocket now. I assumed it was some kind of igniting mechanism that would start the fire.

"Did you happen to see Kim Kardashian outside when you came in before?" I blurted out.

"What?"

"Kim Kardashian? Is she outside?"

"What in the hell are you talking about?"

"I sure hope Kim Kardashian is out there somewhere."

Suddenly, I heard sirens.

Then the sound of footsteps rushing up the front steps.

And Scott Manning—along with a half dozen men wearing FBI jackets—burst into the house with guns drawn.

CHAPTER 61

EVERYTHING WAS PRETTY much a blur after that.

Even now, after talking about it endlessly on the air and in interviews and trying to replay it all in my mind as I lay awake at night hoping to fall asleep without the nightmares, I never totally am sure of exactly what happened.

There are Manning and his people pointing their guns at Steve Healy. Healy whirling around to face them with a shocked look on his face. I'm not sure what Kyle and Ortiz were doing at that moment. But Healy was a pro. He quickly recovered enough to do the only thing he could think of that might give him a way out of this.

He took a hostage.

Me.

He grabbed me—the one standing closest to him—with an arm around my neck, pulling me as close to him as possible with the gun pressed against the side of my head. He still had the detonating device in his hand that held me.

"Anyone moves a finger on those triggers, and she's the first to die," Healy said. "Is that the way you want this to end? I don't think so."

He didn't know about my relationship with Manning, of course.

He assumed no FBI agent would want to be responsible for the death of a famous TV reporter.

That was enough.

But, for Manning, it was different. It wasn't just any hostage Healy was threatening with death unless he got what he wanted. That hostage was *me*.

"Put down your guns," Healy said.

No one put down their guns.

Everyone still had their guns pointed at him. And he had his gun pointed at my head. A Mexican standoff, I guess is what they call it. I'd heard about it, but never was in the middle of one before.

At some point during this, the woman came out of the basement and saw what was happening. She had her gun pointed too. They were outgunned—but it was still a standoff. With me in the middle. Healy realized the situation and desperately tried to negotiate a way out for them.

"Let us walk out of here," Healy said.

"What about Carlson?" Manning asked.

"She comes with me."

"No way."

"I'll let her go once I get away from here."

"How do I know I can believe you?"

"You have no other choice."

"You're the one out of choices," Manning said.

"Actually, I do have one choice left. But it's a big one. I have something with me that can level this whole place, along with you and her and everyone in it."

"What are you talking about?"

Healy looked down at the device he was holding.

"He's got a detonator," I yelled out. "He was going to use it on us before you showed up. He said it will ignite a massive fire here.

I can't be sure if he's telling the truth or not. But I think I believe him."

"If that is true, you'll kill yourself too," Manning said to Healy.

"Maybe. Or maybe some of us will survive. Could be me. I'm willing to take that chance. I'd rather go up in flames than go to prison. I don't really have much of a choice here. But you do. You've got a lot more to lose than me if I press the button on this ignition device. Not just your own life. But also, the lives of Carlson, Kyle, Ortiz, and your men. Are you ready to take that chance, Mr. FBI agent?"

"And, if that happens, Magnuson would walk free too."

"You know about him?"

"We listened to your conversation. Carlson was wired for sound. I guess you didn't know that, huh?"

"If you die here, no one else ever finds that out. If you let me walk out, you can bring down Magnuson later—even if you don't get me. You really want Magnuson more than me, don't you? Well, that's the trade-off for you here. What's it gonna be?"

I wondered if there were rules in the FBI guidebooks on what to do in situations like this. I assumed Manning had read whatever rules there were and knew what he was supposed to do here. But I couldn't be sure about his decision. Not then, not even now. Even after it was all over, I never directly asked Scott Manning what he was thinking at that moment. Maybe I didn't want to know. I like to think he'd have done whatever it took to save my life. That sure worked out better for me than any of the other alternatives.

Instead, though, it happened like this.

I realized at some point that Healy had the detonation device in the same hand he was using to hold onto me. I looked down and saw it. I wasn't sure what might detonate it. But I had to take a chance, I decided. I bit down hard on his hand that was holding me. He screamed and the detonator dropped to the ground. Nothing happened. He still had the gun pointed to my head and held on to me, but he was confused and in pain.

That gave Wendy Kyle the opportunity she was looking for.

She suddenly lunged across the room at him, knocked the gun out of his hand, shoved him down, and began pummeling him in a fury of blows and screaming at the suddenly defenseless Healy.

At this point, Ortiz raced toward the woman and began wrestling with her for the gun, eventually getting it away from her after a struggle.

Meanwhile, Kyle kept hitting Healy with her fists, kicking him, using some kind of martial arts moves that looked lethal—and basically beating the crap out of Healy until he was a bloody mess trying desperately, but unsuccessfully, to crawl away from her vicious assault.

Maybe she was thinking about Warren Magnuson while she did it, and was taking out her anger on Magnuson as well as Healy.

Or maybe she was thinking about Troy Spencer, and trying to avenge her murder by Ronald Bannister and the whole police cover-up.

Or maybe she was thinking about all the terrible things she had seen other men do over the years—and she wanted Steve Healy to pay the price for that.

Manning could have stopped her—should have stopped her, I suppose.

But he didn't.

Not for a long time.

I'm happy about that.

"You sure cut it close," I said to Manning afterward.

"A simple 'thank you' for saving your life would suffice."

"Thank you."

"You're welcome."

"How much did you hear?"

"All of it."

"Why didn't you come in sooner?"

"We weren't sure what was happening. Well, until . . ."

"Until what?"

"Until that last Kim Kardashian reference you made." He smiled. "That one convinced me."

"God bless that Kim Kardashian," I said.

CHAPTER 62

THERE WAS ONE big question that was still unanswered on the story.

Who killed Ronald Bannister?

Oh, the operative theory with the authorities was still that it must have been Magnuson and Healy because they were worried that Bannister might crack under all the media pressure and finger them for taking all that money from him to cover up the Troy Spencer murder.

Which sort of made sense on one hand. But then it didn't. Not really. Why would they get rid of their golden goose—the source of all their illicit income? For two guys like Magnuson and Healy, who were all about the money, it didn't make sense to me.

Also, both Healy and Magnuson continued to insist they had nothing to do with Bannister's death. Of course, they could be lying. But Healy had decided his best option was to try to make a deal with authorities, and he was talking freely to them about a lot of things.

He admitted he and Magnuson were responsible for the bombing of Kyle's car, setting up her ex-husband to make it look like he did it in a murder suicide, and killing Becky Ayers in the subway station because she knew too much and they were afraid she might go to the authorities. Magnuson wasn't saying anything about those crimes on advice of his high-priced lawyers. But he, like Magnuson, profusely denied knowing anything about Bannister's murder.

For some reason, I believed them. Their denials seemed real. It didn't make sense to me that they murdered Bannister too.

Okay, if Magnuson and Healy didn't kill Bannister, then who did?

And why?

Well, not unlike with Wendy Kyle, there was a long list of people who were probably mad enough at Bannister to want to see him dead.

Starting with all the people he did business with. You don't become a mega-billionaire like Bannister without screwing a lot of people along the way. And, from what I knew, Bannister had a reputation for unscrupulous business deals. There were many people on Wall Street and financial markets around the world who didn't like him and might have even resorted to murder. That was an option to consider.

Then there was his controversial personal life too. I saw him in action that night at the bar, and he played the role of the ladies' man all the time. Any angry husband or boyfriend or maybe a jealous woman he spurned could have done it. Wendy Kyle had talked about the one angry woman who had hired her to investigate him and find out if he was cheating on her. He was even sleeping with Wendy Kyle herself. What did this woman do then? Did she go out and buy a gun to shoot him? I tracked down the woman at one point and asked her about it. But she denied having anything to do with Bannister's murder, and I had no way of proving anything different.

There was something else bothering me too. No one saw a potential suspect carrying a gun to Bannister's office that night.

There was nothing on the security cameras either. Which suggested it was someone Bannister knew well. Someone familiar with getting in and out of his office late at night without drawing any attention.

But who knew him that well and had a reason to be angry enough to kill him?

Well, his wife, of course.

He humiliated her over and over again by cheating on their marriage and having very public affairs with lots of women.

That was a pretty good reason for her to be furious with him.

Except she didn't care about him cheating on her with other women.

How did I know she didn't care?

Because she told me so.

I remembered seeing her being interviewed on camera after he died, and the emotions she showed. The anguish and the crying over losing her husband of twenty-nine years. I thought at the time it was a pretty good acting job from her that day. But maybe she wasn't acting after all.

I decided it was time to pay another visit to Eleanor Bannister.

*   *   *

The doorman at the Brantley House didn't seem any happier to see me than he was the last time I was there. But he remembered that Eleanor Bannister did want to see me then. So he called up to her phone to say I wanted to talk to her again. He came back and reported to me there had been no answer.

"Any idea where she might be?" I asked.

"That's none of my business."

"Have you seen her recently?"

"No, not for a couple of days."

"Is that unusual?"

"Yes, but maybe she went on a trip somewhere. I mean, her husband just died."

"Or she could simply be not answering the phone. Or taking a nap or something. Could I go up and knock on her door?"

"No, you cannot."

There didn't seem to be any point in continuing this discussion. I glanced at the building listing in the lobby and noticed that the place had a garage. Sure, they did. These people needed some place to park their Mercedes and their Rolls. There also was a phone number listed to call the lobby. I memorized that, said goodbye to the doorman, and left.

When I got out of sight, I took out my phone, changed the setting so it didn't display my name to anyone I called, and dialed the number. The doorman answered.

"Hey, I'm down in the garage," I yelled, trying to disguise my voice. "There's some woman down here—says she's from a TV station—and she's harassing me. Trying to get me to talk about Eleanor Bannister. She shouldn't be here. You need to get her out of our building."

"Who is this?" he asked. "What apartment do you live in?"

"You better get down here fast!" I screamed into the phone, then hung up.

It worked. When I went back to the front door, there was no one there. I rushed to the elevator and rode up to Mrs. Bannister's apartment on the penthouse floor.

I wasn't exactly sure what I hoped to accomplish. But I'd had a feeling—actually more of a concern—about Mrs. Bannister before coming here. Now that concern was even stronger. I didn't like the fact that no one had seen her for a few days. I rang the bell and knocked on the door loudly several times. No answer. Sometimes the simple solution works. I turned the knob on the door. It was open. I went inside.

The apartment looked the way it did the last time I had been there. The big living room and dining area. Hallways leading off to various bedrooms and other rooms throughout the place. Everything was exquisitely furnished and clean and neatly in its place. But yet . . . something seemed different.

I made my way through the apartment and eventually into the master bedroom. That's where I found her. She was lying on the bed in a nightgown, almost as if she had simply gone to sleep. On a table next to her was an empty bottle of vodka and an empty bottle of sleeping pills. Enough to kill her.

There was an envelope on the table too. It said: *To Whom It May Concern.* I opened it and read what was inside:

Yes, I killed Ronald. I was the one who murdered my own husband. I wasn't sure I could get away with it. I was afraid of being arrested and going to trial and then being sent to jail for the rest of my life. But now I really think there's a worse punishment for me to endure. Looking at myself in the mirror and facing my own self-judgment for the terrible thing I have done.

Why did I kill Ronald?

Out of love, as crazy as that sounds.

Oh, I know I always pretended that I didn't care he was spending his time with other women instead of me. And, for a long time, I convinced everyone—even myself, I guess— that was true. But no woman can suffer that kind of humiliation and rejection in her marriage forever. And, when I saw those pictures of Ronald and everyone found out about what he was doing with the girl at that hotel, it was too much for me to bear.

I didn't go to his office that night planning to kill him. At least, I don't think I did. But I did bring the gun with me. And when I told him how much he had hurt me and how much I wanted his love, he laughed. He laughed at me. Suddenly, I was filled with such an uncontrollable rage—a violent rage like I'd never felt before. It only lasted for a few seconds, but it was enough for me to pull the trigger.

I loved Ronald.

I really did.

Despite all those other women, I was the one who loved him the most.

And—even though he'll never know it—I forgive him for everything he did to me.

I only hope that now—wherever I am going next—God can forgive me.

I reread the letter several times. Then I took notes on it. I was going to have to do a story on this. My last big story about Ronald Bannister and Wendy Kyle and all the rest.

Finally, I took another look at Eleanor Bannister lying so peacefully on the bed—a woman who desperately wanted love from her husband, but never got it from him—and then called the police.

I punched in the number for Sam Markham, my ex-husband.

It was going to be another high-profile case, and I wanted Sam to be able to be a part of it.

I figured I owed him that much.

CHAPTER 63

"Happy birthday, Mom! Happy Fiftieth!"

"Fifty years old," I muttered.

"Hopefully, the next fifty years will be just as good."

"Wait a minute—there's more?"

I had flown down to Virginia to celebrate my milestone birthday with my daughter, Lucy. Yes, I know her name is Linda now. But she'll always be Lucy to me.

We were having a birthday lunch at a restaurant in Winchester, VA, not far from where she lived. There were other people I could have been with on my birthday. Janet. Maggie and the people in my office. Maybe even Scott Manning. But I wanted to be here with my daughter to share the moment. Besides, she needed my support too.

Emily was with her father, Greg. We were going to pick her up after our lunch. I looked forward to that. Emily had recently gotten a new Zelda video game for her Nintendo Switch. I used to be pretty good playing Zelda on the old Nintendo when I was younger. I promised her I'd play along with her on this one too. Maybe some of my old Zelda tricks would still work.

"I miss her when she's with Greg," my daughter said. "But he's been very cooperative, very good about everything. Sharing time with Emily. And including the divorce. I think it will go pretty smoothly. Although no divorce happens without a lot of problems along the way. You must know that better than anyone."

"Because I'm a three-time loser?"

"You'll find someone for you."

"When?"

"Give it time."

"Time? I am fifty years old."

She laughed.

"You'll find the right man one day."

"I'd settle right now for Mr. Sort-of-All-Right."

She wanted to know all about the details of the Wendy Kyle story. I went through it all. Including the stuff that had happened since the arrests of Healy and Magnuson.

"Do you want to hear something wild?" I said at one point. "Wendy Kyle has closed down her Heartbreaker Investigations business. She said she didn't want to do that kind of work anymore. And she said she's not sure she wants to write a tell-all book anymore. Instead, she's going to reapply to get back on the police force. Wouldn't that be something. I hope she makes it. I think she'd be a terrific cop again."

"You like her, don't you?"

"I do. I like to think we could be friends. Maybe we could be. We've talked about having dinner when I get back. Stranger things have happened. I think Wendy and I are a lot alike in some ways."

"Except you never kicked your boss in the balls."

"I might have except my boss these days is a woman."

She asked me what was happening at Channel 10 News. I said Susan Endicott was still there as executive producer, and she and I continued to have an uneasy relationship. As for the sale of the station, it was in limbo now. Kellogg and Klein had pulled out after the delay by Kaiser and the much bigger bid from Bannister before he died. Theoretically, the station was still up for sale. But I had a feeling Kaiser might decide to hold onto it. Especially after this story. He likes to be a part of a big story, just like me.

"What about you and Scott Manning?" she finally asked.

"What about us?"

"Why aren't you together?"

"Why would we be together?"

"He saved your life."

"That's his job."

"He also has the hots for you."

"True."

"And you have the hots for him."

"Also true."

"Then why are you not together?"

"Because he's married."

After everything that happened, Scott and I wound up back at my place that night. Just the two of us. He kissed me. I kissed him back. We repeated this several times. The next step was to move into the bedroom. But we never did.

"I asked him to leave," I said.

"Why?"

"I've been thinking a lot about marriages. Marriages that have gone bad. Wendy Kyle's marriages. All the women in marriages where she was investigating their husbands for cheating. Ronald Bannister's marriage. And your marriage, too. I thought you had the perfect marriage with Greg, but then another woman came along and . . . well, your marriage was destroyed. I don't know that *other woman*. But I hate her for doing what she did to you and Greg. I know it wasn't all her fault; it was Greg's, too. But if she hadn't been there, maybe you'd still be together. If there were no *other women* like that, maybe a lot of marriages would be saved."

"And that's why you told Scott Manning to leave before you had sex?"

I nodded.

"I don't want to be that *other woman*. I don't want to be the one to break up his marriage and leave his wife alone and his children without a father in the house. Maybe one day he will leave her on his own, and Scott and I will get together. But not right now."

"That might be the most mature thing I've ever heard you say."

"Words of wisdom from my own daughter. Hey, as long as I have a big story to chase, I'll be all right."

"A big story always makes everything better. That's what you say all the time, isn't it? Well, maybe that's just like men. Like chasing after Scott Manning. Maybe it's time to think about some other priorities in your life."

I suddenly didn't like the way this conversation was going, so I changed the subject. We talked for a while more about other stuff over coffee and dessert. Until my phone rang. I looked down and saw it was from Maggie in New York.

"There's a big murder breaking," she said. "A fashion heiress shot and killed her fiancé when she caught him in bed with another woman. This is a biggie. If you get on a plane right now, you can be back here in time to go on air with it for the evening newscast."

I started to say yes. I almost said yes. I normally would have said yes. But instead, I looked over at my daughter. She was there waiting, no doubt wondering if I was about to run off on another story again. I was fifty years old, and I'd spent most of those years chasing stories like this. I'd only spent a handful of years being with and getting to know my daughter. I thought about how my daughter needed me more than ever right now. I thought about my granddaughter, Emily, and her new Nintendo Switch game waiting for me.

"Give the story to Cassie or Janelle," I said to Maggie. "I can't come back now. I'm busy here."

"Busy doing what?"

"I'm going to play Zelda with my granddaughter."

There'd be other stories. There'd be other men too. One of them might even be Scott Manning. But maybe my daughter was right. Maybe it was time for me to look at other priorities in my life.

What the hell, my fiftieth birthday sure seemed like a good time to give it a try.

AUTHOR'S NOTE

Broadcast Blues is the sixth book in the Clare Carlson series, and I've gotten to know Clare pretty well. Hopefully, you readers have too.

But—even though she is still the same person—a lot of things are changing for Clare in her life now.

For one thing, she has a new boss these days. Susan Endicott. Or, as I like to describe her, The Boss From Hell. I created ambitious and scheming executive producer Susan Endicott by combining the worst qualities of all the bad bosses I've had in my own media career over the years—I've had plenty of good ones too!—into one character. Which makes her a lot of fun to write.

Other changes Clare has to deal with in *Broadcast Blues* are a potential sale of the TV station to a bottom-line new owner. Clare is approaching her fiftieth birthday, which leaves her worried about the impact her age will have on both her TV news career and her personal life; the dissolution of what she thought was the perfect marriage of her daughter; and, of course, the three-times-divorced Clare's continual romantic search for the right man.

The one thing that remains consistent in this book for Clare, though is the chaos that goes on around her in the Channel 10 newsroom. All the newsroom stuff I write about in *Broadcast*

Blues—the traffic reporter who wants the station to buy him a helicopter; the personal and professional battles between the married man and woman co-anchors; the sports reporter who wants to talk more about her political views on air than give baseball or football news. These are all based on my own real-life experiences in colorful New York City newsrooms as a journalist for the *New York Post*, the *New York Daily News*, *Star* magazine, and NBC News. These newsroom scenes are the most fun for me to write about in the Clare Carlson books.

The bottom line here is that—after six books—Clare is still pretty much the same as she was at the beginning.

Terrific reporter.

Great newsroom leader.

And a woman with a big mouth whose personal life too often turns into a train wreck.

Yes, that is our Clare Carlson.

No matter how much change goes on around her.

I wouldn't have it any other way.

BOOK DISCUSSION QUESTIONS

1. Clare Carlson is willing to push the envelope, break the rules, and do whatever it takes to break a big story. How far do you think a journalist should go to get the truth?

2. When Clare first broke the Wendy Kyle case, had you any inkling of the ultimate outcome of the case? When did you first suspect that all was not as it seemed?

3. Clare works for what she thinks is the worst boss in the world. Have you encountered a boss as unpleasant as Susan Endicott?

4. Clare is stressed out over turning fifty and worried about what that might mean for her career as a woman TV journalist. Do you agree with her that ageism and sexism threaten a woman's career in the media?

5. Did you find Wendy Kyle a reprehensible character? A sympathetic one? Or somewhere in between? Any reservations about Wendy's investigative techniques when spying on cheating husbands?

6.   Ronald Bannister's wife says she's willing to look the other way when it comes to her rich husband cheating with other women because of the wealthy lifestyle she's able to lead with his money. Did you find it believable that a wife would be that forgiving?

7.   Clare's own love life continues to be a train wreck. Why do you think that is? Will she ever find the right person for a relationship?

8.   What advice would you give Clare on how to help her daughter deal with the breakup of her marriage?

9.   Janet, Clare's best friend, is almost an exact opposite of her in personality and lifestyle. Do you find this is common in women with challenging careers?

10.   What do you think will happen to Clare and her career at Channel 10 News?

NOTE FROM THE PUBLISHER

We trust that you enjoyed *Broadcast Blues*, the sixth in the Clare Carlson Mystery Series. While the other five novels stand on their own and can be read in any order, the publication sequence is as follows:

Yesterday's News (Book 1)

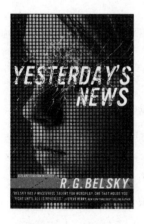

"Tell me what happened to my daughter!" For fifteen years this anguished plea has haunted reporter Clare Carlson.

"Belsky's *Yesterday's News* elicits all parents' deepest fear—the disappearance of a child. But this intelligent, gripping novel is about so much more: ambition, secrets, and, most shocking of all, truth."

—REED FARREL COLEMAN,
New York Times best-selling author

Below the Fold (Book 2)

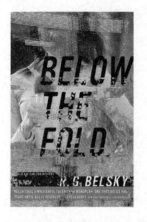

Murdered on the streets of New York: a homeless woman who called herself Cinderella—and how quickly the tragic murder of a "nobody" falls *below the fold*.

"In an era of 'fake news' and political attacks on the free press, reporter-turned-TV news director Clare Carlson personifies the best in journalism—tenacious, honest, and relentless in her pursuit of the truth and to giving a voice to those who can't speak for themselves."

—LEE GOLDBERG,
New York Times best-selling author

The Last Scoop (Book 3)

News director Clare Carlson stumbles onto a serial killer no one knew was there—and no one can stop her from pursuing the killer, exposing the truth, and finding justice for her beloved mentor.

"Belsky's experience as a journalist provides fascinating insights and a sense of authenticity. Readers will look forward to seeing more of doggedly determined Clare."

—*Publishers Weekly*

Beyond the Headlines (Book 4)

She was a mega-celebrity—he was a billionaire businessman—now he's dead—she's in jail.

"A complex and deftly written mystery replete with unexpected plot twists and darkly memorable characters, *Beyond the Headlines* by novelist R. G. Belsky is a mystery lover's delight from cover to cover."

—*Midwest Book Review*

It's New to Me (Book 5)

Dashed dreams—she wanted to run for president one day, now she's dead at twenty.

As soon as Clare Carlson tackles the story, she knows Riley Hunt's death is more than just a simple murder case—and that more lives, including her own, are in danger until she uncovers the true story.

"Clare Carlson's irreverent comments and dogged reporter's instincts make for a propulsive ride as she races from the chaos of a newsroom's inner sanctum to the dangers of a murder victim's deepest secrets."

—LISA GARDNER,
New York Times best-selling author

We hope that you will read all the Clare Carlson Mysteries and will look forward to more to come.

If you liked *Broadcast Blues*, we would be very appreciative if you would consider leaving a review. As you probably already know, book reviews are important to authors and they are very grateful when a reader makes the special effort to write a review, however brief.

For more information, please visit the author's website: www.rgbelsky.com.

Happy Reading,
Oceanview Publishing
Your Home for Mystery, Thriller, and Suspense